ROSE OF ANZIO BOOK TWO
JALOUSIE
A WWII EPIC LOVE STORY

ALEXA KANG

Copyright © 2017 Alexa Kang
ISBN-13: 9781656242266
All rights reserved.

Cover art by Adam Wayne
https://adamwayneart.com

No part of this book may be reproduced in any form or by any electronic or mechanical means, including information storage and retrieval systems, without written permission from the author, except for the use of brief quotations in a book review.

This is a work of fiction. All names, characters, businesses, places, events and incidents are either the products of the author's imagination or used in a fictitious manner. Any resemblance to actual people, living or dead, or actual events, is purely coincidental. The author has made every effort to ensure that major historical facts are accurate, but has taken some artistic license for fictional purposes. This book is not intended to be used as reference material and in no way should it be treated as an authority on any subject on any account.

PART I
DEPARTURE

CHAPTER ONE

Alone in her art studio, Tessa stood in front of the painting of Nadine and Laurent embracing each other in a state of rapture. Months ago, when she had painted this, she had thought this was what love would be like. Passion. Euphoria. Everything that would bring one to the epitome of happiness in this world. How could she have known then that love could come with so much pain even when the two people in love wanted nothing more than to be with each other?

She had meant to give the painting to Nadine as a gift, but she never found the time to bring it to her. So many things had happened that got in the way. First, it was Jack's return from the war, injured. And then, Anthony.

Anthony…

Emptiness gripped her. She stood staring at the painting for a long time without seeing it. A maze of other thoughts occupied her mind. She tried to remember every sensation she felt in every moment when she was with Anthony, starting from the stroke of midnight when the New Year arrived. That was the moment when all the barriers, confusions, and misunderstandings between them disappeared, and a new beginning full of promises unveiled itself.

That night, when they kissed, he had opened his inner world to her. In his arms, she felt close to him in a way she had never felt with anyone else. In that moment, she belonged to him, and he belonged to her. She felt as if they were the only ones in the entire ballroom. No one else mattered. Nothing could come between them.

In the small hours as the lights dimmed, he kissed her again and again. Everything felt so right. There at the top of the Allerton Hotel, he had given her the most beautiful memories of her life. There was no other place she would rather have been that night.

She remembered looking into his eyes. Such beautiful blue eyes. So deep, she wanted to lose herself in them.

She could still feel the warmth and tenderness of his touch. His breath on her lips, on her cheeks, and on her neck. All those sensations still felt so real, so tangible. She could almost reach out her hand and touch him as if he was right next to her.

She tried to remember all these feelings as she stared at the painting before her. Her memories took her back to New Year's Day.

It was Friday, the first day of 1943 and the day after the Fur Ball, the day after they danced deep into the night and discovered paradise at the top of the world. As in all the previous years, the Ardleys hosted a New Year's Day brunch for their close friends and neighbors. By noon, everyone in the Ardley household was dressed and ready.

She didn't get much sleep the night before. She and Anthony had returned home well past midnight. Back in her room, all she could do was lie in bed and think about everything that had happened. For hours, waves of sweetness flowed in her heart and it was impossible for her to fall asleep. Finally, when dawn broke and the morning light crept through the slits between the curtains, she dozed off and drifted into a series of dreams. She couldn't remember what she had dreamt about, but they were good dreams.

Despite having only a few hours of sleep, she did not feel tired. Her whole being was bursting with blissful energy. She would rather be awake and be with Anthony than be asleep, unconscious and away from him.

She came downstairs just in time. Uncle William and Aunt Sophia were leading the guests into the dining room. Aunt Sophia had planned for the brunch to be informal and relaxed, but the maid had nonetheless put out the fine china and silverware. Fresh flowers filled the vases on the table, making even this cold winter day cheerful and bright.

Quickly, Tessa took a seat. When she looked up again, Anthony had entered. Her heart skipped at the sight of him and she looked down at the plate set in front of her. When he walked past her, he ran his fingers lightly across the nape of her neck and down her hair. She gasped at the feeling of his touch. Such a small, subtle gesture, but so filled with meaning. Sweet paralysis spread through every inch of her.

He took the seat next to her and turned to look at her just as she turned to look at him. Excitement rushed through her core the moment their eyes met. Embarrassed, she turned away. She could feel Uncle William and Aunt Sophia watching them even as they continued speaking with the guests. She tried to act normally, but inside, she was exhilarated.

At the table, the surprise appearance of Celeste Le Vonne at the Fur Ball the night before dominated the conversation. Uncle Leon had pulled off a huge coup. The actress's attendance at the event would surely be the talk of the town for months to come. Celeste had wowed everybody with her fantastic singing and their guests could not stop raving about it. But for Tessa, the only music she could hear were the blissful melodies flowing between her and Anthony.

Sitting on the carpeted floor in his room, Anthony put his arms around Tessa as she leaned back against his chest. All he wanted this afternoon was to be alone with her, but the New Year's Day brunch went on and on for what felt like an eternity. He could not wait for the last remaining guests to leave. Now, away from everyone, he could at last bury his face in her hair and breathe in that sweet scent of her rose perfume. He brushed her hair to one side and kissed the back of her neck. She turned around and smiled. Her smile was so endearing. Her affection was so genuine. He leaned in closer and kissed her again.

If only they could remain in this moment. He looked at Tessa smiling and gazing at him with her bright, spirited eyes. What he wouldn't give to remain in this moment forever.

He didn't know it would be so hard to follow through with what he had resolved to do. He could only blame himself for being so simple-minded. He thought if he confessed to her, he would be able to do what he should have done months ago, to enlist. So many of his classmates had done it. They made their promises to their girlfriends and left to answer the call of duty. He thought he could do the same. He only hoped Tessa would accept him and not laugh in his face.

A year ago, after Pearl Harbor, he had let his parents and Uncle Leon convince him to wait until his draft number came up. Now, his civilian status marked him like a badge of shame. Everywhere, men of drafting age had taken up the military uniform. The absence of young men at the Fur Ball was impossible to miss and he had felt entirely out of place. Even worse, the handful of young men who had attended were 4-Fs rejected by the military for physical or other health reasons. Unlike them, he had no excuse for being there.

Things could not have been more awkward than when he met the lieutenant who came to rally for the war bond drive. All night long, the guests' eyes were on the decorated young soldier, praising him for the two years he had already served. Anthony couldn't tell if he had imagined it, but he thought he saw the young lieutenant giving him a derisive look when Uncle Leon introduced them. He thought he heard a tone of contempt from their valiant guest when they exchanged greetings and shook hands.

There was no point in waiting anymore. The military spared no one who qualified. Sooner or later, his number would come up. He had escaped the odds for too long. Every passing day, the shame of remaining a civilian weighed heavier on him. A liaison officer from the Marine Corps visited his school two weeks ago, requesting to meet with students who wished to serve with them. After hearing the liaison officer speak, his decision was clear.

That was how, when New Year's Eve ended and the clock struck midnight, he gathered all his nerve and kissed the girl he loved. How was he to know that when she returned his feelings, it would tear his heart to think he would have to leave her?

What an idiot he had been! Did he think he would ride off to battle while the fair maiden bid him farewell like he was a knight in a fairy tale? Did he think he could just leave and everything would be fine?

He looked at the girl in his arms, happy and unaware of all that was going through his mind. How could he have not foreseen that if she had felt the same way about him, it would only be that much harder for him to leave? How thoughtless of him to let her know he loved her, only to bring her disappointment in the end.

He hadn't told anyone, but before he left school for the holidays, he had made up his mind not to return. He meant to contact the Marine liaison officer. Once he did, he would be inducted as soon as the Marine Corps issue their first call for draftees next February.

But now, he hesitated once more. Should he continue to stall and prolong the inevitable? Return to school and continue to wait until he was drafted? He could extend whatever time he could have with her that way. Or should he remain steadfast and do what he had set out to do?

In two days, the spring semester would begin. One way or

another, he would have to make a choice. If he chose to follow through with his plans, what would he tell her?

He hadn't even left yet, but the ache of being apart from her already hurt. He tightened his arms around her, wishing he could hold on and never let her go.

For Tessa, the New Year holiday was ending all too fast. Sunday afternoon was almost over. Tomorrow, she would have to return to the hospital, and Anthony would return to school. How sad that this weekend must end.

In the parlor, she played the piano while he straddled the bench seat watching her. His eyes never left her the entire time she played. What a wonderful feeling it was to have him so near her. How could it be possible to like someone this much? Not in a million years would she have thought that the someone she would fall in love with would be Anthony. And yet, it was him. The more she looked at him, the more she liked him. His eyes, so full of intelligence, reflected a world of integrity. His body was such a figure of strength, he could take any girl's heart. But these were not the only reasons why she found herself falling hopelessly in love.

Last night, he had come by her room after everyone had turned in. On impulse, she took his hand and led him into her room to let him steal a kiss goodnight. He surprised her and gave her a kiss so passionate, it left her breathless. They were so close, she felt his body rousing against her. It left her confused, then amazed. It sent her heart racing.

With great reluctance, he tore himself away from her, kissing her once more on the forehead before he left her room. Afterward, she lay on her bed, staring at the ceiling and realizing for the first time the kind of feelings he had for her. He longed for her. And now, as he sat listening to her play the piano, it was all so obvious.

His every look made her feel wanted. His every touch made her feel desired.

The new intimacy between them thrilled her. She finished the final notes of their song, "Liebestraum," and turned to return his gaze. He reached for her hand and kissed her. When their lips touched, she felt her heart could erupt and melt into streams like lava flows.

They were still holding hands and gazing into each other's eyes when Uncle William entered with a sullen look on his face and an envelope in his hand.

When his father came in, Anthony quickly let go of Tessa's hand. She looked as embarrassed as he felt. They hadn't said anything to his parents yet about what had changed between them, but from the way his parents had looked at them these last two days, his parents no doubt already knew and had given their tacit approval. Still, how awkward it was to have his father walk in on them.

Oblivious, Tessa couldn't stop smiling. His own feelings of joy, though, vanished the instant he saw his father. He could guess already why his father looked so grave.

"I haven't told your mother yet." His father handed him the letter. "I only realized a moment ago this was among the pile of mail that came in on Friday."

Anthony took the letter. The envelope's upper left corner showed the County Draft Board as the return addressee. To his own surprise, he felt calm. Even relieved. He had expected this for a long time. Now that it had come, at least he would no longer have to make a choice.

But he would never forget the crushing look on Tessa's face.

CHAPTER TWO

THE FOLLOWING week went by like a blur. Back at the hospital, Tessa went through the motions of everything required of her at classes and work. She didn't even have much private time with Anthony. He had only one week before he needed to report to the County Draft Board for his qualifications exam. If he passed, and surely he would, he would not return. The army would take him directly from the place of the exam to training camp.

He had so many personal matters to attend to before he left, taking a leave of absence from school, terminating or passing on the academic projects he was working on, and last goodbyes to his friends and classmates. Most importantly, his time belonged to his parents and family. One afternoon, he sat with Aunt Sophia and listened to radio programs she liked. Another morning, he accompanied her to a meeting with Philip Wrigley to talk about giving their support to help fund a new girls' softball league to keep baseball alive at home. Uncle William changed his week's schedule and cut short his work hours to be home to help Anthony with whatever he needed. Uncle Leon too came by with Aunt Anna every evening after work. On the weekend, Katherine and Alexander joined them.

The entire family took the news hard. Uncle Leon went into

hysterics when he first heard about it. He called every government official he knew, but nothing could be done. Aunt Sophia tried to put on a brave face, only to tear up whenever she thought no one was looking. Uncle William, who everyone normally relied on for assurance and comfort, seemed lost too.

Ironically, it fell to Anthony to try to cheer everyone up.

"It's still possible they won't assign you to combat," Uncle Leon said when the Caldwells came for dinner the evening before Anthony left. "With any luck, they might assign you to a staff position. Didn't you take classes in military shipment and logistics? And you've had two summers of work experience with me on imports and exports. What you should do is tell them you can help them plan military logistics. You'll be more valuable to them that way. Make sure they know that."

"Logistics?" Anthony said. "Sounds good. Maybe I can be the delivery guy or the mail guy." He pointed to his plate. "Or I can cook. Maybe they'll make me a cook." Everyone laughed except Tessa. She looked down without saying anything.

"Not a chance," Uncle William said. "The troop would starve to death from bad cooking."

"It's not bad cooking they gotta worry about." Leon served Anthony another slice of pot roast. It was a special treat made for Anthony. Aunt Sophia had saved their entire week's meat rations for it. "What they got to worry about is that fool in the White House…"

"Leon," Aunt Anna interrupted him, "don't start."

"What? If there's anything I worry about, it's that fool of a commander in chief. Why are we still short on weapons? You'd think we would've churned out a mountain of tanks and guns to crush the fascists by now. We should be wiping the Germans and the Japs off the map. Especially the Japs. How big is Japan? It's not even the size of California. We can bomb that whole country to its knees overnight. We wouldn't even have to send thousands of boys there to do the job. I'll tell you what the problem is. The problem is we got that New Yorker sitting in the White House.

What does a New Yorker know about manufacturing and production anyway?"

"Fine, you know better. You know everything about wartime production. We'll call Senator Reinhardt tomorrow and he'll tell Roosevelt to appoint you the Secretary of Factories."

Anthony, Katherine, and Alexander all laughed. Even Uncle William and Aunt Sophia couldn't hide their smiles, but Tessa only felt her heart sinking further and further.

In her room afterward, Tessa sat on her bed, crying silent tears in the dark. Not wanting anyone to know she was still awake, she had left the lights off. The view outside the windows was pitch black. There was no moonlight and the government-imposed blackout had taken all the neighborhood lights away.

She felt engulfed by darkness.

In the dark, she heard a light knock on the door. She knew it was Anthony, but she could not bring herself to answer it. He opened the door and peeked in, then closed the door behind him and came to sit with her on the bed. She pulled her knees up and wiped her tears away with the back of her hand.

"I never meant to hurt you." He put his arm around her.

"It's not your fault," she said. "You're being drafted. You don't have a choice."

"That's not entirely true. This would have happened even if I hadn't gotten that draft letter."

"What do you mean?"

"I don't want to lie to you. Before I left school for the holidays, I had already decided I would enlist. I just wanted to come home and let you know how I feel about you before I leave."

She couldn't believe what she was hearing. "You planned on leaving?"

"I can't stay. I can't watch everyone else go to war and stay behind. People won't forgive me. I won't forgive myself."

She didn't know what to think. He had planned on leaving her. He could leave her behind. She pulled herself away from him.

"I'm sorry. I swear I didn't know it would hurt so much. I…I didn't even think you would like me back."

She slumped against the headboard. He didn't think she would like him back? What did he think would happen the way he had led her on?

"I didn't want to leave without letting you know how I feel. If I didn't tell you, I would regret it. But now, I regret telling you. If I had known this would hurt you so much, I would've kept it all to myself. I'm an idiot."

Her heart softened. She took his hand and kissed it. "Don't say that."

He drew her closer again. "For whatever it's worth, when I found out you felt the same way about me, it was the happiest I had ever been in my whole life. I'm so sorry I hurt you. It hurts me too, but I don't regret hurting myself. I would take all the hurt and more if that's what it takes to have what we have together."

She held his hand up against her face. No. She wouldn't trade what they had for anything either.

"I kept asking myself, would it have been better if we never got started so you wouldn't be so hurt?"

She shook her head. "Would you have stayed if you weren't drafted and I asked you to stay?"

"No." His answer surprised her. "If I stay, we may be happy for the time being, but after a while, we won't be. Almost everyone I know who's qualified to serve is gone. If I stay behind for selfish reasons, I wouldn't be worthy of you. You wouldn't want to be with someone who stayed home like a coward. You want to help. That's why you became a cadet nurse. How could you work day and night to help everyone who had gone to war, and then come home to a boyfriend who wouldn't share the burden?"

She held him tighter and buried her face against his chest. She didn't want to hear all this, but he was right.

"If I stayed, you would eventually think less of me, and I would resent myself too. Isn't that true?"

She couldn't answer. There were no answers to anything. All she could hear was his heartbeat.

"I'll write to you. I promise. I'll try to write to you every day." He kissed her on the head. "And you'll write me too?"

She nodded. He squeezed her shoulder and gave her a soft kiss on the lips, then started to get up to leave.

"Don't go." She pulled him back.

He stopped.

"Stay with me for a while. Stay with me till I fall asleep."

He sat back down next to her while she snuggled up against him. She felt so tired. Everything about the war had tired her out. The warmth of his body comforted her. Her eyes felt heavy and her mind dulled. In his arms, she found the calm she needed to get through the night.

Early the next morning, seven o'clock, they took off; Anthony, Tessa, Uncle William, and Uncle Leon. Uncle William had relieved the driver and was driving the car himself. The icy winter air chilled them to the bone as they left the house. Aunt Sophia remained behind. At breakfast, she broke down. She had kept up a brave front all week, but today, she could no longer restrain her tears. Not wanting Anthony to see her so devastated, she kissed him goodbye quickly and returned to her room. Aunt Anna had to stay behind to console her.

Last night, she had tried to pack for Anthony. She wanted to make sure he had everything he needed when he went away, but Uncle William kept telling her to put everything back. The draft letter told Anthony to bring no more than three changes of clothing.

"He can't bring all this stuff. They'll make him throw everything away," Uncle William told her.

Leaving Aunt Sophia and Aunt Anna behind, the four of them drove along in silence. In the backseat, Anthony held Tessa's hand the entire way.

The car pulled up to the intersection at 79th Street and Exchange Avenue. The moment Tessa had dreaded had arrived. They were here. The offices of the County Draft Board. Helpless, she looked at Anthony. Their time had run out.

He gave her a quick kiss on her forehead and got out of the car. Uncle Leon hugged him. Uncle William gave him a hug goodbye, then stroked his head as though Anthony was a child. "Take care of yourself," he said to his son.

"I will, Father." Anthony turned to look at Tessa one more time, then without saying another word, he walked off to join the group of draftees gathered on the sidewalk. An official in charge began to direct the men to line up.

"Let's go." Uncle William put his hand on her shoulder. There was nothing left for her to do but to get back inside the car. As they drove away, she looked out the passenger window and watched Anthony until he disappeared out of her sight.

The three of them drove on silently on the way back. From the reflection in the rearview mirror, Tessa could see Uncle William's melancholic face. Next to him, Uncle Leon pretended to wipe his eyes to hide his tears. It was so disconcerting to see a middle-aged man cry. Anthony's departure had brought back to him all the sad memories of the loss of his brother, Lex.

She stared out the window. She herself couldn't cry anymore. She had cried enough last week and her tears had dried up. Now that Anthony was gone, what she felt was not sadness, but rage. Red, fiery rage that burned. This damn, bloody war. Once again, it had separated her from someone she loved.

For what reason must she be parted again and again from people she loved? Why must she put up with this?

When they reached home, she went straight to her art studio without saying a word. She was enraged and she couldn't unleash her anger. Everyone else was upset enough already without having to worry about her feelings. She needed to be alone. She needed to think.

In her art studio, Tessa stood in front of the painting of Nadine and Laurent. She stared at it for a long time, but it was not the painting that she saw. In her mind, she replayed every moment and every memory of her and Anthony together. She tried to feel again the sensation of his touch and the sweetness of his kiss. She wanted to recapture the smell of his scent. Everything felt as tangible as yesterday. How long could she hold on to these sensations before they became distant memories? How many days or months would pass when, all alone, she would feel these sensations no more?

This despicable war. It kept separating her from the people she loved. It kept putting those she cared most about in harm's way. She had been away from her parents for years. Jack had been crippled. And now, it took Anthony away. It kept ruining everything good in her life. The more she thought about it, the angrier she felt.

Must she remain passive and helpless while the events of the war dictated how she must live?

No. She would not yield so easily to the demands of this war anymore. Two years ago, she had no choice but to do as her parents wished and come to America. This time, she would take her life into her own hands. If she must live with this war, then she would live with it on her own terms.

If Anthony must be sent off to war and couldn't remain here, then why couldn't she go too? Maybe she could even find a way to go to him.

She didn't know how she could make this happen. The prospect of going to him was so daunting. If anyone knew what she was thinking, they would think she was mad, but she must try. Yes. She would try. She would do everything she could to find a way. Certainly, it would be better than to stay here and wait. For all she knew, she could be waiting and waiting for years with no end in sight, just like she had been waiting all these years to return to her parents. And heaven forbid, if Anthony got hurt like Jack did, well, then…maybe she could be there for him.

Coming out of her thoughts, she took the painting off the easel, wrapped it up, and headed out of the house to Murphy's.

CHAPTER THREE

When Tessa walked into Murphy's in the late afternoon, Nadine was surprised to see her. The last time Tessa had come to Murphy's, Jack was still a patient at the Veterans Hospital. She had come with Henry to pick up the beer Mr. Murphy had wanted to give to Jack. That was a long time ago.

"Honey! Where have you been? I haven't seen you in months." Nadine put down the glass she was wiping and gave Tessa a warm smile.

"I'm sorry," Tessa said, her voice more reserved than usual. "Couldn't get away from the hospital." Knowing she was here now only because she needed something, she shifted her eyes away.

"Can I get you anything?" Nadine leaned over the bar counter toward her. "I've been experimenting with a new cocktail recipe. It's a variation of the French 75. Want to try one?"

"No, thank you." Tessa shook her head. "I can't stay long. I came to ask you a favor."

"Sure," Nadine said, still not noticing how tense Tessa looked. "What do you need?"

Tessa tightened her lips. "I know the Colts come to you when they need forged identification documents. And since Pearl

Harbor, some of the boys around here younger than eighteen come to you if they want to join the army."

Nadine raised her eyebrow with a wry smile. "You're more observant than I thought," she said. "So what can I do for you? Someone you know needs a new birth certificate? Passports? A driver's license maybe?" She winked.

Tessa took a deep breath. "Can you help me get an American birth certificate to prove I was born in 1923?"

"You want…" Nadine said, confused. Then, eyeing Tessa with suspicion, she asked, "Why?"

"I want to transfer to the special training program for American military nurses for service overseas. I need to meet the age requirement."

"You want to serve overseas? How come?"

"Because if Anthony is sent overseas, I want to go with him," Tessa said without hesitation.

"Go with him?" Nadine's eyes widened. "Your family is okay with that?"

"They don't know I'm doing this," Tessa reluctantly admitted, but seeing Nadine's doubts, she pressed on. "You have to help me. You're the only one who can help me. I have to do this."

"Tessa, honey," Nadine touched Tessa's hand on the bar counter. "Are you sure? We are talking about the war. You could be sent to a combat zone."

"I don't care," Tessa said, determined. "If that's where Anthony is going then that's where I'll go."

"I don't know. This could be dangerous…"

"Nadine, please. It's dangerous for the boys too and you do it for them."

"That's different. Those boys would have no future here anyway. The army gives them something to do. It's not the same with you."

"So what?" Tessa asked, frustrated. "I shouldn't be treated any differently. I wish everyone would stop trying to protect and shelter me all the time."

Nadine still looked hesitant. Feeling desperate, Tessa said, "You would do the same if you were me. I know you would. If Laurent was being taken away somewhere, you would go with him no matter what. Wouldn't you?"

"Yes, of course, I…"

"So please. Help me."

"Tessa, the army doesn't let people pick and choose where they go. Even if you are qualified to be a military nurse to go overseas, how could you be sure you'll be sent to wherever Anthony would be?"

"I don't know." This problem weighed on Tessa's mind too. She had no idea what she could do. "I'll figure something out. There's a dire shortage of nurses serving abroad. Maybe I can find a way. I want to try. Would you please help me?"

Nadine crossed her arms and thought for a while, then sighed and relented. "I hope I won't regret this, but all right. If you are sure this is what you want."

"Thank you! Thank you so much," Tessa said, relieved.

"Come back tomorrow afternoon and I'll have it ready then."

"I know I can count on you."

Feigning disapproval, Nadine started wiping the glass again.

"By the way, I have something for you." Tessa took out the painting she brought and showed her.

Amazed, Nadine gasped. "You painted this?"

Tessa nodded.

"It's beautiful!" Nadine dried her hands with a towel and took the painting from Tessa.

"I'm glad you like it."

"Laurent will love this."

"I hope so," Tessa said. "I have to go. Need to get back to the hospital. I'll see you tomorrow." She picked up her purse and started to leave.

Still admiring the painting, Nadine called out after her, "Tessa."

"Yes?"

"I would try to do the same thing if I were you."

Tessa smiled as she left the bar. At least, she had Nadine on her side.

The day she got the forged birth certificate from Nadine, Tessa set her alarm clock an hour earlier than usual. When she woke up the next morning, everyone else in the house was still asleep. She looked at her reflection in the mirror and knew exactly what she had to do.

Carefully, she rolled her hair back and pinned it in place the way so many women were doing these days. The thought of having to spend extra time to fix herself up like this every morning from now on annoyed her, but the hassle was a minor nuisance to put up with if it could help get her what she wanted.

With her hair set, she dabbed water on the sides to keep the curls in place, then applied the lipstick. She was not used to seeing herself like this, but it worked. Yes. She could pass for someone older. If she acted correctly, no one would suspect she wasn't at least twenty years old. Satisfied with how she looked, she left the house.

Please, she thought on her way to the hospital. *Please don't let anything go wrong today.*

In the office of the chief nurse, Tessa stood at attention as she tried to gauge what Lt. Jean Carlson might be thinking. Outwardly, Tessa did her best to appear detached and emotionless, but inside, her stomach churned. Why was Carlson taking so long to review her performance records? America was gearing up for war. There weren't enough nurses to meet the military hospitals' demand for them overseas. Everyone knew that. That was why the hospitals at home were all staffed with student nurses. Carlson should be rolling out the red carpet to accept her request to transfer to the Nurses Specialized Training Program.

"Your performance record is fine," Carlson said.

Tessa felt slightly relieved.

"Your bedside manner could be improved, it seems." Carlson continued to examine her records. "The doctors and senior nurses you've worked with have all noted you need to show more compassion at times."

Tessa didn't say anything. She didn't know her superiors thought that of her. How annoying. Just because she didn't always smile at everyone like Ellie or chat them up like Sarah didn't mean she did not care about the patients. She took good care of them.

"But that aside, you're clearly qualified," Carlson said.

Good, Tessa thought. *So far, so good.*

"You grew up in England?"

"Yes. But my mother's American," Tessa said. She hoped Carlson would not ask her any more questions about that.

Carlson finally closed the file. "The program you're asking to be transferred to is very demanding. It's highly selective because of the accelerated training time. You'll have to undergo training for many subjects in just twelve months. Being a transferred trainee, you're already behind. You'll have some serious catching up to do."

"I can handle it, Ma'am. I'll work hard. I won't fail."

Her determined insistence seemed to be working. Carlson looked impressed.

"You are aware that the sole mission of this program is to train nurses for service overseas. Are you absolutely clear you understand what that means?"

Tessa clutched her hands. She understood Carlson was asking whether she was up for the risk of the dangers ahead, but the risk that weighed on her mind was something else. This was a huge gamble. "I understand clearly, Ma'am."

Carlson nodded. "We do need nurses at home to care for the veterans and civilian patients too," she said, almost as if she was testing Tessa's resolve and at the same time giving her another chance to back out. "There are enough returning veterans who need our help. Your services would be equally valuable here. With the Nurses Specialized Training Program, once you've completed it, you will receive an assignment, and there will be no turning back."

Tessa felt her chest tighten. If she were to serve abroad but couldn't find a way to join up with Anthony's unit, she would be doubling down on the risk of her and Anthony being separated even further. But if she did nothing, if she didn't try, then she would have no chance of joining up with him at all.

What should she do? She couldn't change her mind now.

She looked up. Carlson was watching her, observing her.

"I'm ready." The words slipped from her mouth before she could sort out her own thoughts. The firmness in her voice surprised even herself. "I want to be available and ready for service overseas. This is what I want to do."

Her apparent conviction must have swayed Carlson. The corner of Carlson's lip turned up ever so slightly and revealed she was pleased. Tessa felt a bit guilty. The chief nurse probably thought her conviction was a testament to her commitment to serving and helping injured soldiers, but she couldn't tell Carlson her true motivation was to be with Anthony.

"Very well, then. Your request is granted," Carlson said. "You may start and join the classes already in progress and train with the student nurses preparing for overseas assignments. You can go to the registrar's office today and submit all the proper paperwork."

"Thank you," Tessa said, glad that another hurdle was over.

"I'll remind you, though," Carlson warned her, "you're already three months behind everyone else. The classes and work will not be easy. This program is not for the faint-hearted."

"I understand, Lieutenant."

"All right. You're dismissed." Carlson handed Tessa's personnel file back to her. Tessa took it and left Carlson's office.

Out in the hallway, Tessa folded her arms and held the file close to her chest. She couldn't believe she had jumped and taken the chance. For a moment when Carlson warned her about being assigned overseas, she became unsure. But when she saw the skepticism in Carlson's eyes, she felt as if she was watching hope slip away. All she could think of was that she had to grasp it before it was lost.

On reflection, she wished she hadn't hesitated at all. Yes, she might be out of her mind. Maybe the whole idea of joining up with Anthony's unit was an absolute fantasy. In the big scheme of the war and the U.S. Military, she was so insignificant. But she was done letting the war determine her fate. If Anthony was being sent to war, then she would go too. Whether or not she could find a way to join up with him, they would now be in this together. She had made her own choice. That, at least, was a private battle she had won over this war. She felt liberated. The triumph had set her free.

The clerk at the personnel office barely looked up at Tessa when she entered. The scrawny, balding man had worked at the hospital, pushing files and papers day in and day out for more than twenty-five years. The tedium had sucked all the life out of him. His face registered no emotion or interest in anything under the depressing office light.

"Hello." Tessa placed her personnel file on the clerk's desk along with the notice of program transfer which Lt. Carlson had given her. The clerk scanned the notice, his lips moving as if reciting the words he was reading. Then, bored by the message, he set it aside and took a drag of the cigarette burning in his ashtray. "Your proof of identity please." He hadn't looked up from his desk once.

Tessa handed him the falsified birth certificate she had gotten from Nadine. The clerk copied the information from the document onto an application form, then gave it back to her along with a duplicate of the form he had just filled out. "Goodbye."

Tessa took the papers and walked out. She couldn't believe her luck. That was much easier than she had expected. Her biggest worry had been the clerk questioning her age. Well, she doubted the clerk even remembered who she was.

If only it would be half as easy to figure out how she could join up with Anthony. The idea was far-fetched. She had no idea what to do or where to start planning her next move. The possible outcomes before her now were endless.

Would it be possible for her and Anthony to be sent some place in England? There were American troops stationed in the UK. What if they got lucky and she and Anthony could both somehow end up in London?

Or would everything go to hell and she would be sent to a foreign country in Asia or Africa while he was sent to Europe? Or vice versa? How would she find her way to him then?

She felt lost like a needle in a haystack, trying to find her way out.

And then, there were her parents, and Uncle William and Aunt Sophia. They couldn't know about this. They would never let her get involved with the war. She could hide her plans from them for a while, but eventually, she would have to leave them behind. How would she explain this to them?

All at once, every prospect overwhelmed her.

Small steps, she told herself. *One step at a time. You'll figure something out.*

PART II
THE HOME FRONT

CHAPTER FOUR

Riding on the bus on the way to Camp Grant at Rockford, Illinois, Anthony watched the other draftees strike up conversations with one another. They were all boys and young men like himself, except most of them appeared to have come from more humble backgrounds. Caught up in the new experience of being away from home for the first time, many began sharing stories of where they were from and what they did. They reminded him of his first trip to summer camp.

The bus driver steered off the freeway onto a back road toward the suburbs, hitting a bump along the way that bounced the passengers off their seats. The stack of boxes that took up the two front passenger seats rattled. What was in those boxes, Anthony wondered. Something government issued, obviously.

Government Issued. Or G.I. as everybody called it. He, too, was now also Government Issued. Everyone on the bus was Government Issued. Freedom was no longer theirs. The government had summoned all of them to give up their freedom in the name of fighting for freedom.

A funny vision came to him. Once, he had gone to the university's biological science lab to meet a classmate. Before they left, his friend had put away a transparent plastic box of healthy, white laboratory mice. The box had holes on the side to enable air to pass through. Trapped, the mice clustered around and on top of each other, their squeaks not unlike the animated chitchat on this bus. The unfortunate rodents had no idea what was coming to them.

What was coming to them?

As his thoughts ran, the humor in his vision ceased. This bus was not a simple means of transportation. It was a trap.

He tried not to think about it. No use thinking too much about it.

What was it like for Uncle Lex? How did Uncle Lex feel when he first embarked on his journey to fight in the Great War? Lex must have gone with much greater enthusiasm. In fact, he was sure of it. Over Thanksgiving weekend, he had gotten Alexander to find all of Lex's old letters which Uncle Leon had kept in storage in the attic. He read all the letters Lex had sent home while he was at war. For the most part, Lex wrote about his life in the military and how much he missed everyone. But behind the recount of day-to-day events, his words revealed a latent tone of conviction of someone who believed in the cause for which he fought. Lex was no mere idle young man looking for ways to rebel against his family. He went to war because he felt it was the right thing to do.

Thinking of Lex's letters, Anthony felt ashamed. If only he could be as great a man as Lex. Everyone had such great expectations of him because he was William Ardley's son. In truth, he never felt the drive to do greater things than what his father had done. Sometimes, he thought he wanted to break free of the life his family had already set before him, but he had never found a direction he felt passionate enough to follow. After reading Lex's letters, it occurred to him he had never committed himself to doing something truly good and worthwhile either. Even after his own country was attacked, it took him a year to finally answer the call of duty. He looked out the bus window. He would never measure up to his father or Uncle Lex.

· · ·

When the recruits arrived at the camp, a sergeant marched them to a warehouse. There, Anthony picked up his uniform and his "dog tag." Engraved on the tag were his name, his army identification number, his blood type, and the letter "C" denoting his religious faith. The tag weighed on his hand like a bad omen. He put it away and tried to put it out of his mind.

They followed the sergeant to their barracks. No one would ever mistake this place for home. The barracks had no furniture except for the metal bunk beds with footlockers in uniform rows down the room. They didn't even have decent lights. Everything in there felt sterile and depressing.

What bothered him, though, was not the lack of comfort and luxury. Homesick. Already, he felt homesick. His family, Tessa, school, they were all now out of his reach. Their lives would go on and they would make new memories without him. He felt cut off and cast out. This was his new life, one which would take him farther and farther away from everyone and everything he cared about.

He could hardly believe how much his life had changed in just a span of hours.

January 29, 1943

Dear Mother, Father, and Tessa,

How are you all? It has been three weeks since I began my army life. I am trying to adapt but it will take some getting used to. I had wanted to write home sooner but this is the first time I have been able to write with a clear mind after processing everything that has happened since I left home.

It was a very long day I spent at the County Draft Board after reporting for duty. I passed my qualification exams, then waited for hours for my branch assignment. At the time, all the recruits were very anxious. There were a lot of theories being talked about as to how the assignments would be made. Everyone thought that those who voluntarily enlisted would get to choose which army branch to join and even request for a position they wanted, while those who were drafted would be out of luck. You know how Uncle Leon wanted me to tell the authorities I had special skills in logistics so that they might assign me to a safer position? I thought that since I didn't enlist but was drafted, I was in for the worst.

I never got to find out if that rumor was true or not. When my turn came, I was simply assigned to the army and was sworn in. The official in charge never gave me a chance to bring up the subject of a specific position either. I guess Uncle Leon's scheme didn't work. That was fine by me. Army or not, I don't want to make a career out of logistics anyway. (I'm only joking. I know he wants me to be safe, that's all.)

Later on, I was taken to Camp Grant. This is where they send all the new recruits from Chicago. We spent two weeks there, learning the basics of drills, marches, and formations. Most of these are fairly easy to follow, and I thought two weeks were excessive for such simple exercises. But even into week two, some recruits were still falling out of formations. One of them continuously messed up. Our squad leader got so frustrated, he made the guy carry a bag of garbage at all times for the remainder of our stay there. The guy had to carry it wherever he went, and whenever he met someone of superior rank, he had to explain that he was carrying a bag of garbage because he was a piece of trash.

Aside from drills, we had to do a lot of camp maintenance and housekeeping, as there were no civilian employees to keep up the camp's operations. That meant we cleaned a lot. I've gotten very good at sweeping, mopping, and folding clothes and sheets. Several times, they assigned me to kitchen duty (we call it KP duty) and I cleaned pots and pans all day. They even had me cook once. I was never asked to do that again, so I guess they weren't very impressed with what I cooked up. (I thought the meatloaf I made turned out okay, considering it was partly burnt.)

I've since left Camp Grant and am now in Camp Dover in California. We took a very long train ride to get here. On this endless ride, I got to know many of the new recruits in my group. One of the boys is from a rural farm in Wisconsin. A few others are factory workers. I'm the only college student among us who wasn't working before joining the army. The guys give me a pretty hard time about it sometimes, but it's all in good fun. Really, it doesn't matter where we are from. We are all privates now and all in the same boat. I tried to mingle and get along with all of them.

At Camp Dover, my day starts at 6 am sharp. We begin the morning with physical training. The guys who are not in good shape have a very tough time with it. In the afternoon, the noncomissioned officers (everyone calls them noncoms) teach us about weaponry. It is strange to be around so many guns and artillery. I've never held a gun before. It is odd to think that I might one day have to use one for real. They teach us battle formations, different models of planes used by the Allies and the enemies, and how to recognize different tank models. All these are new to me and fascinating actually. Besides, these training sessions are the closest things to being in classes again. I kind of like them because of that.

I won't talk about the food here. The thought of army food is enough to ruin my appetite. I want to ask you to send some Reese's Butter Cups, but on second thought, please don't send any. One of the guys received a package of candy from his girlfriend for an early celebration of Valentine's Day. Our captain made him dig holes in the yard and bury each piece in a hole. The sergeant said since the guy liked candy so much, he should try to grow more. So now, the guy has to water the candy every day until they grow. (It's too bad. With the sugar ration, his girlfriend must have gone through some trouble to find those candies. Oh well, I'm waiting to see if the fruit of their love will blossom.)

By the way, they told us all our letters are censored. They read everything that goes out and comes in. The censor is to prevent us from sharing and writing anything that might compromise military secrets. Honestly, it's not as if I know any secrets to tell. Here, no one ever tells us anything. Speaking of not knowing anything, can you send me some magazines? None of us here knows what's going on outside of camp. No one in my squad has a radio and, with this camp being in the middle of nowhere, we have no access to any newspapers. We're completely cut off from the rest of the world. You probably know more military secrets than I do.

I miss you all. Please tell Uncle Leon, Aunt Anna, Katherine, and Alexander I'm thinking of them. I will write again very soon and will write them too when I get a chance.

— Love, Anthony

Tessa held Aunt Sophia's hand as Uncle William read Anthony's letter aloud. When he finished, he gave the letter to his wife. Grasping it as if she was afraid she might lose it, Aunt Sophia reread every word. When she finished, she put down the letter, looking drained and defeated. "He's in the army."

"Don't upset yourself, Sophie." Uncle William put his arm around her, but she was still distraught. They both looked so sad. Tessa wished she could say something to comfort them, but she didn't know what. She never knew what to say to make people feel better. Words always felt so useless. Words could never really help or change anything.

"We'll have to hope for the best," Uncle William said with resignation.

"I thought I'd be happy to get his letter." Aunt Sophia's face fell even more. "But...I don't know. I don't like hearing about him handling guns."

Tessa didn't find it as difficult to imagine Anthony with guns. He was always so strong. What she couldn't imagine was him in the kitchen. "They had him doing other things," she said. "He said he cooked and washed pots and pans." She didn't mean to joke, but Uncle William chuckled. Even Aunt Sophia cracked a smile.

"Tessa," Uncle William said, "you don't have to sit with us." He glanced at the letter on her lap. Anthony had sent a separate letter addressed only to her. "I know you want to read that."

Embarrassed, Tessa picked up the letter. She still hadn't gotten used to being Anthony's girlfriend in front of Uncle William and Aunt Sophia. She wished Anthony were here. If he were here, she might not feel so awkward. But she had no time to dwell on that now. Uncle William was right. She couldn't wait to read what Anthony had written to her. "Thank you," she said. "Excuse me." She left the parlor and ran upstairs to her room.

In her room, Tessa closed the door behind her and tore open the envelope. She scanned the entire letter quickly all at once, then read it more slowly a second time, then a third time, then again, and again, savoring every word.

January 29, 1943

Dear Tessa,

Forgive me if I can't put into words very well everything I want to say to you. I've never written a love letter before. If I hadn't joined the army—no, if I had never met you—I don't think I would ever have written one. When I picked up the pen and wrote your name, I realized that nothing in my entire life—not all the years of school, not the education I got at the best academies in Chicago, nor one of the finest universities in the country—had prepared me to write a simple letter to the girl I love. I worry you will find whatever I write to be inadequate to express how much I really miss you and how often I think of you.

If it were up to me, I would have every country at peace, and you and I would be with each other without a care in the world. I'm afraid your boyfriend (me) is not a very impressive man. Would your ideal boyfriend be a hero who would stand up for righteous principles and make honorable sacrifices? If so, I'm afraid you will be disappointed. Do you remember my friend Brandon Lowe? Our neighbors Mr. and Mrs. Lowe's son? Brandon's a real hero. He always talked with passion about fighting against the evils in this world. He wanted to make a difference, so he joined the Navy. Me? All I want is to have my life back to the way it was. Go to school, swim, and be with you. I wish we could walk along the beach and watch the sunset. I want us to lie on the grass outside and watch the clouds move in the sky, or sit by the fireplace in the winter and watch the wood burn. Better yet, I wish you would play the piano while I listen all afternoon and all evening.

I've been thinking about Uncle Lex a lot. He was a hero too. Mother and Father, Uncle Leon, and everyone are now calling me that, but I don't deserve it. I have no aspiration to be a hero. I'm here because it is the right thing to do. There are close to a hundred thousand men at Camp Dover. Most of them too wish they were somewhere else, so it is only right that I'm here. I would never forgive myself if I stood by and not share the burden with everyone.

But I will take comfort in knowing that what I am doing now may contribute in some small way to make the world safer for you. And dare I think that maybe by being here and being a part of the military, I may even help, however insignificantly, to defend your country? To make England safe again for you and your parents? I hope so.

I'm sorry I haven't been able to write to you every day as I said I would. I feel terrible about it. The army's schedule is out of my control. There are days when I am exhausted from training. I promise you though, I will write you every chance I get. Please write to me. Every day, I think of the day when I will see you again. I'm so lucky. I have the most wonderful, most beautiful girl in the world at home waiting for me to come back.

Again, I hope this letter is acceptable to you. I feel like such a dunce. I don't know how to write anything romantic. I should have taken poetry classes.

I miss you. Take care of yourself.

— Love, Anthony

After reading his letter for the fifth time, Tessa folded it and held it against her heart. This was the closest she could get to Anthony. She could almost feel his warmth through his letter.

She turned around and ran her fingers across the words "Dream of Love" on the "Liebestraum" poster on the wall. When Anthony came back, she would play this music for him again. She would play this for him as many times as he wanted. She would play all afternoon and all evening anything and everything he wished to hear.

She read the letter one more time, then went to her dresser and emptied out the top drawer. She needed a special place to keep his letters.

Deep in the drawer, she found a small jewelry box. She flipped it open, revealing the rose pendant inside. Dear Lord. How could not she have thought of it? Anthony had given this to her for her sixteenth birthday. She held up the pendant by its chain. Sweetness filled her heart again.

She put the letter into the drawer and placed the jewelry box with the rose pendant carefully on top. From now on, this would be the drawer for Anthony's letters and all their secrets.

CHAPTER FIVE

"This is incredible!" Sarah Brinkman jabbered on in the hallway as she and Tessa headed to their rounds to check up on the patients. Their shift had barely begun, but Sarah was already bombarding her with all the details of the news. Upon learning Tessa had transferred to the Nurses Specialized Training Program, Sarah had decided to do the same.

"I'm so glad you thought of transferring. I don't know why I didn't think of it. Ok, that's not true. Actually, I did think of registering for that program when I signed up to train as a nurse. I guess I was afraid I couldn't handle the pressure. But then you did it. You asked to be transferred and it gave me the shot of confidence I needed to go for it. I told myself, try it. Try it like Tessa did. Still, I can't believe they accepted me. My brothers will be so proud of me. Do you think I'll do okay? Do you think I can manage the workload?"

"You'll do fine," Tessa said and went into the patients' room on the opposite side of the one Sarah was entering. It was a relief to get away from Sarah's incessant chatter.

The patients stirred when Tessa entered. Generally bored at the hospital, they were always excited to see a nurse walk in. Anything to help them pass the time was good, and the younger nurses were of special interest to them. How the nurses looked, how they worked, what they did in their private lives. Tessa had never seen a gossipier bunch of men.

When the men saw that it was her coming to do their check-ups, their enthusiasm evaporated. Among the ones who had been recovering at the hospital the longest, Tessa was known as the Ice Queen. They gave all the nurses nicknames. Sarah was "Sweetie Pie," a nod to her pie-baking skills, and Sarah did often bake pies for them. Ellie was "White Angel." Tessa, though, was "Ice Queen." They did not care for a visit by the Ice Queen. No fun there.

This was the part about her job that Tessa could do without. Not the part about being given a nickname, but being the subject of idle gossip. Back in London, her mother tended to all sorts of patients—men, women, the elderly, children. Those patients never made the nurses into subjects of amusement. Here, the boys had too little to do and too much time. She was here to work, not to be their entertainment.

She checked on the patients one by one. Everything was routine until she reached Bed No. 10. The bed, the last in a row near the wall, was empty. Where had the patient gone?

She checked the patient's chart on the clipboard hanging at the foot of the bed. There, between the bed and the wall, lay a man curled up in a fetal position on the floor.

"What are you doing down there? Are you all right?" She crouched down. The man didn't answer. He had a glazed look in his eyes and didn't seem aware of her. She looked around the room. No one was paying them any attention. The other patients were carrying on as usual, reading on their beds or talking with each other. She checked the man's medical chart again. Captain Ron Castile. U.S. Marine Corps.

"Ron? Captain Castile?" She put her hand on his arm. He flinched, then yelped. Startled, she yanked her hand back and stood up.

She took a closer look at his chart. His medical records said he had been hit by a bullet once in the leg and returned to battle after he recovered from that injury. He was subsequently injured again from exposure to shrapnel, suffering external cuts and wounds for which he underwent surgical operations at a field hospital. He recovered fully from that incident, but had been sent back home because of "nerves." The final assessment on his chart: "Patient unable to mentally operate."

"He's been like this since he got here last night," said Tommy Ross, the corporal in the bed next to them. Tommy had gotten shot in the stomach at a battle in Africa and had since been honorably discharged. He liked to joke and tell an exaggerated story about how he "lost his guts."

"He slept on the floor all night last night," Tommy said. "No blanket, no pillow, nothing. The nurses tried to put him back into bed a couple of times, but after they left, he would go right back on the floor. The third time, a doctor came with them and they tried to force him to sleep on his bed. He started squealing like a pig being slaughtered. Woke everybody up. They had to give him a shot of tranquilizer. He woke up later and went right back onto the floor."

Tessa listened, trying to make sense of what he said.

"I thought I lost my guts in the war. He really lost his guts." Tommy laughed. "Get it? Lost his guts? Ha ha."

Not amused, Tessa crouched back down next to the man lying on the hard floor. "Captain Castile? You can't be on the floor. Can I help you get back into your bed?"

The man turned his eyes to her as if coming out of a trance. He looked disoriented and confused. Unsure how to get him to understand her, Tessa said the first thing that sprung to her mind. "May I hold your hand?"

He looked as though he was struggling to understand what she had asked, then looked away. Tessa reached out and gently touched his right hand. Her touch seemed to comfort him as he closed his own hand around hers.

"Ron?" she asked as softly as she could. The man nodded.

"Captain Castile?" The man winced when he heard the word

"captain." Noting his reaction, she said, "Ron then. I'll call you Ron."

Ron Castile closed his eyes, then opened them again. His lips curled up slightly, almost a smile.

"Can I take you back to your bed?" she asked.

He shook his head. In a whisper she could barely hear, he said, "No. I don't deserve it."

"You don't deserve it? Why?"

"They died," he said, looking into space. "They all died. I should be in the ground with them, not lying comfortable in bed."

This was more complicated than she could handle. She needed to finish her rounds, but she couldn't leave the man like this here. Anxious to find a quick solution, she scratched the back of her neck and thought about calling a doctor, but then changed her mind. She didn't want to interrupt the doctors on duty without an emergency. She must try to resolve this herself.

"I see," she said to him. "How about you don't lie down comfortably? What if you sit on the bed? Can you sit on the bed?"

Ron's eyes came into focus. "If I sit, would you stay with me?" He tightened his hand around hers.

"I have to check on the other patients."

"Then I can't sit," he said, distraught. "I have to stay down here. I'm not worthy to show my face." He was clinging on to her now. "Please don't leave."

He looked so pitiable, she couldn't ignore him. She glanced at the clock on the wall. "How about this? It's ten o'clock now. My break is coming up at eleven-thirty. Would you sit on your bed until then? It'll be temporary. I'll come back during my break, and you can decide then whether you can continue to sit on the bed or not. Surely no one would blame you if you were only sitting there for a little while, and only because I told you to wait for me."

The option of sitting on the bed temporarily seemed to have never occurred to him. But to her relief, he accepted her suggestion and nodded. She came closer and helped him up to the side of the bed. He sat down, but would not let go of her hand. He looked frightened.

Digging deep to think of what to do to make him let go, she took a handkerchief out of her pocket with her free hand and squeezed it into a ball. "Ron, listen. I have to go away for a little while. Just a little while." She showed him the balled-up handkerchief. "This is mine. If you hold onto it, it would be the same as if you're holding on to me. Can you hold this for me until I come back?"

Ron looked at the handkerchief. As if intrigued, he let go of her and took it. For the first time since they had spoken, he looked her in the face. "Who are you?"

"I'm Tessa. Tessa Graham. I'm a nurse here."

"Pleased to meet you, Tessa." His politeness surprised her.

"Pleased to meet you too, Ron." She tapped him on the shoulder. "You sit here and wait for me, okay? I'll be back very soon."

He seemed more grounded now, and she took her leave. As soon as she finished her round, she caught up with Ellie Swanson in the administrative office.

"Have you seen the patient in Ward 6? The one named Ron Castile?" she asked Ellie.

"The one who was admitted last night and caused all the commotion? Yes. I haven't checked on him myself, but don't worry. The doctors said there's nothing wrong with him."

"How can they say that? Something's clearly wrong. He's acting very strange."

Ellie put down the file in her hand. "All his wounds are healed. We didn't find anything wrong with him."

Tessa wasn't convinced.

"Don't worry, Tessa. That patient is fine. We normally don't admit someone who isn't still in recovery, but he said he has back and hip pains. The doctors decided to admit him and run a few more tests because he's the son of someone important in the army. A major general or something. So you see, he's already getting special treatment. Anyway, he probably has a bout of battle fatigue, that's all. He'll come out of it."

Tessa wasn't so sure, not with that hollow look in his eyes and the desperate way he held on to her hand.

At break time, she returned to his ward. Ron Castile was sitting on the bed in the same spot as she had left him. But at least, he looked more alert.

"Hello, Ron," she said. He was still clutching her handkerchief. "See? I'm back. Just like I promised. I brought you orange juice. Would you like some?" She gave him the glass of concentrated orange juice, which she hoped would cheer him up. He took the juice but only held it and didn't drink any. "How are you doing?" she asked.

Instead of answering her, he asked, "Where am I?"

"You're in our hospital."

"The evac hospital?"

"No. The Chicago Veterans Hospital."

"Chicago…" He looked confused.

"Yes. Chicago. You're home."

He lowered his head and furrowed his brows as if trying to think. "My hip hurts. My back hurts too."

"Yes, I heard." She didn't tell him his medical files showed no record of back or hip injuries. "Was it gun shots?"

"I think so." He sounded meek and unsure.

She decided to see for herself what was wrong with him. "Let's take a look. Would you please lie down on your stomach?"

He put the juice down and did as she instructed. She lifted the top of his gown. Other than scars from shrapnel, she could see no obvious injury that would cause him pain. "Where exactly does it hurt?"

"Right here." He pointed to a spot on his lower back above his left hip. "I can't walk right because of it."

She touched the spot where he had pointed. No sign of any injury. Not even a scar. She pulled his gown back down. "Okay, you can sit back up now." Again, he did as she told him as if he had no will of his own. "When did the pain start?" she asked.

"In Guadalcanal," he said. "I was leading a troop of thirty marines on a reconnaissance mission. We were ordered to make contact with the Japanese troops stationed west of the Lunga perimeter." His lips stiffened as he spoke. With so much tension in his voice, he could hardly get his words out. She thought he might stop talking, but he continued. "We were sure the Japs would surrender. All the intelligence reports said they were isolated. We landed by boat between Point Cruz and the Matanikau River. We landed, and they had reinforcement. A platoon of Japanese naval troops surrounded us. I had no idea where they came from." He stared at Tessa with terror in his eyes. She took his hand again to encourage him to continue.

"I screamed for my men to retreat. Then I ran. I ran and ran until I got back to our boats. I had to get my troops out of there. I thought all my boys were with me. I kept yelling for them to run, to run. I shouted as loud as I could. I didn't know if they heard me. There were grenades and bombs exploding all around us. They were firing at us with machine guns from behind every tree. I kept shouting for everyone to run. Then, I got to the boats. The bombing and shooting stopped. I thought we'd gotten away. I looked behind me, and…" He stopped. His face scrunched together and he started to cry. Tessa tightened her grasp of his hand to give him support.

"I looked behind me, and there was no one there," he whimpered. "I ran back. I shouted everyone's name. Slater. Kent. Harrison. No one answered me. I looked for them for a long time. Then I saw their bodies. They were all dead. My entire troop. They were all killed." At this point, he choked and threw up. Nothing came out. He hadn't eaten breakfast, it seemed. Tessa grabbed the towel on the cabinet stand next to his bed and wiped his mouth.

While she helped him, she considered the possibility of his account. His story did not sound right. It made no sense that he could escape the Japanese when the rest of his troop didn't. And how could he have run back to look for everyone without being caught? The Japanese couldn't have left so quickly. She watched him more closely, but he didn't appear to be lying.

"I failed them. I don't know why the Japs didn't see me. I didn't know how I was the only one left. I didn't know what else to do, so I got back to our boats and went back to the base. Then, in the boat, I felt a sharp pain shooting from my hip up to my spine. I was sure someone had shot me. I turned around and shot back. I must have scared him away. I don't know how I made it back to camp. I try so hard to remember but everything is so hazy. They took me to the field hospital. I was sedated for days and I thought they had put me through surgery. But when I had my wits about me again, the medical staff denied it. They said I wasn't shot. How could that be? My back still hurts." He pulled her hand and shook her arm. "They wouldn't treat me. They think I made everything up because I came back uninjured but everyone else died. I told them I was in pain, but no one would believe me."

She thought about what he said. Whatever really happened, clearly these were his memories of the events. Moreover, the incident had traumatized him. She sat down next to him. "I believe you."

He looked at her. More tears fell from his eyes.

"You're here now." She smiled. "We'll take care of you. We'll find out what's wrong and make the pain go away. I promise."

He took a deep breath and loosened his body.

"But you must promise me one thing in return."

"What is that?"

"Will you sleep on the bed from now on? Not on the floor? If you do that, I'll come see you every day during my break."

He looked down and rounded his shoulders like he wanted to hide. "I don't deserve the bed."

"Maybe, maybe not. But it is okay because I told you to do it. You are not choosing to sleep on the bed. You're only doing it because you owe me a promise. So that's okay. Don't you see?" The reason she gave sounded ridiculous even to her. She made it up because she thought something incomprehensible which he could not dispute might be the only way to convince him.

He thought for a moment, then nodded. She breathed a sigh of relief. At least that problem was solved.

The bigger problem was, what could she do for him?

"How about you get some rest? You look like you could use a little sleep. I'll be back later." She got up and patted the pillow. Following her instructions, he lay down and she put the blanket over him. She couldn't help but feel sorry for him. Here he was, a grown man—a Marine captain no less—letting her tell him what to do as though he were a child.

Tessa soon found out, making a promise was one thing. Delivering one was another. When she tried to talk to Dr. Donovan about treating Ron the next morning, Donovan showed little interest.

"I sympathize with him, Tessa, I really do." Donovan looked up from the heap of papers on his desk. "But we're buried with work as it is. We have new patients coming in every day with much more serious injuries. Obviously, Castile has some mental issues, but those aren't life threatening and right now, he is simply not our top priority. Besides, this is a veterans hospital, not a mental institution. Our purpose here is to treat veterans wounded at war."

"But Doctor, he is this way because of the war," Tessa said, remembering how Ron, muscular with no physical handicap, had curled up on the floor, completely broken.

Donovan would not be convinced. "To be frank, Tessa, if he weren't the general's son, he would've been discharged already. We need more beds available. All I'm doing is waiting for the general to get here to take him home."

Disappointed, Tessa left Donovan's office. She would have to try to help Ron herself.

At break time, she visited Ron again. This time, she found him in bed covered under the blanket from head to toe. "Ron." She touched him on the arm. "Are you cold?"

He curled up a bit more under the blanket.

"I'm on a break now. I brought you orange juice again. Would you sit up and have some?"

He didn't respond, but she took it as a positive sign that he didn't refuse. "I'll leave it here then. I'll let you rest." She put the juice on the cabinet next to his bed and started to walk away.

"Please don't go." he said, his voice faint and muffled under the blanket.

"All right." She halted. "How can I help you?"

"I can't move."

"You can't move? Do you feel pain anywhere? Shall I get the doctor for you?"

"I can't get up. I can't get out of bed. I want to hide and disappear."

From his voice, she could hear him weeping. She didn't know what to do except to sit down and stay with him for the remainder of her break.

After work, Tessa remained at the hospital searching for answers in the medical library. Two hours later, she still hadn't found anything. How could it be that none of the books said anything about Ron's condition? There was no mention of his ailment in any medical journal, let alone a diagnosis.

"Tessa? You're still here?"

Tessa looked up. It was Ellie. Ellie picked up one of the medical books on the table and read its title.

"I'm trying to find out what's wrong with Ron Castile," Tessa said. "I've been looking for hours. I can't find anything. Nothing at all."

"Everyone said there is nothing wrong with him." Ellie sat down across the table.

"It doesn't matter what everyone says. Something is wrong." Tessa closed the book she was reading. "You can see that, can't you?"

Ellie gave her a sympathetic smile.

"What will happen to him if they release him like this?" Tessa asked.

Ellie didn't answer. She didn't know either.

"We have to find out what's wrong with him and help him before they make him leave," Tessa said. "Will you help me? There's a section of books about mental illness over there that I haven't looked at yet."

Ellie looked over to the section where Tessa was pointing. "Of course." She nodded. "I'll help. Let's ask Sarah too. Maybe she can cheer him up."

"That's a good idea!" Sarah's endless blather would probably work better to cheer Ron up than Tessa herself sitting with him in silence.

They were wrong. Ron didn't want Sarah's company, nor Ellie's. At break time the next morning, Tessa brought Ellie and Sarah along to visit Ron, hoping his spirits would rise if he saw more that people cared about him. But when he saw Tessa coming with other nurses, he cowered into hiding under his blanket. Helpless, the three nurses looked at each other. Ellie and Sarah could do nothing except leave.

"It's okay, Ron." Tessa patted his shoulder. "They're gone now."

His body relaxed under the blanket. She sat down on the chair beside him. Although he was calm now, this was not a solution. Her sitting here in silence would not make him better. She tried to say something, but couldn't think of what. She wasn't a talker to begin with. She couldn't carry on a conversation by herself like Sarah.

She tried to think of what to do. Tommy, the not-funny joker who "lost his guts," tossed the newspaper he was reading to the end of his bed. It gave her an idea. "May I?" she asked Tommy.

"Go ahead," Tommy said as he picked up a magazine.

She opened the newspaper and scoured it. So many stories and reports on the war. She glanced at Ron. These stories would not do. She flipped through more pages. Movies! What movies were showing? *Sergeant York.* Maybe not. *Caught in the Draft.* No. *They Died with their Boots On!* Dear God! No. These won't do either.

She flipped a few more pages. "Zielinski and the Chicago Symphony Brought Beethoven to New Heights." It was a review of the Chicago Symphony's performance last night.

"Ron," she asked. "Do you like Beethoven?"

He didn't answer. She continued anyway. "Old Ludwig's Fifth Symphony finally received the treatment he deserved with the buoyant performance at the direction of guest conductor Viktor Zielinski yesterday evening." She checked on him, then read on. "Too often, this gem has been ruined by its own grandeur, as conductor after conductor repeated with the same tired seriousness…" She proceeded to read the entire article out loud while eyeing him every now and then. The blanket slipped from his head, revealing part of his face. "It was refreshing to hear Zielinski push the tempos and toss the motives…"

She glanced at him again. For the first time since she met him, his mind looked to be in the present. The article had caught a hold of him. It was bringing him out of the horrific world in which he was trapped.

She read on, careful not to alter her tone or rhythm in case she might lose him. But inside, she could hardly sit still. She couldn't wait to tell Ellie and Dr. Donovan about this.

CHAPTER SIX

February 13, 1943

Dear Anthony,

Words cannot describe how happy I was when I received your first letter. I miss you so much. You are so silly to think the letters you write have to be romantic. The truth is, I am happy to see your words no matter what you write. Every day, every moment you are away, my heart is empty. Your words and letters are the only things that can fill that emptiness.

I don't care whether you are a hero or not a hero. Perhaps the world thinks of all the men fighting in the war as brave heroes, but when I look around at the wounded veterans at the hospital every day, my first thought is never whether they are heroes. I see victims. Men who are caught in an uncontrollable catastrophe and suffering for it. I look at them and I fear what might happen to you. I hope and pray you will return home safe. That is all that matters. I only wish to have your arms around me again.

I hate this war. I hate that it's taken you away from me.

Anyway, your letter was romantic. At least it was to me. You said such nice and beautiful things about me. I tell you, my patients would definitely disagree with you. They call me the Ice Queen behind my back. They think I don't know, but I do.

I can't stop thinking about you whenever I'm alone. I'm so glad for the Liebestraum poster you gave me. Every night, I stare at it while I'm in bed. I pretend you are in the room with me, then I can fall asleep and dream of you.

Tomorrow is Valentine's Day. I wish you were here.

I'm always with you in spirit. My heart follows you wherever you go.

— Love, Tessa

TESSA FOLDED the letter into the envelope. Funny he said he did not know how to write a love letter. She didn't exactly have a way with words either. She hoped her letter sounded uplifting enough. His life at training camp sounded tough, and she wanted him to think happy thoughts of his girl waiting for him at home. Good thing he couldn't see how upset she looked now, thinking of him. Being away from him hurt. It hurt even more than being away from her parents. Every night when she read his letter, her heart ached.

Seeing injured veterans at the hospital every day didn't help. They reminded her constantly of what could happen to Anthony. What if he came back maimed like them? What if he came back mentally destroyed like Ron Castile?

She pressed her hand against her forehead. These thoughts could drive her insane. She needed to stop thinking.

Ron. She must help Ron. He had to heal. She had to keep hope alive, for herself and for everyone. It was the only way they could get through this war.

That was it. She would fight this war her own way. She would not let this war ruin the people around her, including Ron.

But how? She had exhausted all avenues and resources at hand. No one at the hospital had any more ideas what they could do for him. She wondered if the doctors in England might know more. They had been at war longer than the Americans. Could they know things the Americans didn't?

Maybe her mother would know.

She picked up the pen and started writing again.

February 13, 1943

Dear Mother,

I hope you are well. How is Father? Have you been busy at the hospital? I have been entirely preoccupied with a new case myself. In fact, I wonder if you could help me.

We have a new patient. His name is Ron Castile and he is a Marine Corps captain. He has been with us for several weeks. He has no physical injuries, all of his war wounds healed before he came to our hospital. His mind, however, is in a very bad state. Most of the time, he is in a daze. When he is more alert, his memories are fragmented. He thinks he was shot in the back, but he was not. Still, he complains of back and hip pains where he thought he was shot, and he says he cannot walk.

I don't know what to make of it. When he first arrived, he slept all night on the hospital's concrete floor and refused to sleep in his bed. It took a Herculean effort to convince him to rest properly in his bed. Even then, all he wanted to do was to hide under his blanket. He said he didn't deserve to be a part of this world. It is awfully sad to see him like this. From the look of his body, I can tell he was once a tough, strong Marine captain.

He and I have a routine now. Every day during my break at eleven-thirty, I visit him and read to him. If I don't go, he becomes very frightened. I bring him a glass of orange juice each time and he seems to like that. He is calmer when things are consistent and stable.

I wish I could do more. The doctors aren't taking his case seriously enough. They diagnosed his condition as war neurosis, or battle fatigue.

But since his condition is not life threatening, they assume he will recover on his own and they aren't doing much to help him.

Have you ever seen anything like this? Are there similar cases with the soldiers and veterans you see in London? I tried to search for information but came up with nothing. If you have any ideas or advice, please write and let me know.

On a brighter note, we finally heard from Anthony. His letters arrived earlier this week. That made Uncle William and Aunt Sophia very happy. This whole situation has been very difficult for them. It's been difficult for Uncle Leon and his family too. The house feels dreary and empty without Anthony. I don't know why that is, because he wasn't around much either while he was at the university. But now, we really feel his absence. Odd, isn't it? Uncle William and Aunt Sophia took me in to keep me safe, but they have to send their son to war. It is so unfair.

I hope you are not too lonely while Father is on tour again. Please give him my best when he returns to London. I will write again soon. I miss you both.

— Love, Tessa

She laid down the pen. Should she tell her mother she and Anthony were seeing each other? She couldn't bring herself to write about such things to her parents. What would she write? *Dear Mother, Anthony and I are now in love...*No! That would be so embarrassing. *I met a nice young man...*But she didn't meet him. She had known him for almost two years. She wondered if Uncle William and Aunt Sophia might tell them.

And her father. How could she tell him such things? He was always protective of her. He probably wouldn't take the news very well.

She glanced at the letter she wrote to Anthony.

What would they think if they knew of her plan to follow Anthony to war?

No doubt, they would be shocked. They wouldn't want her to go. Better keep that a secret for as long as possible.

She tucked the letter into her purse along with her letter to Anthony and took them to the post office.

CHAPTER SEVEN

Late afternoon one day, while Tessa was assisting with the preparations for a surgical procedure in an operating room, Sarah Brinkman came running in looking for her. "Ron Castile is demanding to see you," Sarah said. "He woke up from a nightmare and asked to see you. When we told him you were busy and couldn't come, he started throwing a fit. You need to come and calm him down."

The nurse in charge came over to them. "Can't you give him sedatives? I need Tessa's help here."

"No one could go near him," Sarah said. "He's yelling and crying. One of the attendants tried to give him a shot of sedative and he punched him."

The nurse shook her head in exasperation. "All right, go. Go."

Tessa put down the surgical equipment and followed Sarah to Ron's ward. Even in the hallway before they got to the ward's entrance, they could hear Ron shouting. Inside, a group of nurses and attendants, including Ellie, surrounded him while he cowered in a corner on the floor with his arms covering his head. Tessa pushed her way through them to Ron.

"Tessa," Ellie said. "Be careful."

Tessa ignored her and came close to him. He was hyperventilating. "Ron?"

His breathing slowed and his arms dropped slightly.

"Ron, it's me." She leaned in closer. "You asked for me. I'm here."

He lowered his arms and gazed at her. "I thought you wouldn't come back."

"What a ridiculous idea. Why wouldn't I come back? I work here." She turned her head and signaled the others to move back, then said to him, "Come on. Let's get you back in your bed." She lifted him by the arm. Still disoriented, he nonetheless got up.

In the bed, he held on to her hand. "Don't go away." He said it like a small child pleading with his parents not to leave him.

"I'm not going away. I'm right here." She let go of his hand and put a blanket over him. Quietly, Ellie handed her a needle filled with sedative. "I'm giving you a shot. Okay?" Tessa said to him. "It'll make you feel better."

Once he calmed down, the other nurses and attendant left, leaving only Ellie and Sarah with them. Moments later, the sedative started to work and Ron fell asleep.

"You're the only one he trusts," Sarah said.

"I don't understand," Tessa said. "Why me? You're a much warmer person than I am. He should've befriended you instead. Or Ellie. Ellie is nicer than me and she has more experience than either of us."

"But you were the first person to reach out to him," Ellie said. "His mind's fallen apart. You're the only constant thing he can hold on to."

Tessa sighed. Ron was deep asleep now, languishing on the bed. "I wish we knew how to treat him. How could someone who had won two purple hearts and is decorated with so many awards become so broken?"

Neither Ellie nor Sarah had any answers.

. . .

On her way out, the nurses and attendants who had been at the scene earlier were still in the hallway talking about Ron.

"... they should transfer him to a private room. He's disturbing all the other patients," one of them said.

"Or discharge him. I've never seen a grown man behave like such a crybaby," another one answered.

"They can't discharge him yet. His father's an army general. The general only has to give an order..."

Annoyed, Tessa turned the other way and left.

The events of the day had drained every last bit of energy out of Tessa. But when she returned home, she found the excitement of the day hadn't ended yet. In the parlor, she came upon the shocking sight of Aunt Sophia kneeling on the floor peeking under the sofa. She had never seen her aunt in such an unladylike position.

From under the couch, a little ball of orange fur darted out, crying, "Meow!" and jumped on top of the piano, then back on the floor and snuck under the liquor cabinet. Aunt Sophia got up and wiped the dust off the front of her trousers. "That little devil."

"Where did it come from?" Tessa asked.

"William brought her home this morning. I can't get her to come out of hiding." She kneeled down on the floor again and tried to coax the kitten to come out from beneath the liquor cabinet.

"Maybe you should let her be for a while. She'll come out when she's more familiar with this place."

"I suppose." Sophia gave up. "But I can't let her run around without supervision. What if she messes things up while I'm not looking?"

Tessa smiled and didn't say anything. Although Sophia sounded like she was complaining, Tessa could tell by the happy look on Sophia's face that what she really wanted was to play with the kitten.

"Does she have a name?" Tessa asked.

"Muffin."

"Muffin?"

"She looks like a muffin…oh, there she goes!" The kitten darted out from under the liquor cabinet and out of the parlor. Aunt Sophia ran after it. Tessa followed her to the parlor entrance and watched her chase Muffin. This was the liveliest Aunt Sophia had been since Anthony left. Uncle William sure knew the right medicine to cheer her up.

While she watched her aunt, Uncle William opened the door and walked into the house. "I'm home."

"Uncle William," Tessa greeted him.

"You're back?" Uncle William took off his coat and hung it in the coat closet.

"I don't have night class or night shift today."

"They're finally giving you an evening off, huh?" He went to the liquor cabinet and poured himself a drink. "This Cadet Nurse Program sure is demanding. I don't remember you being so busy last fall."

"Mmmm…yes…it's all right. I'm learning a lot," Tessa mumbled. She didn't want to talk about her classes or her work in case it raised any suspicions about what she had been doing at the hospital. They would be so alarmed if they found out she was training to serve overseas. She changed the subject. "You gave Aunt Sophia a cat? It's raising hell. Aunt Sophia's chasing it all over the house."

Uncle William laughed. "Is that so? I'm glad to hear it." He took a sip of his brandy. "Sounds to me like the beginning of a wonderful friendship."

"Here, kitty kitty. Here, kitty kitty…" They could hear Aunt Sophia trying to lure the kitten from the den.

"Come here," Uncle William said to her. "Sit down and tell me how you've been lately."

She took a seat next to him.

"How are you doing?" It was a casual question, but from his concerned tone, she knew what he was asking her about.

"It's hard," she said. "I miss him." She looked down to the floor.

"I know."

"It must be worse for you and Aunt Sophia."

"It's been tough on all of us," Uncle William admitted, "but your Aunt Sophia and I take a lot of comfort in knowing that you care for him."

"Me?" She looked up, puzzled. "I don't understand."

A gentle smile came onto his face. "He misses us, his parents, of course. He misses Leon and Anna too, and Katherine and Alexander. Leon, especially. They are very close. And I'm sure there are many other friends and people he misses. But I also know that far away, wherever he is, if he is feeling lonely or having a particularly bad day, and he really, really needs to think of something happy, it won't be us he'll be thinking about."

Uncle William's words were a revelation to her. She had never thought of it that way.

"One day, when they send him overseas, when he'll have to face whatever danger or disaster that comes his way, it won't be us that he'll think of to motivate himself to fight his way out."

It never occurred to her that Anthony needed her. She held her hands together, trying to understand what it all meant.

"Because he's in love with you, he has a much greater chance of staying alive. He has something to live for." He turned the glass of brandy in his hand. "Love, it's an extraordinary thing. It's a strong motivator. Of course, there's no guarantee. There are some things nobody can control, but the fact he has you waiting for him, it'll give him the inner strength to go on and come through, if it ever comes to that."

What an odd turn of events. As improbable as it was, she had become the ray of hope for everyone.

"So your Aunt Sophia and I feel very fortunate that you love him too."

Feeling awkward to admit her feelings, yet unable to deny it, she said, "I do." She thought of Anthony, his positive smile and his straightforward ways. "Very much."

Just then, Aunt Sophia came in holding Muffin in her arms. "Look! I caught the naughty little rascal." She sat down, stroking the kitten on her lap.

"Sophie," William said, "I've been thinking, now that spring's coming around, why don't we plant a garden?"

"A garden?"

"Yes. A victory garden. The ones they've been writing about in the newspapers. We can grow our own vegetables, do our part to help reserve farmed food for feeding the troops. We have a sizable yard. We can convert half of it into a vegetable garden. We might even have extras to give away."

"I like that idea," Aunt Sophia said, rubbing Muffin's head. The kitten started purring. "Anthony's in the army. It'll be a little something we can do to help with the war effort."

"Let's make it a family outing this weekend. We'll go look for seeds," Uncle William said. "Does that sound good?"

"Sounds perfect," Tessa said.

Uncle William relaxed back into the sofa, sipping on his drink. Aunt Sophia smiled at Tessa, then continued to play with Muffin.

They all missed Anthony, but life went on.

Spring was coming again.

In her room after dinner, Tessa sat on her bed and continued to search for answers in the books she had brought back from the medical library. She still hadn't found any information on Ron's afflictions other than general references to battle fatigue in psychiatric journals. Even those mentions had no information about treatment. Finding nothing that could help him in the books on battle-related syndromes, she moved on to the books on ordinary neurosis. The one she was reading now recommended electroshock, and in severe cases, lobotomy. Halfway through, she couldn't bear the ghastly descriptions anymore and closed the book. She was about to turn off the lights and sleep when the sidebar of an open page of a medical magazine caught her attention.

… Originated in China in 1368 A.D., the stress balls, also known as Baoding Balls, are used for tension relief and help relieve stress by rotating them in one hand, usually in pairs, which is believed to stimulate acupressure points in the nervous system. Stress balls can be made in flexible forms so that they can be repeatedly squeezed, held closed in the hands and released to relieve muscle tension…

She put the magazine back down and turned off the lights. *Stress balls*, she thought as she lay in bed. She wondered how Ron might react to them. She could stop by Chinatown tomorrow and buy some on her way to work.

PART III
BOOT CAMP

CHAPTER EIGHT

Fifteen miles.

They had been hiking in the mountains for fifteen miles with their full field packs on their back. Even for Anthony, this was torture. His back ached. His boots rubbed against his heels and his feet hurt.

Five more miles to go. It would be another two hours at least before they would be done. He felt so thirsty, but he was running low on water. He must reserve the little he had left and make it last.

He wished they didn't have to carry their full packs. When they went on their last twenty-mile hike, they only had to wear their gun belts, helmet liners, gas masks, and rifles. Why did they have to carry a full load today and not then? He had no idea. If there was any logical reason for how their training was conducted, he did not see it. As far as he could tell, everything was done on the whim of the noncoms in charge of their training.

And it was best not to ask why. One time, a recruit had the audacity to ask why they were carrying different loads each time they hiked. He wanted to know if there was any system or method behind it all. The recruit was only curious, but the army did not like questions. One was simply to do as he was told. As a punishment for asking, the noncom made the recruit fold and unfold his uniforms over and over again for four hours. When the recruit was finally relieved, the sergeant told him the reason he had to be punished this way was because the sergeant said so.

Since then, Anthony had learned, it was best to keep his head down and mouth shut.

Obviously, the military training program was set up to train the recruits to follow orders and to never ask questions. Every drill and exercise they did was to teach them to conform and to break down their resistance. No one could have any deviating thoughts. No one could have any individuality. They were to behave as a unit. Their actions must be uniform and predictable. They must only do as they were told. There could be no surprises.

Deviation included having special skills or being excellent. Being excellent at anything was an invitation for trouble. He had had to learn that the hard way.

Right off the bat, Sergeant Hinkle had it in for him. A career noncom officer who had risen through the ranks after he had left behind a glorious career as a kitchen appliance salesman to join the army, Hinkle had a penchant for calling all the recruits "fucking retards" and "pieces of shit." It didn't matter that Hinkle himself had never been in battle. As far as Hinkle was concerned, all recruits were pathetic ninnies who weren't real men because they hadn't been in the army for years like him. Poor him. Now he was stuck with the wretched job of whipping a bunch of milksops into shape. He must perform the impossible and turn them all into real soldiers just like him.

And he held a special contempt for Anthony.

Anthony being a university student, or more precisely, a University of Chicago student, irritated him to no end. "You're not special," Hinkle never failed to remind him. "Whatever they taught you at that hoity-toity school's got no use around here. You should be thanking your lucky stars the army made you come here instead. Now you'll learn what it takes to be a real man."

Sure. Anthony thought. A real man like him. Who wouldn't want that?

And yet, he had no choice but to put up with Hinkle. One afternoon, Hinkle came to their barracks looking for him. "Ardley. Does that fancy school of yours teach you people anything about art?"

Unsure of why he asked, Anthony made the mistake of being honest. "Yes."

"Good. Let's see you do some painting then. We might as well put your education to use."

Next thing Anthony knew, Hinkle had made him spend the entire rest of the day painting the laundry room's walls. Painting the walls would have been fine, except what he had to paint with was not a paint brush for wall painting, but a small artist's brush for watercolor painting like the brushes Tessa used in her art studio.

It wasn't only his education. The fact that Anthony didn't smoke was a problem. That Anthony didn't curse like the rest of them was another problem. By Hinkle's standard, he could do no right. It was a no-win situation.

Having to put up with Hinkle was a special kind of hell of its own.

"… so I got her right where I wanted," Hinkle chortled while gloating about his previous night's conquest at the noncom officers' table in the mess hall. "And let me tell you, she's got a fine pair of titties. You scum would never get your hands onto boobies like that. Not in your wildest dreams…" The more he talked, the more excited he got. His voice was so loud, everyone could hear him. All Anthony wanted to do was to finish eating and get out of there.

"The way those titties bounced, I tell ya, it got me all hot and going. So I pushed her down and…hey, Ardley!"

Anthony cringed.

"What the fuck is wrong with your face? You look like you're gonna puke. What's the matter with you? You don't like girls?"

Anthony kept his face straight and didn't answer.

Hinkle got up from his seat and came over to him. With Anthony sitting down, Hinkle, all five-foot-five of him, hovered over Anthony. "You got a problem?"

"No, sir."

"Fuck, you need to man up, you lousy scum. Get up. Give me fifty push-ups, now!"

Anthony got up and did as he ordered. As unfair as this was, it was better than listening to Hinkle's obscene, dirty talk. Hinkle stood in front of him, clearly enjoying having his feet just inches away from Anthony's face.

"We'll make a man out of you yet, Ardley," Hinkle said while his fellow officers chuckled.

When Anthony finished, he stood up at attention, hoping to be dismissed so he could get away. Hinkle wrinkled his eyes and scrutinized him. "Where's your button?"

Anthony frowned. What was Hinkle talking about?

"Where's your button?" Hinkle poked him at the top of the chest.

Anthony looked at where Hinkle was pointing. A button was missing. It must have fallen off somewhere.

"How many times do I have to tell you people to follow the dress code? What am I? Your mother? How dare you show up dressing like a bum? This is the army, not your bedroom. Don't they teach you any respect at that snooty school of yours? Huh? Goddamn it. That's it. You're going to be the one to cut the grass today. Report to me after lunch."

"Yes, sir." Whatever. Cut grass. Sure. He could mow the lawns.

Or that was what he thought until he got to the field. Hinkle handed him a small pair of scissors. "I want all the grass on this field trimmed nice and neat."

Anthony held the scissors. Trim the grass with these? He looked at the field.

"Fucking faggot," Hinkle sneered and walked away.

And so went the days at Camp Dover. It did not pay to be someone with a superior educational background.

Or, one could say, being excellent in any way was a gift that kept on giving. One time, he accidentally showed he was excellent and dearly paid the price.

An army general had come to camp that day for an inspection. For once, the noncoms had all put on their best behavior. Anthony had hoped Hinkle might be distracted enough to give him a break, but he should've known better.

"I expect each and every one of you to perform to the best of your abilities," Hinkle hollered before the obstacle course race. "If any of you screw up and embarrass me before the general, you'll all pay for it tomorrow. Twenty-four-mile hike up the mountains, full pack. You all got that?"

Yes, they got it. Underperform, and there would be hell to pay.

But the other groups must all have gotten the same warning. Anthony had never seen the recruits take an inter-camp competition so seriously. His own unit was performing well, but others could edge them out anytime.

"Not looking forward to that twenty-four-mile hike tomorrow," someone in his unit said.

"We're doing fine," he told the others.

"I'm not so optimistic," another recruit chimed in. The units were running against each other neck-and-neck.

When his turn came, all Anthony could think of was to not let his unit down. He would not be the cause for everyone to have to do an all day hike carrying their heaviest load. With that thought in mind, he dashed through the track and came to the six-foot high wall. He jumped, grabbed the top and hauled himself over to land on the other side, then crawled through the mud field. Approaching the end of the field, he grabbed the rope hanging before him and climbed up. He was pulling so fast, his arms burned. The roughness of the rope scraped his hands, but he couldn't worry about that now. After reaching the top, he lowered himself back down, ran past the hurdles ahead and through puddles of water and mud. He felt like a thousand pins were stinging his thighs. By the time he reached the monkey bars, his legs were heavy as lead, weighing him down as he swung from one bar to the next. His entire core hurt.

One last obstacle to go. He focused on that thought to turn his mind off from the pain. Back on the ground again, he hopped onto the log, doing his best to concentrate and not lose his balance even though his legs now jellied. As he came to the end of the course, the recruits in his units who had finished before him were all shouting and cheering him on. He didn't know why they were so excited, but for a brief moment, he felt like he was back at school at a swimming competition.

"Ardley, Ardley," one of the recruits yelled out to him after he crossed the finish line. "You broke the time record!"

He did? He had no idea. But it sure felt good. His fellow recruits surrounded him and congratulated him. He thanked them, but more than feeling victorious, he was glad he probably saved everyone from the prospect of a twenty-four-mile hike.

On the far end of the obstacle training course, the army general was staring at them. Major General Frank Castile. He had come to inspect the camp's training operations. Anthony could feel the man's imposing presence even from where he stood. Castile remained for only a brief moment before he was driven away.

Meanwhile, his good feelings from winning the obstacle race lasted only until they returned to their barracks.

"Great job, Ardley. Great job." Hinkle said as he swaggered in. "A job well done."

Although Hinkle was giving him praises, from the sarcastic tone of his voice, Anthony knew he was in trouble. The only thing he did not know was what kind of trouble.

"Everyone, let's give Private Ardley a round of applause for showing the other units what real soldiers are capable of. Private Ardley sure did us proud today, didn't he?"

The barrack turned silent. No one dared say a word.

"Well, aren't you proud, Ardley?" Hinkle came up close to him.

"No, sir."

"You're not proud then? You're not proud our unit won?"

"Yes, sir. Of course I'm proud, sir."

"Ah, I see. You are proud. You think you're better than the rest of us?"

"No, sir."

"No? You're sure about that?"

"I'm sure, sir."

"Good. That's good. Then you'll take one for the team, right?"

"Yes, sir."

"Very well. You can report for latrine duty tonight. I'm sure your fellow soldiers would thank you for saving them from having to clean up after the tough race today. We all need a good night's rest, don't we? Now we know we can count on you." Hinkle smirked and left.

Latrine duty, Anthony thought. The job that nobody wanted and one that he could do without. He took a deep breath and fell back on his bed.

As if that wasn't bad enough, when he showed up for the miserable task, the noncom in charge gave him a toothbrush and a piece of soap. "Sergeant Hinkle's order," the noncom said.

He took one look at the toilets. The place was beyond filthy. Everything stunk. How was he supposed to clean these? He threw the toothbrush against the wall.

When he got back to the barracks, he had made up his mind he would never outperform anyone or show excellence in any way again.

Do not be exceptional. Do not distinguish yourself. Be mediocre. Be ordinary. If that was what the army wanted, that was what the army would get. He was sick and tired of all the pointless punishments with small tools.

To his own surprise, being mediocre didn't turn out to be such a bad thing after all. All his life, people had expected him to do great things. His swimming coached had wanted him to be the team captain. Uncle Leon had wanted him to lead America First on campus. His father had wanted him to take over their family business. When he was drafted, everyone at home treated him like a hero, even though he hadn't the faintest clue what the army was about and he hadn't fought a single battle. He had always tried to live up to what they wanted of him. He couldn't disappoint the people he loved.

For the first time, the world wanted him to do less, not more. Here, no one wanted anything from him. He didn't have to think. He didn't have to carry anyone's hopes. All he had to do was to follow orders.

A new path opened before him like an epiphany. What did he care anyway? He never wanted a military career. Why did he have to be good at anything? From now on, he would strive to be the least he could be.

A weight of burden fell off him. Happy, he sat back in his bunk and began reading the copy of Timely Comic's *Human Torch* someone had left in the next bunk.

CHAPTER NINE

THE CALIFORNIA DESERT sun beat down on the recruits as they repeated another round of target practice. Sitting on the ground as the temperature approached the high nineties, Anthony waited for his next turn. He felt hot and tired. He didn't feel like moving another inch, let alone getting up to shoot his gun.

"You think we can fry eggs on our helmets?" the recruit next to him asked. Anthony glanced at the recruit, too dispirited and weary to laugh at his joke.

His group had left Camp Dover more than a week ago. The noncoms had selected his squad to come out here for a training excursion. Why here? As usual, no one gave them any explanation. They simply had to endure it.

He loathed this place and so did everyone else. Compared to where they were now, Camp Dover was as good as a luxury hotel. This place was dead. Dry, hot, and dead. Not a single sign of life could be found anywhere, but this was the place where they were told to stay. No information was given on when they could leave either.

Who came up with these plans anyway? Why must they train in this oven? Did some bored bureaucrat dream this up for no reason other than to amuse himself by making them miserable?

When it was his turn to shoot, Anthony mustered every ounce of strength he could and pulled himself up to perform the task. Drenched in sweat, his shirt stuck to his back and his armpits felt wet. His hair was soaked inside his helmet too, but taking it off would be worse with the sun smoldering above.

Standing in line with the other recruits, he aimed his rifle. Don't deviate, he reminded himself. Be mediocre like everybody else. It was the army way. The only way.

He pulled the trigger. The bullet hit two inches north of the bulls-eye.

When target practice finally came to an end, the recruits could not wait to head back to their tents. Without being told, they all lined up in formation, wanting nothing more than to finish and leave to get some rest. Hinkle, though, had a different agenda. Hinkle wasn't satisfied with their performance. Not at all.

The blistering heat, the drudgery, the mind-numbing repetitions of all their drills and routines, the grueling training, the annoying noncom officers making their lives hell. It finally got to everybody. They had all reached their limit. This was the worst target practice they had ever had. No one did well.

Anthony himself had performed worse than usual. For the first time since coming here, Anthony received the "fail" grade. During the first round, he made an honest attempt to hit his own intended spots off the mark. As the day dragged on and the sun began to burn, he gave up. He made his shots without caring what results he would get. He only wanted the day to end.

"This kind of lazing off is not acceptable! Not acceptable! Do you all hear me?" Hinkle hollered. "How are you going to fight a war like this? You lazy scum! The Gerrys and the Japs will eat you alive. You are all a national disgrace!"

Why couldn't he stop shouting? Anthony wondered in exhaustion. How could this buffoon still have so much energy after spending the entire day out here? It was unbelievable.

"Ardley!"

What now? Anthony winced at the call of his name.

"Your regression was the worst. You'll handle target duty on your own today."

That was enough to make Anthony almost utter a curse word. Now he had to stay in this goddamned place even longer.

But Hinkle wasn't through. "You all see that?" He turned to the rest of the group. "If you don't keep up with your practices, if I see any of you screw around like this again, there will be punishment. I will not allow you people to treat training like a game. This is not child's play."

Anthony watched the trucks drive everyone else away and began to clean up the practice area. What choice did he have? He picked up the targets one by one and rebuilt the target line stations for the next practice session. When he finished, he checked his watch. With the time it would take for the unit to get back to their tent, a jeep likely wouldn't return to pick him up for another half an hour. He sat down and took a drink of water from his canteen. The water quenched his thirst but he wished it wasn't so warm. How he missed having ice. He swore he would never take ice for granted again.

He closed the cap of the canteen and stared mindlessly at the target station. A sudden inspiration overcame him. Up to this point, he had always aimed to miss. What if he were to try to hit the target itself?

He reloaded his rifle and positioned himself two-hundred and fifty feet in front of the line.

At practice, he had almost got it down to an art how to intentionally miss, or near miss. In fact, nine times out of ten, he could hit his own intended targets as opposed to the ones he was supposed to hit.

He aimed at the first target and pulled the trigger. Bull's-eye.

He aimed at the second target, then the third, and the fourth, hitting the mark on each of them until he demolished the entire line. He walked back to the station and lined up a second set of targets. This time, he walked back further and positioned himself at five hundred feet, then aimed and shot again. He hit the mark on all except one, and even that one barely missed.

Great shots. He could do this. If the army wasn't run by morons like Hinkle, he might put in some real effort. With the way everything was run, the U.S. Army probably wouldn't even win this war. But what could he do? He was nothing but a lowly grunt. If the army preferred incompetent people, then fine. Their loss.

A jeep pulled up behind him. Thank God. His ride was here. He turned around. To his surprise, sitting beside the driver was Major General Castile. Immediately, he straightened up and stood at attention.

Castile got out of the jeep. For a man in his fifties, he was exceptionally fit with a steely build. His full head of silver hair made him look younger than his age while lending him an air of distinction.

The general sauntered over to the target station. He eyed each of the shot targets, then looked Anthony once over. Anthony stood still as the Army had trained him to do. Nonetheless, the general's intimidating presence unnerved him.

"Tell me, Private," Castile said. "I've been coming off and on to watch you all practice for several days now. Did you suddenly acquire an expert level of shooting skills? Or have you been faking your shots all along, playing your officers for fools?"

"No, sir."

"Then how do you explain this?" Castile looked at the targets.

"Luck, sir. Dumb luck," Anthony said, hoping his answer would be enough.

"Luck? Are you playing me for a fool too?"

"No, sir!"

Castile moved closer. Anthony wondered how he could get himself out of this. He thought the general might punish him, but instead, Castile backed off. "I know what you're doing." Castile walked to the spot five hundred feet from the target line. "I know what you're all doing and all your little shenanigans to get past Hinkle, that sorry excuse of a captain." He mumbled the last part of what he said.

Anthony couldn't believe his ears. The general had just openly criticized a captain in front of him, a mere private. He stole a glance at Castile, who looked annoyed at the thought of Hinkle.

"Line up the targets again," Castile ordered.

"Yes, sir." Anthony did as he said.

"Is your rifle loaded?"

"Yes."

"Give it to me."

Anthony handed him the gun. Castile grabbed it and aimed. "Gonna do some target practice myself." Before Anthony could react, Castile fired the bullets in rapid speed, hitting all the targets without a miss. Anthony's ears rang from the successive blasting sounds of the gunshots, but he dared not move.

"That felt good." Castile handed the rifle back to Anthony. "I've been watching you. Don't you think for a minute I don't know exactly what is going on."

Anthony held on to his gun. The general was making him feel very, very small.

"Where are you from, Private Ardley?" Castile asked.

"Chicago, sir. Evanston just outside of Chicago."

"Chicago." Castile raised his eyebrows. "What do you know? I'm from Chicago. I'll be heading back there in a couple of weeks." He looked out into the distance at the desert. "Got some unpleasant business to take care of," he muttered under his breath, more to himself than to Anthony. Anthony wondered how much longer he had to remain here in this uncomfortable situation.

Castile looked at the targets. "I see thousands of men in training every day. Not everybody is gifted. It's rare to be gifted." He came close to Anthony. "You know how good you are, don't you?"

Anthony didn't feel right answering one way or another.

"Or maybe you don't know. If you don't know, would you push yourself to find out? See if you can stand head and shoulders above the rest?"

Stand above the rest? He thought the whole point of their military training was to blend in.

"Or would you waste everything you got that others don't, all because you hold a grudge against a little man like Hinkle? You can't take a little insult? Is that all it takes to stop you?"

Now the general was making him feel petty.

"Is Hinkle going to define who you are?"

Hinkle? Of course not! But...Anthony lowered his head. He did let go because of Hinkle. At home, he achieved because of his family, teachers, and coaches. Here, he underachieved because of Hinkle. He had let everyone else define him except him.

"Next week," Castile said, looking directly at Anthony, "All you recruits will be taking the Army General Classification Test. Assuming your scores will meet the requirements, Private, I'm going to personally recommend you to the OCS after you're through with basic training."

"The OCS…"

"Officer Candidates School. I came to scout for candidates to train to become commissioned officers."

Stunned, Anthony didn't know what to say. He didn't know he was being observed. He never thought someone from the army would notice anything special about him, not after what he had been experiencing all this time since boot camp started.

"Keep up your training and finish your time here," Castile said. "When you're done, the OCS is the next place where I want you to be."

Anthony stood still. He hadn't thought at all about moving up the rank, but he dared not show any excitement, as Castile warned him, "Don't disappoint me." The general looked stern and dead serious. "You'll do yourself a favor to remember I don't take disappointment kindly. When you take that test, I don't want to see any of this faking and underperforming monkey business. I want to see what you're really made of."

Ashamed to have been caught in the act, Anthony almost forgot to respond until Castile glared at him. "Yes, sir."

"Now clean all this up and get into the car," Castile said and walked away. Anthony hustled to clear the target station, then climbed into the back of the jeep. The general didn't say anything more on their way back, so neither did he nor the driver.

Approaching camp, he hoped Hinkle wouldn't be there to see them when they returned. He couldn't believe he was riding in the same vehicle with a general. If Hinkle saw him and thought he was getting special treatment, that nitwit would make him pay dearly later for sure.

Wait. Why did he care what Hinkle thought?

What was he really made of? He didn't know. So preoccupied with doing what others wanted of him all his life, he never thought to stop to find out.

The OCS. Maybe now was his chance.

Back in his tent after supper, Anthony sat on his cot and turned on his flashlight. His tent mate was already asleep and snoring like a hog. Quietly, he took out a notebook and a pen from his duffle bag. He opened the cover of the notebook where he kept the photo of him and Tessa taken by the Christmas tree at the Museum of Science and Industry. The theme for the tree's decorations was Christmas Around the World. The tree was a beacon of hope and peace. Smiling, he ran his finger over Tessa's face, then put the photo back inside and began to write her a letter.

CHAPTER TEN

March 12, 1943

Dear Tessa,

I'm now in the California desert on a training excursion away from Camp Dover. We are camped out here, not in barracks but in tents. We have no light and no bed. I'm sitting on my cot holding my flashlight and it is very hard to write, but I don't want you to think that I've forgotten about you. I won't be able to send this letter until I return to Camp Dover. By then I'll be sending you all the letters that I've written since we got to this God-forsaken place. It's so hot and dry here.

A general came to me today and told me he will recommend me for Officers Training School after I finish basic training. You know something? I'm actually quite excited about it. The OCS training program is three months long. If I complete the program without fail, I will be assigned a second lieutenant ranking. Mother and Father will be happy to hear about that, don't you think?

I really want to think of you more often but sometimes it's very hard. To me, you are everything that is beautiful in the world. I don't like to mix up memories and images of you with the ugly, dreary views of the desert here.

Don't be too bothered by your patients thinking you're a cold person. For me, I'm happy to know your patients call you the Ice Queen. That way, I know they are not trying to come after you when I'm not there. Anyway, it gets so miserably hot here every day, I would love myself an Ice Queen right now.

When you send me letters from now on, will you spray your letter with your rose perfume? I long to hold something that makes me feel like you're right by my side.

I'm going to sleep now. I miss you.

— *Love, Anthony*

IN HER BED, Tessa finished reading the letter and put it next to her pillow. Now, she could feel his presence next to her all night.

He said he was in a desert. She wondered where.

Officer Candidates School? Of course. Anthony was smart and strong. It didn't surprise her someone would pick him out from the pack. No doubt, he would make an excellent lieutenant.

And he would look so good in an officer's uniform.

She put her fingers to her lips to hide her silly smile.

Today was a good day. Not only did she receive Anthony's letter, her mother's letter had arrived too.

March 2, 1943

Dear Tessa,

I am so sad to hear Anthony has been called to service. I had been worrying about that, and now it has happened. I wish I could come at once to America and be there with you all, especially William and Sophia. As a mother myself, my heart goes out to them. I cannot imagine what Sophia must be going through right now. I hope my letter to them will offer some words of comfort.

And Leon? How is he holding up? He must be so upset. I shall write to him too. You were too young to know this, but after Anthony

Browning passed away and then Lex died in the Great War, a part of Leon was destroyed. For a long time, he lived with a wounded heart. He was still that way when I left America. But William told me young Anthony had filled the void that left him feeling so empty, and having Anthony around had made up somewhat for the losses he had suffered. Anthony being drafted must be very hard for him to take. With the memory of what had happened to Lex, Leon must be worried sick. Please watch over Leon for me if you can. Be there for him as I would.

As for Ron, the patient you wrote to me about, I think the medical establishment here in Great Britain may have more experience dealing with his condition. The Great War has had a much greater impact on everyone in Europe. His condition is not unheard of. Your colleagues have correctly diagnosed it as battle fatigue. During the Great War, the condition was known as shell shock. In 1917, a doctor named Arthur Hurst pioneered a treatment programme at the Seale Hayne Agricultural College to treat soldiers suffering from this illness. He persuaded the government to convert the College into a hospital. I've gathered for you copies of journal articles detailing records of his patients and the results of his treatments. He recorded his patients and his films have been very useful for educating the public and persuading the government to provide help to the patients with this condition.

I wish you could see the footage. I have watched the films. His treatments included something he called "occupational therapy," which was giving the patients jobs to do to reorient them to normal life. He also did a fair amount of therapy sessions using hypnosis and sometimes, reenactment of the traumatic events. I asked Dr. Lawrence and Dr. Mansfield what they thought. (You remember them, don't you? They asked about you. They are very pleased to hear you have joined the nursing profession. They send you their regards and wish you good luck.) Anyway, they suggested you experiment with occupational therapy and give your patient a work routine so he can have some sense of normality. For his phantom pain, hypnosis or massage therapy are possible options. You can find more information in the articles I am sending you.

I know you are doing all you can. The best way to help him is to be compassionate and find ways to make him feel safe. Above all, don't forget to treat him with dignity. It's what all patients need.

Your father and I are very proud of you. He is on tour again. His troupe has been traveling incessantly to perform for the soldiers all around the country. I know he will try to write to you whenever he can, but it may be hard while he is traveling.

Let me know if your patient makes any progress. Take care of your Uncle William, Aunt Sophia, and Uncle Leon for me.

— Love, Mother

Occupational therapy. That was worth trying. The hospital wouldn't object to that. There must be something Ron could do in the hospital. Maybe she and Ellie could think of something together.

The journal articles her mother had sent her looked helpful too. They were in-depth analyses of battle neurosis. She had found nothing like these in their own medical library. Tomorrow, she must show these articles to Dr. Donovan.

She put the letter away in the drawer of the nightstand, then turned off the lights and lay down on her side.

Take care of your Uncle William, Aunt Sophia, and Uncle Leon for me.

Yes. She must do that. They miss Anthony so much, and they were so worried about him going to war. Most of the time, they couldn't even talk about it.

Maybe she should spend Saturday afternoon with Aunt Sophia and listen to the radio with her. She hadn't done that in a while.

Please watch over Leon for me if you can. Be there for him as I would.

Be there for Uncle Leon. She would, for as long as she could, but this could not be if she had it her own way. She wanted to be there for Anthony.

When Anthony completed his training and was assigned, she

would do everything she could to join him. She had already looked into how the army departments were organized, which offices handled military assignments, and whom she might be able to contact. Being a nurse for the veterans paid off too. Those boys who had returned home sure gossiped a lot, but they were a fountain of information. They told her more than she could ever have discovered on her own how to reach the army officials who were in charge.

She would do this. She would go to Anthony, no matter how hard she must try.

PART IV
THE SHELL-SHOCKED PATIENT

CHAPTER ELEVEN

"Good morning, Ron." Tessa came by for her daily visit with Ron Castile during her morning break. His face brightened the minute he saw her. She noticed the stress balls in his hand. Since receiving this gift, he had not had any more episodes of hysteria. That little device had helped him.

The information her mother had sent her about Arthur Hurst's experiments helped too. They piqued Dr. Donovan's interest. After reading the medical journal articles Tessa had given him, Donovan's attitude changed a hundred and eighty degrees, and he decided Ron would be his prize patient for potentially pioneering a field of medical treatments for veterans in the United States. Tessa was thankful for that. Whatever Dr. Donovan's motivation might be, at least the medical staff was now taking Ron's condition seriously and was trying to help him recover from his illness.

One of the ways they attempted to treat Ron was occupational therapy, which Arthur Hurst had tried. The job they gave him was easy. They assigned him to help the kitchen staff distribute meals to the other patients during lunch. His "work" became part of a routine they had prescribed for him. The routine also included Tessa's daily visit and his daily afternoon walk. With his life now more stable and his focus away from the war, he had shown a marked improvement. He could now interact with people. He still had nightmares, but those had become less frequent. When the nightmares woke him, he knew to calm himself with the stress balls and ring for help without causing a scene.

But his deepest wounds remained. He still complained of back and hip pains no matter how many times they had explained to him he had no back or hip injuries. When they said his pains were not real, he would become distraught and fall back into depression. As they could not give him medications nor perform surgeries for imaginary pains, no one knew how to treat this problem. All they could do was to arrange for a physiotherapist to give him weekly massages.

His case, thus, continued to be a challenge.

"How are you today?" Tessa gave him a glass of orange juice as usual.

"I'm doing good. How are you?"

"I'm fine, thank you." She handed him a book. "Look what I brought you today."

He took it and looked at the book's title. *A Scandal in Bohemia.*

"It's one of my favorites. I think you'll like it."

"Thank you. I've never read Sherlock Holmes before." He turned the pages.

Their conversation was interrupted when all of a sudden, the other patients stirred and the room turned quiet. Dr. Donovan entered with a tough and steely-built man in military uniform and several nurses and attendants behind them. The man commanded everyone's attention as soon as he walked in. Despite his white hair, he moved as briskly as any man half his age. His presence had an immediate impact on everyone. Those who could move stood up. Even the ones who could not move their legs but had upper body mobility straightened up in their beds. Only those who were too sick, asleep, or sedated by medicine stayed as they were.

Ron's face turned ghastly white at the sight of the man.

"Ron, are you all right?" Tessa asked, nonplussed. Ron didn't answer.

"Holy Bejeezus," Tommy Ross in the next bed whispered to her. "It's Major General Frank Castile."

"Major general?"

The distinguished man approached her and Ron while ignoring all the other patients. Ron tightened his fist around the stress balls.

"Do you know him?" Tessa asked Ron.

"My father..." Ron said. His voice was meek and barely audible.

"Your father?" Tessa asked. "He's come to see you then? That's wonderful."

But Ron shook his head. His expression turned more and more agitated.

"What's wrong?"

Before Ron could answer, the general was standing before them. Tessa politely stepped aside.

"Captain," the general said to Ron.

Ron did not answer but stared at him.

"Why are you still in the hospital?" The general glanced at Ron from head to foot. "I don't see any injury on you. What are you here for?"

Ron inhaled and took a deep shaky breath, then lowered his eyes and looked away. "My nerves."

The general glowered at him.

"The war..." Ron's voice quivered. "I couldn't take it anymore."

Before anyone could see it coming, the general raised his arm and slapped Ron hard on the face. Ellie, who had come in with the nurses following Dr. Donovan, covered her mouth while the other nurses and attendants gasped. Ron's cheek turned scarlet red.

"Nerves?" the general shouted. "Nerves?" He pointed at the rest of the patients in the room. "Look at these men here. Look at the ones who lost their limbs and how their bodies were shattered. Do you know how many millions of men are out there in battles right now, risking their lives? And you're hiding here because of nerves?"

Ron squinted his eyes and teared up, but the general was not moved. "Do you know how many parents are sacrificing their sons to the front line, while you, my own son, are hiding here because you can't take it anymore? You coward. You're a total disgrace," he roared and raised his arm again.

Without thinking, Tessa threw herself in front of Ron. All she knew was she had to shield and protect him.

"Tessa!" Ellie screamed, while Dr. Donovan and the other patients watched in horror.

The general caught his arm just in time before he brought his hand down on her. He, too, looked as shocked as everyone else. Seeing Tessa throwing herself in front of Ron threw him into a momentary state of confusion.

"Move away, nurse," he said when he regained his composure. "This is none of your business."

"No." Tessa glared at him. She felt as angry as the general looked. "I won't let you hurt him."

"He's my son and a soldier under my command. I can discipline him if I want to," he said, although his voice wavered slightly as he sized Tessa up.

"And he's my patient," she stared him in the eye in defiance. "It's my duty to protect him."

Taken aback, the general observed her more closely. Tessa felt as if the man was reading her, but she refused to back down. The general took a step toward her. She thought he might strike again and squeezed her eyes shut.

"Then do your job right and fix him," the general hollered. His thunderous voice boomed in her ear.

He then left them and marched toward the exit. As he passed by Dr. Donovan, he said, "I give you one week to cure and discharge him."

The entire room was stunned into silence. Cowering in his bed,

Ron cried. Tessa grabbed his hand and held it as the general walked away.

Ron fell into a helpless state of depression after his father left, crying uncontrollably in the corner of the room on the floor next to his bed. Nothing could calm him. No one could coax him out. Dr. Donovan decided to give him a shot of sedative to make him fall asleep. "We'll review and discuss his case tomorrow morning," the doctor told the nurses and attendants.

After the staff left, Tessa pulled the blanket further up over Ron's shoulders and tucked him in. Even asleep, his face showed such anguish.

One week. How could he possibly recover in one week?

The next morning, when she came to make her morning round, she found Ron back on the floor. The vacant look in his eyes had returned. All the progress they had made had been wiped out.

"Ron?" She kneeled down next to him. "Ron, are you all right?"

He didn't respond. He languished there without an ounce of vigor.

"Would you please come back into the bed?" Tessa shoved him lightly.

"I can't move." His lips drooped and tightened. He was about to cry again. "My back and hip hurt so much."

"It won't get any better by you lying on the floor," she said. "Please. Let me help you. Please stand up. Do it for me? Please?"

He nodded while trying to hold back his tears. She grabbed his arm and helped him up. When he stood up, his waist twisted in an odd way that made his hip protrude to the left side and his body contorted as he walked. Tessa's heart sank as she helped him back into bed. He was now even worse than when they started.

At least Dr. Donovan still cared. She had worried he might give up after what had happened yesterday.

"I've been contacting doctors in veterans hospitals in other states these last few weeks," he said to Tessa, Ellie, and Sarah later in his office. "Ron Castile isn't the only one suffering from severe battle neurosis. I sent them copies of the journal articles Tessa gave me. There are people who would like to help patients with this syndrome."

Tessa was happy and surprised to hear that, considering Dr. Donovan's initial resistance to her request for help. There was even a tone of genuine concern in his voice which was not there when he first agreed to try to seriously treat Ron. Perhaps he had come to care more about Ron after spending weeks trying to help him.

"The problem is, none of the veterans hospitals is equipped to provide the proper treatment," Donovan continued. "We don't have the right resources. Personally, I would like to do what Hurst did, set up a specialized department for treating battle fatigue here in our hospital, but I highly doubt the military or the government would give us the funding we need. You saw the general's reaction. I don't know how to convince the military this is a real war-related illness that requires medical attention."

"If you could open a specialized department," Ellie said, "what would you do?"

"Well," Donovan said, "I would begin a small pioneer program and arrange to transfer a group of patients with this condition to us. We could put them under close observation, document their symptoms. We would try out different experimental treatment methods and record the results. Then we would have concrete data to present our case to change people's minds and expand treatment to even more people." He sounded as enthusiastic as if he had set up the program already. "But of course, even a small program would still need funding, and we don't have that." He took off his glasses and his eyes showed his disappointment.

Tessa knew how they could solve that problem. "Doctor, if I may...there is a possible source of funding. My family is a long-time supporter of the Chicago Hospital. Maybe they would be interested."

"Really?" Donovan straightened up in his seat.

"I can't guarantee it, but I can ask."

"That would be fantastic," Ellie said. "And I'd be happy to volunteer my time beyond my work hours and classes to help."

"Me too," Sarah said.

Encouraged, Donovan smiled, but then looked troubled again. "Even if we can get the program started, it won't help Ron. General Castile wants him released next week."

"That brute." The thought of that nasty man made Tessa angry all over again. "Doctor, he can't be serious. You can see Ron is not well. Do you have to release him?"

"We can't go against his family's wishes," Donovan said. "Ron doesn't have any physical injuries to justify us keeping him here. Unless we can convince the general to change his mind, my hands are tied."

Frustrated, Tessa tried to think of a solution. Any solution. She glanced around Donovan's office and noticed one of the articles about Arthur Hurst on the desk. The article had a black and white photo of Hurst filming one of his patients. "Maybe…" she said. Thoughts raced through her mind as she tried to grasp the scheme forming in her head. "Maybe…if we can show the general that Ron really is sick. What if…," she picked up the article she was staring at, "what if we take photos of Ron when he is in a state of paralysis, like when he won't get up from the floor? Or maybe we can film him?" She looked at Donovan, Ellie, and Sarah. "What if we show him Ron does have physical problems? Ron says he can't walk, and it's true. He can't. Ever since that brute's visit, Ron's body has been all contorted every time he tries to walk. I've never seen anything like it. It's painful looking at him. If we can show Ron in his worst state, maybe we can persuade his father this is not a simple case of Ron being afraid and unwilling to fight."

Donovan reclined in his seat and considered the suggestion. "It's worth a try. We've got nothing to lose."

"Can we invite the general back to see for himself in person?" Sarah asked.

"After the awful confrontation they had yesterday?" Ellie asked. "It's probably not a good idea. We don't want to upset Ron again. It's better if we photograph him," Ellie said. "But how would we be able to film him?"

Tessa crossed her arms. If she was back in London, this would have been easy. Her father or someone in his theater troupe could easily arrange that. They knew people in the movie industry.

In the industry…She glanced over at Sarah. "Sarah! Your father works in advertising, doesn't he? Would he know anyone in advertising who has access to recording equipment?"

"I don't know," Sarah said. "He might. I'll ask him."

There was hope after all. "Tell him this is very important and ask him to inquire with as many people as he can until we can find someone who can help."

"Sure. I'll do my best."

They could do no more for now. Tessa prayed everything would work out. For better or for worse, she had taken it upon herself to help Ron. Because of that, she had become the only one he trusted. She felt responsible for him. Besides, he was a nice person. On his good days, he was always polite and respectful. A perfect gentleman. She couldn't imagine that only recently, he had been at war in combat. She didn't want him to remain in that dark place in his mind.

CHAPTER TWELVE

April 5, 1943

Dear Tessa,

This is the last letter I'll be writing to you from Camp Dover. Tomorrow, I'll be heading to the Officer Candidates School (the OCS) at Fort Benning, Georgia. I can't tell you how glad I am training camp is over. It was not the most pleasant experience for sure. I suppose war won't be a pleasant experience either, so maybe I better get used to misery being a permanent state of things. Still, I hope the OCS will be an improvement. I've been reading books on military strategies and battle tactics in my spare time. Being an army officer and leading a unit of men in war situations is a serious job. I've never done anything where people's lives depended on me. I want to be ready. I want to prove to myself that I can do this.

I got a three-day pass this past weekend. It was a godsend to be able to get away from training camp and back into the civilian world. I joined some fellas who also had passes and we hitched a ride into L.A. again. One of my deepest regrets about the OCS is that I won't be serving in the same unit with these guys when my training is over. We've formed a close bond at Camp Dover. When I complete my OCS training, they will have moved on, and I'll likely be assigned to another unit. Even if by chance we end up in the same unit, things wouldn't be the same because officers are not allowed to fraternize with enlisted soldiers, so this really was the last weekend I could spend with them.

Like last time, we went to see a movie and visited the USO Center for our free meals. We went to some bars too. (Some of them were Irish pubs like Murphy's and I wished you were there with me.) We were having a good time but one of the guys insisted there was a famous cocktail lounge that was the ultimate place to be. He heard movie stars go there and insisted we must go, so we went, except we never found the place. He either remembered the name of the place wrong or he got the streets and address confused. We walked around the streets for a long time looking for it but never found it. Eventually, it got very late and we went back to our hotel.

On Saturday night, the fellas decided to go to a dance club. I had never gone to dance clubs back in Chicago. It wasn't something my friends and I did. The closest I came to being in one was the time when I saw you at the Melody Mill. The dance club we went to was way bigger than the Melody Mill. There must have been a mass of over a thousand people inside and the place was very cramped. Everyone tried to dance but I couldn't even get through the crowd. I was squished every which way I turned. People spilled drinks all over each other and the music blasted so loud we had to scream at each other to be heard. There were many servicemen there, even some foreign ones. Later on, one of our boys got very drunk and I had to leave to take him back because all the other guys were talking to girls (I didn't) and wanted to stay. That was all right. By then, I had had enough of the noise and the crowd.

Sunday we hung out at the USO center because the place was buzzing with rumor that Katharine Hepburn would come by for a surprise visit with the troops. She showed up early in the afternoon. It was quite something to see her. She was even more beautiful in person than in the movies, and she was very nice and gracious, signing autographed photos for all of us. It was a huge morale boost for everyone. In the end though, L.A. has a tad too much excitement and glamour for a Midwestern boy like me. I rather prefer the weekend I had when I came here four weeks ago, when I went to the beach. I thought about you, about us, when I looked at the ocean. The ocean was so beautiful. The world is a beautiful place. I can't wait for the day when we can put the world's worries aside, and you and I can be alone and listen to the ocean waves.

What I really wish is that the weekend passes could've been longer. Then I could come home and spend time with you instead.

I received all your letters from the last two weeks. Thanks for sending me photos of you too as I asked. Seeing you, Jack, Henry, and Ruby at Marconi's made me very hungry for Italian beef! I'm so envious.

But will you please send me a pocket size photo of you alone like I've been asking? Otherwise, I'll have to cut out everyone else from one of the photos you sent me just so I can have a picture of you to keep in my pocket.

How is everything going for you at the hospital? You never tell me anything about your work. I hope it's not because the work is too much for you. Take care of yourself. Don't work too hard.

I love you and miss you.

— *Love, Anthony*

ALONE IN HER room late at night, Tessa kissed the letter she received from Anthony and read parts of it again. He always asked her about her work, but her work was the last thing she wanted to talk about with him. Why tell him all the horrible injuries her patients had suffered? It would only remind him of the dangers he might face. Besides, there was her plan to complete her specialized training to serve overseas. She wasn't about to tell him she was doing that.

April 15, 1943

Dear Anthony,

She sat down at her desk and started to write while Muffin rubbed her head against her shin. When did this cat come in? Her door was closed but Muffin had pushed it open and entered anyway. This cat thought she owned the house. No place was off limits to her. She came and went wherever and whenever she pleased, the same way Anthony used to do when he came home from school.

The thought made her smile. What would he think if he saw how this cat had taken over his place at home? She even liked to hide in his room and sleep on his bed.

> ... *By now, you must be at the Officer Candidates School. I hope all is going well there. I had so much fun reading about your excursions in L.A. The actors and actresses my father worked with used to tell me stories about that city. So many of them dreamt of being a part of Hollywood. It must have been something to meet Katharine Hepburn. Did you ask her for an autographed photo too?*
>
> *I'm happy to hear you were able to take breaks and enjoy your time off. So you wish I was at the bars with you now? I see the army training might be a good thing after all! — No. I'm only joking. I, too, wish we could be on a quiet beach, enjoying the peace and beauty of the scenery just the two of us.*

Muffin jumped up onto her lap, disrupting her.

"You bad moggy!" She tapped her on the head. The cat raised its nose and rubbed it against her fingers. She chuckled while the cat settled herself comfortably on her lap.

> ... *Muffin is getting big now. She grows so fast. Aunt Sophia loves her, but she's a very naughty cat. Yesterday, she knocked over and broke the 18th-century antique vase Uncle Leon gave Aunt Sophia for her birthday. Uncle Leon is going to be very upset when he finds out.*

Muffin started purring. Tessa stroked her fur and her purrs grew louder.

... You should see this cat. She's a little rascal. Actually, I wish you were here and could be a part of everything we are doing. Uncle William converted a large part of the yard into a vegetable garden. Everyone whose home has a garden is now planting victory gardens. We planted more seeds last week. This is the time of year when you usually come home from school for spring break. If you were here, you would've been helping us to break ground and plant seeds.

She stopped. If he were her... If he were here, on school break instead of away with the army, he would be reading in the den after dinner or listening to music or radio with her. Sometimes, he even listened to the president's fireside chats, although he made sure Uncle Leon never knew about it.

How she wished he were here. It hurt to be away from him. The darkness of the night outside the window and the silence of the room made her feel even more alone. When would they see each other again?

She continued writing.

... I miss you so much.

She stopped again. Anger started to fill the hole in her heart. The rage that gnawed and ate at her on the day she saw Anthony off to training camp had returned.

... I hate this war. I hate that it's taken you away.

Without realizing it, her hand tensed against Muffin's back. The cat hissed and leaped off her lap and sprinted out of her room. She watched the cat run away. Her eyes lingered on the "Liebestraum" poster on the wall. The anger in her heart subsided, replaced by a wave of tenderness. When she closed her eyes, she could remember him kissing her next to the poster, and the way he pulled her body close to him. She could still feel his soft caresses.

She opened her eyes and picked up the pen again.

… I'm sorry I didn't send you a photo of me last time. I don't know how my father could stand to have his photo taken so often. I feel self-conscious seeing myself in photos. I never look right. At least I don't think I do. But I finally had one taken by a photographer because you've asked several times already. I'm enclosing it with this letter. I guess this one doesn't look too bad. I'm sending you photos of Muffin too so you can see what she looks like.

I will try to write again tomorrow. Take good care of yourself. My heart is always with you.

– Love, Tessa

CHAPTER THIRTEEN

"We're here, Ron." Tessa leaned down to Ron in the wheelchair. Along with Sarah, Ellie, and Dr. Donovan, they had arrived at the studio where Sarah's father had arranged for them to film. Ron showed no reaction. His head dropped to one side and he didn't look interested in anything.

"Hello," a chunky man with a round face like Sarah's opened the door.

"This is my father," Sarah introduced them.

"Please, please. Come on in." Mr. Brinkman welcomed them and stepped aside to let them in. "Let me introduce you to my friend Ted Barnaby. Ted owns this studio. He'll be doing the film recording today." He brought them to a man with a long but jovial face sitting behind a desk.

Ted Barnaby quickly wiped his mouth with a napkin. "Sorry. Just finishing my lunch." He got up to greet them, leaving behind his unfinished bottle of Coca-Cola and sandwich.

Tessa glanced around the studio floor behind the staging area where Ted sat. The recording camera was already set up. Ted turned on the studio lamps and invited them to come closer. "This camera records in color. It's a fine piece of equipment. State of the art, if I do say so myself." He patted the camera. "How shall we do this? Do you want me to film you while you ask him questions?" he asked Dr. Donovan.

"We want you to start by recording what happens when we ask him to walk," Donovan said. "He has no sign of physical injury, but he has trouble standing up and he can't walk properly. It's difficult to explain but you'll see what we mean."

"All right," Ted said. "Let's have you and one of your nurses take him to the studio floor. I'll start the camera."

Donovan nodded at Tessa. She took the cue and said, "Ron, I know this is difficult for you, but will you please stand up?"

Looking lost, he gazed at Tessa. "You can do this," she said. He lowered his head and pushed against the arms of the wheelchair to get up. Ellie quickly moved to hold the wheelchair in place from behind while Tessa helped him. "That's it." She encouraged him. "You're doing very well," she said, even though he was not doing well at all. He was having difficulty standing up. Once on his feet, his back curved sideways to the left.

Donovan took his left arm and they walked him to the studio floor. There, they let go of him. "Ron," Donovan said, "can you turn to your right and take a few steps forward?"

Ron turned to the right and took several deep breaths as he stared straight ahead. "I can't." He looked at the doctor, helpless.

"Give it a try," Donovan said. "We're here to help you if you need it."

Ron curled his fingers. His face tensed.

"Small, easy steps, Ron," Tessa said. "One step at a time."

Looking ahead, he pressed his lips together and took a step forward. As he did, the contortion of his body worsened. His waist shifted unnaturally to the left while his hip pushed to the right. His body was crooked like a broken puppet. He couldn't bend his knees. All he could do was force his rigid right leg forward by pushing down on his right heel and dragging his left leg along.

"That's it." Donovan glanced over at Ted, who had started filming Ron. "Keep going that way."

Ron continued. The look of excruciating pain on his face was hard to watch. When he reached the end of the studio floor, Donovan told him to turn around and walk back to the opposite side. He did as Donovan asked, but he tensed up further and his back twisted even more. After another repetition of this walking exercise, he collapsed. "I can't. I can't." He kneeled on the floor and cried. "My back hurts." Tessa and Sarah rushed to console him.

"Shall we continue?" Ted asked Dr. Donovan.

Donovan crossed his arms. "I'm afraid this will have to do. I don't want to upset him anymore today. If you don't mind helping us, we can arrange another session later this week."

"No problem," Ted said. "I'll be glad to help."

Donovan joined Tessa and Sarah. "Let's get him back to the hospital." He lifted Ron up on one side while Tessa supported him on the other. When they came back to the staging area near Ted's desk, Ron's eyes bulged and he screamed. Hysterical, he flailed his arms, knocking both Donovan and Tessa off balance. Ellie ran to them and tried to help Donovan restrain him.

"What's wrong?" Tessa asked. "Ron! What's wrong?"

"The fly!" Ron slurred between his screams. "The fly! The fly!"

Tessa looked around. A fly hovered over Ted's leftover sandwich, then landed on the uneaten bit of food. Ted started to walk toward the desk. "No!" Tessa said. Her instinct took over. "Keep filming. Record him."

Deferring to her, Ted went back to the camera and turned the lens toward Ron. Dr. Donovan and Ellie had now managed to hold Ron down. Tessa took the stress balls from her pocket and put them into his hand. He closed his hand around them. They calmed him and he stopped screaming.

"What happened, Ron?" Tessa asked gently. "Why did you scream when you saw the fly?"

He sniffed. His body slumped to the floor. "The fly was on his eye socket."

Tessa gagged at the grotesque image that came to her mind but held back from showing her disgust. "On whose eye socket?"

"Pete Whitfield. We fought together in the Solomon Islands. He was my first lieutenant." He talked as if he was in a dream.

Seeing Ted was still filming, Donovan moved back out of the camera's view and signaled Ellie to do the same.

"Can you tell me more?" Tessa asked.

"We made an amphibious landing at Gavutu. We parachuted down. Some men never made it to the shore. They drowned. The waves were so high. Our gears were heavy." His body deflated further.

"Go on."

"We got to the land and the shelling and bombing came right away. It was chaos all over. Pete was running next to me. I knew when he was hit. I felt it. And then I saw it. He fell down right beside me. I wanted to help him but I couldn't. Everything was exploding around me and shots were flying everywhere. I pressed on ahead." He tugged his arms into his chest and curled up. "The fighting went on and on. When we finally took the beach, I went back to look for him. He wasn't at the field hospital so I went back to the beach to look for him. And then, I found him. He always wore this Navajo hemp bracelet on his right wrist. It was orange and turquoise. Diamond-shaped patterns. He said they have protective powers. His sleeve was rolled up and I recognized it as soon as I saw it." He stopped talking. He had a faraway look in his eyes as if he was somewhere else, perhaps back on the beach at Gavutu where his deceased comrade lay dead.

"Do you want to stop?" Tessa touched him on the shoulder. "We can stop now if you want."

He didn't seem to hear her. "I walked over to him. He was dead. One of his eyes was blown out by a sniper shot. All that was left was an empty socket. There was a fly on top of it."

Behind them, Sarah let out a gurgling sound from her throat.

"I couldn't save him. I didn't save him. I knew he was shot and I couldn't and didn't save him." Ron blinked and tears fell down his cheeks.

"That's enough." Donovan held up his hand. Ted turned off the camera. "Ellie, Tessa, let's get him back into the wheelchair. We'll take him back and let him rest."

Tessa and Ellie did as Donovan said. Ron, despondent, let them handle him without any resistance. He looked weak and frail despite his muscular physique.

"I'll deliver the footage to you as soon as I can," Ted said. His voice choked.

"I wish we could help more." Mr. Brinkman opened the studio's door, his face full of sympathy.

"Thank you." Donovan shook his hand goodbye. "You've both been a great help already."

In the ambulance on their way back, none of them said a word. Tessa reached for Ron's hand. What place had he withdrawn himself into? She wondered. She wanted to pull him out.

Back at the hospital, Ron lay listless on his bed for hours. Tessa stayed by his bedside as long as she could so he wouldn't be alone.

"You should go home," Ellie told her. "I'll keep an eye on him this evening."

"Do you think his father will change his mind and let him stay so we can treat him?"

"The general?" Ellie asked. "Let's hope so." Her face showed only doubt.

CHAPTER FOURTEEN

FRANK CASTILE STOOD at the center of Dr. Donovan's office in front of the doctor's desk. Donovan invited him to sit down, but he refused. "I don't have much time, Doctor. I'm here to pick up my son. Can we make this quick?"

Out of courtesy, Donovan remained standing himself. Ted Barnaby stared wide-eyed at the general and shrunk behind the film projector.

"We want to talk to you about your son's condition, sir," Donovan said.

"You're testing my patience, Doctor. My son has no condition other than losing his drive to fight. You can release him. A few weeks with me and he'll be back to fighting form."

"No, he won't be," Tessa interrupted them. She was trying her best not to sound rude to this mean, unreasonable man. "He needs our help. If you don't do right by him and let us treat him, you will regret it."

Castile fixed his eyes on her as if noticing her in the room for the first time. Donovan shook his head at her to warn her to stop, but she wouldn't. She wasn't afraid of this bloke. He was wrong and she meant to set him straight.

"You're the same nurse who got in my way last time, aren't

you?" Castile asked. "Is that what it's come to? My son now needs a woman to protect and defend him?"

Tessa ignored his comment. "Your son is ill. And he isn't a coward like you think. He's a brave man and a hero. You should watch our film and see what battles have done to him. He deserves this much from you."

She was ready for him to argue with her. Reprimand her even. But instead, he asked, "What's your name, nurse?"

"Graham. Tessa Graham," she answered. She wasn't sure what that had to do with anything.

He checked her rank insignia. "Only a cadet."

Defiant, she stood taller. She didn't care if he slighted her. But oddly, his steely demeanor softened. "What do you intend to do when your training is over?"

My training? She thought. She didn't see why he was asking her these questions. Who she was and what she planned to do were entirely irrelevant. Besides, what did he think she was here to do? The more she thought, the more resentful she felt. Men like him were the reason Anthony had to leave. They only cared about the war. They didn't care about what happened to people when they sent young men out to fight. They didn't care that battles destroyed people's minds, or that loved ones had to separate. If it weren't for these men and their war, she wouldn't have been here working to treat wounded soldiers, and Anthony wouldn't have had to leave.

What did she intend to do when she finished her training? Go after Anthony was what she intended to do. She was not going to let men like him or the war keep her and Anthony apart if she could help it.

"I intend to go overseas to where I want to be, Sir," she said. "I'm going to do everything I can to get there, no matter what it takes." She meant every word she said.

The general studied her with renewed interest. "A patriot."

A patriot? Tessa shifted her eyes away from him. What was he talking about? He had totally misunderstood her.

"You know you're crossing the line the way you're behaving, don't you, cadet?" Castile asked. "But you've got a lot of nerve, and you really do care about our soldiers." Castile pulled the guest chair out and sat down to face the small screen hanging on the wall. "All right, Graham. Show me the film."

The general's change of mind surprised her. Before she could react, Donovan seized the chance and waved at Ted. "Mr. Barnaby, can you please run the projector?"

"Uh huh," Ted stuttered. "Sure." He turned on the machine while Donovan switched off the lights. The film began to run. Castile's expression turned to distaste when a fragile-looking Ron appeared on the screen. Donovan's voice echoed in the background. "Ron, can you turn to your right and take a few steps forward?"

While Castile watched the film, Tessa observed his reaction. At first, he appeared confused. "What was the matter with him?" He scowled at the image of Ron walking contorted. "Why was he like this? Can't he walk?"

No one answered. When the film showed Ron collapsing onto the floor, the general's look changed to concern. "He's not faking this," he said, his voice uncertain.

"No," Donovan answered.

"Keep watching," Tessa said. "There's more."

The film now showed Ron screaming while Donovan and Ellie held him down until he slumped onto the floor. In the background, Tessa could be heard asking on the film, "What happened, Ron? Why did you scream when you saw the fly?" Ron began telling the story of his landing at Gavutu.

"I couldn't save him. I didn't save him. I knew he was shot and I couldn't and I didn't save him," Ron wailed.

Castile became visibly upset. "Stop," he ordered. "I've seen enough."

Ted stopped the projector. The frozen image of Ron curled up on the floor remained on the screen while Ted switched the lights back on. Donovan frantically pointed at the screen, and Ted rushed to turn off the machine. They waited for the general's response.

"I know Pete Whitfield." Castile's lips twitched. Tessa thought it even looked like he smiled, a fond smile. "I picked him out and watched him rise through the ranks," he continued. "He was an exceptional young man. I encouraged him to join the Marine Corps. He had a promising military career ahead of him. I'm sorry he ended this way. I wish I could've saved him too."

"You can still save Ron," Tessa said. "You only have to give us a chance."

Castile clasped his hands and listened. He looked less like an army general now and more like a concerned father, the same way that Uncle William looked when he thought of Anthony. "What do you think is wrong with him?" he asked Dr. Donovan.

"Guilt," Donovan said. "He's haunted by guilt. A lot of men under his command died. He cared for them. He feels responsible. His friends were killed in action. It was painful for him to watch his friends die. He says he has back pain, but he doesn't have any back injury. I think his emotional pain is manifesting itself this way so he can share the pain with everyone he lost."

The general considered what he said.

"Ron needs help." Tessa urged again. "We want to help him. Please let us help him."

"Will you be able to cure him?" he looked up to them and asked.

"We can't promise anything. The army doesn't keep very good records of documented cases of battle neurosis. If I may be honest, General, our military and government haven't paid enough attention to this problem, so our information is limited. But we can change that. If we have funding and support, we can start a pilot program here and test different ways to treat this illness." He laid out several documents on the desk. The general picked up one and studied the first few pages.

"If we could have your support, sir, we could be doing a great service for our veterans returning home with this condition," Donovan pressed on.

The general put down the document and straightened in his seat. His moment of introspection had passed. "If you really think you can help him, I'll let Ron remain here under your care."

Relieved, Tessa looked at Donovan. The doctor was clearly pleased. Immediately though, he was disappointed again as Castile said, "But the pilot program won't do. Even if I want to support you, it'd be an uphill battle. It's bad enough our soldiers are coming home shot, maimed, if not dead. The last thing we need is the public thinking they will come home crazy too. If we set up a treatment program, it would mean the military is officially acknowledging that the war is causing mental damage. It would not be good for the army's image or our recruitment efforts."

Tessa could not believe what she was hearing. How could they leave people untreated for the sake of publicity?

As if he read her thoughts, Castile glanced at her, then looked away again and said to Donovan. "I know what I said may sound cold to you, but we are at war. There is a lot at stake. We have to look at the big picture. We could ruin our troop's morale if they think they might lose their minds fighting in the war. Some men will try to use this excuse to get out of fighting. The situation could get out of hand. We cannot have these problems while we're still at war. People's lives are at stake."

"So we sacrifice the ones who are suffering?" Tessa asked.

"It's a sacrifice for the greater good," Castile said. "Anyway, we have to consider our resources. Right now, winning the war and allocating our financial resources to support our troops overseas are our first priorities. We can't spare any financial resources."

Tessa wanted to ask him to reconsider, but Donovan shook his head at her.

"I'm sorry." Castile stood up from his seat. "Take care of my son. I hope he'll be recovered the next time I return."

When he had left, the tension in the room eased and Donovan dropped into his seat. Tessa felt like she could breathe easy again.

"You can treat Ron now," Ted Barnaby said, coming out of hiding from behind the film projector.

"Yes. Thank you, Mr. Barnaby," Tessa said. Ted was right. At least now they could help Ron, even though they didn't get everything they had hoped for.

A few days later, in Dr. Donovan's office, it was Leon Caldwell who was cringing in the seat where General Castile had sat.

"That was the most disturbing thing I've ever seen," Leon said when Ted Barnaby turned off the projector and switched on the lights after the film was over.

"We cannot expect quick results," Dr. Donovan told him. "Our program will require long-term, dedicated commitment to discover what works and what doesn't. Mental illnesses take much longer to heal than physical wounds."

"Yes," Leon said. "Tessa already explained that to me."

"This is our proposed plan and budget." Donovan pushed a set of papers across the desk to show Leon. "We'll start small. We'll try out some of the treatments done by Arthur Hurst. We'll observe and adjust where we need. If we can gather enough empirical results, we can share them with other hospitals even if the Army won't officially acknowledge this is a problem."

Leon nodded in agreement.

"Would you help us?" Tessa asked him.

"We can definitely use your financial support, Mr. Caldwell," said Donovan.

"You haven't told William and Sophia about this?" Leon asked Tessa.

"I don't want them to know. They're worried enough as it is. I don't want them to think something like this might happen to Anthony."

"Yes, you're right." Leon accepted her explanation without a doubt. She glanced away from him. It was true that she thought if Uncle William and Aunt Sophia saw the film of Ron, it would add to their worries about Anthony. What she hadn't told Leon was that she didn't want Uncle William and Aunt Sophia to come to the hospital at all in case they talked to the doctors about her. She still hadn't told them she had switched programs, and she would prefer they didn't find out. She figured that Uncle Leon, not being her direct guardian, would be much less likely to raise the subject.

Besides, Uncle Leon needed a diversion. He had been feeling helpless against every wrath the war had brought that he couldn't control. His isolationist efforts had all but disintegrated. Pearl Harbor broke down everything he stood for. And then, his beloved nephew had gone off to war. Getting him involved with Dr. Donovan's plan would give him something to feel good about.

"I will look at your proposal, Doctor." Leon took the set of documents Donovan gave him. "Assuming your suggestions are sound, I'm ready to pledge my support."

Delighted, Donovan said, "Thank you, Mr. Caldwell."

"I'll see what I can do to round up a group of financial donors to back this program. As I always say, we have to protect and look out for our own."

"Yes. Yes, of course," Donovan concurred. "We most certainly must do that."

Pleased with the outcome, Tessa watched while Dr. Donovan explained the details of the proposal to Leon. Small victories. She smiled to herself. The war may be bigger than her, but she could resist and find ways to win small victories. The idea gave her hope. She might find a way to Anthony after all.

CHAPTER FIFTEEN

ON A SUNDAY AFTERNOON when the sun was shining bright above the sky, Tessa sat alone by the piano, reading the last letter Anthony had sent her. Outside, the trees had turned green and the sounds of birds once again carried through the parlor windows, reminding everyone spring had arrived.

> …It saddens me to hear you sound so upset in your letter. I know how much you resent this war. I don't like being away from you either, and certainly I wish the world were at peace. But the war brought you to me, so it is one good thing that came out of it. I am so happy that we have met…

Anthony. He was always so optimistic. He always saw the good and bright side of everything. She, on the other hand, would always spot darkness. She could so easily succumb to darkness and let rage overtake her.

> …As long as you are in my life, I can face anything. The only thing that matters to me now is that you are in my life…

She raised the letter and caressed it with her lips. By herself, she could never see all the positive sides of things the way he did. Only he could ease their heartaches with his words. In these hard times when they couldn't control their own lives, his optimism carried them through.

How she loved him for it.

A ray of sunlight glinted through the tree branches into the room, shining on the papers with the list of songs he had sent her. She picked up the list from the top of the piano.

> ...I have an idea how we can be together. I know you like to play the piano on Sundays when Mother and Father go on their afternoon walks. Here where I am, Sunday is our rest day. I am sending you six lists of songs. The lists are dated by the Sundays for the remaining weeks I'll be training at the OCS. On Sundays, would you play for me the songs listed for each particular Sunday? If you start at three o'clock and play the songs in the order I have written, I will start thinking of these songs at four o'clock in Georgia in the same order as if I'm listening to you play. This way, we can do something together even though we're apart. We will do this every Sunday for as long as we can.

Today's list contained a mix of classical and contemporary music. When the grandfather clock struck three, she hit the first note. One by one, she played the songs on the list. Was he somewhere now thinking of these songs as he promised? Could he somehow hear the music as she played?

When she got to the last song, her heart tingled and she smiled to herself. "Moonlight and Roses Bring Memories of You" by Ben Black and Neil Moret. Next to the song title, he had scribbled, "Night after the Biograph." That was the night when she swam naked in the lake in front of him after they went to see a movie together. Thank goodness no one was around when she first saw this after opening his letter. Her face burned up even though she was alone. She still could not believe he did this!

Her heart raced along with the melodies. *Can you hear, Anthony? Can you hear this?*

On a Sunday afternoon when the sun was shining bright above the sky, Anthony sat alone in the woods on the edge of the forest near his barracks. He leaned back against the tree trunk and looked up into the sky. The leaves in the surrounding area had turned lush green and the sounds of birds could be heard from all directions. Spring had arrived.

He liked this forest. In the military, no one had any privacy. This forest gave him a place to escape to for a few moments of solitude.

Not that he was complaining. Fort Benning was a huge improvement over Camp Dover and the California desert. The officer trainees must still adhere to a strict military code of conduct, but he no longer had to suffer unreasonable rules, penalties, and punishments designed to break down recruits. There was no more loser captain picking on him and making his life hell. The instructors here had no time to waste on petty nonsense like subjecting trainees to extra fatigue duties or physical exercises for the sake of their own amusement. They had only three months to turn the current class of trainees into qualified officers. They must fill the burgeoning number of officer positions as the U.S military geared up for war. To that end, the classes at OCS were much more focused and organized. Candidates who could not keep up were quickly weeded out, not kept around for disparagements at the higher-ranking officers' whims.

The facilities here were better too, unlike the temporary camps set up to train new recruits. Designed to be a permanent training ground, the living quarters where the officer trainees slept were actual buildings furnished with real beds. They even had shelves on which to store their belongings. Such simple items of comfort made all the difference when they returned from a full day of physical training.

This afternoon, while everyone had gone to the USO center

nearby to catch a movie, read a book, or play a game of cards, Anthony went off into the woods alone. He had been looking forward to this all week. Here, he would be alone with Tessa.

He took her last letter out of his pocket and smelled the sweet fragrance of her rose perfume. She must be in the parlor now, sitting by the piano waiting to start. He felt so happy knowing where she was and what she was doing at this exact moment. Although separated by place, they were together in time.

He glanced at his watch. Four o'clock. The minute hand shifted to the number twelve and he started to think of the music of each song he had asked her to play today. He had made a copy of the list for himself too so he wouldn't forget. Across space and distance, they should still be hearing the same melodies with the passing time.

When he reached the last song in his mind, he thought of her naked silhouette under the moonlight by the lake. He had long stopped caring whether or not it was proper to have these kinds of thoughts about her. Who knew when he would see her again? His thoughts were all he had to go on.

He closed his eyes and imagined what it must feel like to hold her under the moonlight. What was she thinking now? Could she feel how much he wanted her?

PART V
TESSA'S QUEST

CHAPTER SIXTEEN

April 28, 1943

Dear Tessa,

Happy birthday!!! I hope this card gets to you in time. I cannot tell you how unhappy I am to miss your birthday. I can only make up for it with this little gift I'm sending you. I didn't tell you before, but during my last visit to L.A. when I was still back at Camp Dover, I went looking for your birthday present. I found this bookmark with emeralds. Emerald is your birthstone, so I hope you like it. I couldn't get anything too big because I don't have much space anywhere to store my things, and I couldn't get anything too expensive because here with the army, I don't have a lot of money with me. I promise you though, when we are together again, I will get you many many more and better presents. Each year will be a new surprise. I promise you, there will be many good things in store for you in the future.

We will be so happy together when this war is over. God willing, next year?

May all your birthday wishes come true.

— *Love, Anthony*

TESSA GLIDED her fingers across the gold-plated bookmark, careful not to smudge its shiny surface. How long did Anthony look before he found this?

Imagining him picking it out at a shop, she held it up to her lips and kissed it. This was how she could feel him, by touching something he had touched.

Before Anthony, she had always imagined how incredible it would feel to be in love. She had learned now that love could hurt, and hurt so much. Not being able to see him and be with him hurt.

She picked up the birthday card he had sent her and held it close to her heart.

Last year, he gave her a birthday present too. Or, more correctly speaking, a gift to try to make up with her after they had that ridiculous argument about her being at a bar. She took the pink rose pendant out of her dresser drawer. In front of the mirror, she took off the cross she was wearing and put on the necklace with the rose pendant. Looking at her own reflection, she touched the pendant with her fingers. The necklace was quite long. A shorter one would look better and the pendant would not be hidden beneath her clothes, but she actually preferred this length. Now she could have him closer to her heart.

She picked up the cross. Its necklace dangled from her hand. Her mother had given this to her and she had worn it since she was a child. It was a token to keep her safe. After coming to America, she continued to wear it because it was a memento from home. But she still had the Bulova watch her parents had given her when she departed England. More than anything now, she wanted to keep Anthony safe.

She took the cross to her desk and started writing.

May 10, 1943

Dear Anthony,

Thank you with all my heart for the lovely birthday present. The bookmark is exquisite. It is the most delightful birthday present. I will use it and every time I see it, I will think of you. The only gift that could top this would be if you had come home.

On my birthday, Ruby, Jack and Henry came by the hospital and took me out to lunch. Sarah Brinkman, my colleague at the hospital, baked me a birthday cake. Aunt Sophia and Uncle William took me out for a wonderful dinner and gave me a beautiful silk scarf made in India. I also received a telegram from my Mother and Father. That made my day! I miss them terribly. It is horrible to not be able to see my parents for so many years. I hope this will not happen to you. I wish this war will be over soon, and you will be back home with Uncle William and Aunt Sophia.

My parents sent me a photo album of pictures that Father took while he was on tour visiting military troops. There were even photos of Father with the American Army. The American units stationed in London formed an Army Theater Troupe and collaborated with Father's company to perform shows for their fellow soldiers. I am glad to know that American soldiers overseas are able to engage in leisure activities. That means you will be able to find things to do that are not military-related if you are sent overseas.

All in all, I had a wonderful birthday. But still, the day was not perfect because you weren't here. When I blew out the candles on the birthday cake Sarah baked for me, I made a wish that you and I will be able to spend my next birthday together.

Now, to thank you for your beautiful gift, I want to give you something from me. I'm sending you the cross that I have been wearing since I was little. Mother gave it to me for my protection. I give it to you now. May it protect you wherever you go.

— Love, Tessa

She folded the cross into the letter and, after spraying it with her rose perfume, put both the letter and the cross inside the envelope. Now, he could have her close to his heart too.

Before leaving for the post office, she touched the photo of Anthony in a picture frame that now sat on her desk. The photo had been among the ones displayed in the den. Their time together before he left had been so short, she didn't even have her own photo of him.

How she wished she could hold his hand and hear his voice.

A hospital kitchen staff member greeted Tessa and Ron when they returned from their daily afternoon walk. He still complained now and then of back pain, but his condition had improved, as he could now walk in an upright position again without twisting his body and dragging his leg. He had resumed his occupational therapy too. Tonight, they had assigned him to assist with distributing dinners to patients.

Tessa helped him remove his jacket. He thanked her and followed the kitchen staff member away. After they left, Tessa folded his jacket and put it in the cabinet next to his hospital bed. While doing that, she noticed something shiny and silver sticking out from under his pillow. Wondering what it was, she lifted up the corner of his pillow and found a dinner knife, the dull and harmless ones that the hospital cafeteria used. She stared at it, wondering what she should do. He still didn't feel safe when he was left alone.

"Hi, Tessa," Ellie said to her from behind.

Tessa quickly dropped the pillow and turned around to block the knife from Ellie's view. "Hi, Ellie."

"It's good to see Ron getting better, isn't it?" Ellie put a fresh bouquet of flowers into the vase next to Ron's bed.

"Yes," Tessa said. "It is wonderful to see him improve so much."

"He has you to thank for that. Maybe he can be released sooner if his progress keeps up."

Tessa stole a glance at Ron's pillow, then at Ellie. She didn't want Ellie or anyone to discover the knife in case they thought he was dangerous. She wanted to figure out a solution herself. To divert Ellie's attention, she asked, "So, your graduation is in two days. Do you know yet what you'll be doing after that?"

"Funny you asked. In fact, I got my assignment this morning. I've been commissioned to join the 33rd Field Hospital. It's one of the medical units attached to the U.S. Sixth Army Corps. I'll be shipping off at the end of the month."

"So soon? Are you ready for it?" The reality that Ellie would be leaving dawned on Tessa.

"I am," Ellie said as she straightened out Ron's blanket. "Don't look so worried. You're doing the same thing. You're even more eager than I am, switching to the Nurses Specialized Training Program. You fought so hard to help Ron, too. Whichever unit they assign you to will be very lucky to have you."

Tessa looked down. Everyone had misunderstood her. They thought she had switched programs because she was eager to serve. It wasn't her intention to deceive anyone, but she felt guilty nonetheless. Ellie's steadfast belief in her was the worst, as Ellie had supported her from the very beginning.

"Ellie, can I tell you something, if you promise not to tell anyone?"
"Sure. What is it?"
"I'm not the altruistic and dedicated nurse you think I am."
"What do you mean?"
"The only reason I switched programs is because my boyfriend was drafted. I want to join the medical unit that follows his unit. I did what I did for me. I want to go where he goes."

"Tessa," Ellie said, her voice full of sympathy. "It must have been heartbreaking for you to be separated from him."

Tessa didn't deny it.

"What unit is he assigned to?" Ellie asked.

"I don't know. He's still in training and hasn't been given his assignment yet. When he left, I felt so angry. I had to do something. Anything. I wanted to take back control of our lives somehow. So now, here I am."

"You silly girl!" Ellie took her by the hand and led her to sit down on Ron's bed. "How do you think you'll manage to get yourself assigned to follow his unit? The army assigns people. No one gets to make requests. The American troops are spread all over the world. You could be sent anywhere. The chances are minuscule that you'll assigned to serve in the same unit as he."

"I don't know." Tessa raised her hands to her face. "Maybe I can talk to Dr. Donovan and ask him to help me once I know where Anthony's assigned, and I've gathered a list of army officials I would write to." Hearing herself talk, Tessa felt stupid. Ellie must think she was stupid too. What she wanted to do was so unrealistic.

"Tessa, wouldn't your odds of being together with him again be greater if you stay safe at home and wait for him to come back?"

"I'm sick of waiting! I've been waiting for three years for this maddening war to be over. Maybe it'll never be over. Maybe we'll lose the war, then what?" she said, agitated. Some of the patients in the other beds looked over at them. She lowered her voice. "I don't want to be away from him if something should happen to him."

"If you go, something could happen to you," Ellie said. "You'll be doubling the risk that you two won't see each other again."

"There's no guarantee we'll ever see each other again now." A chill ran through Tessa the minute she said that. This thought had haunted her since the day Anthony left, but this was the first time she had said it. Until now, she had avoided bringing this idea into the open, as if by refusing to openly admit it, she could prevent it from ever becoming real. Now that she had said it out loud, it frightened her even more. She squeezed her eyes shut, then slowly opened them.

Ellie put her arm around Tessa's shoulder to try to comfort her.

"The way I see it," Tessa said, "my staying or going has no bearing on the odds of what might happen to him. No one knows for sure what will happen. All I know is, I would rather cast my own lot than leave everything up to fate. If there is any chance at all I could be with Anthony, I'll take it." She must sound to Ellie like a stubborn child throwing a tantrum, but she could not help it. "Besides, why should Anthony have to go to war and I don't? Even if I'm assigned somewhere else, at least he wouldn't be in this alone. I'll be in it with him."

She thought Ellie might laugh at her, but Ellie smiled. "His name is Anthony?" Ellie asked.

Tessa felt her face flushing at the mention of Anthony's name.

"Well then, I'll pray for you and I hope your wish will come true," Ellie said.

"And I wish you the best of luck when you go overseas," Tessa said. "You're a wonderful nurse, Ellie. You'll do a lot of good wherever you go."

"So will you. I know you will."

"I'll miss you." Tessa already felt sad at the thought of Ellie's impending departure. Ellie was the one who had first motivated her to become a part of the Cadet Nurse Corps. The hospital wouldn't be the same without her.

"I'll miss you too. Promise me you'll write me and let me know how everything turns out?"

"Of course. I'll do that." Of course she would write to Ellie, just as she had been writing to her parents, to her friends back in London, and to Anthony.

Letters. These days, writing letters was the only way to keep close to the people she loved.

CHAPTER SEVENTEEN

A LARGE AMERICAN flag above the entrance to the Caldwells' residence greeted the guests as they arrived for the festive Independence Day cookout. The delectable smell of roast ribs and chicken on the grill whetted everyone's appetite as soon as they walked in. Meat was today's special treat. Children's laughter filled the courtyard, bolstering the cheerful atmosphere.

A waiter stepped up to each guest, offering fruit punch and ice tea. Alexander ran by with his friends, nearly knocking him over and spilling the drinks on his tray. "Sorry!" the boy shouted and ran on. His friends followed. Behind them at the putting green, William sunk a ball into a hole. "Good job, Will," Leon said. "Watch me." He took his turn twenty feet away from the hole. The ball rolled straight into the cup and the guests around them cheered. Over by the tent, the barbershop quartet belted out an a cappella rendition of "The Stars and Stripes Forever," delighting Sophia and all her friends at the table.

On the home front, life went on. Life could not stop because loved ones had gone away.

"Aren't they wonderful?" the lady sitting next to Tessa leaned over and asked her. Tessa forced a smile, but couldn't bring herself to join in on the others' lively conversations. She picked at the half-eaten potato salad on her plate. It was useless. She didn't feel like eating. Even among the noise and the music, she felt lonely.

She stared out at the Caldwells' courtyard and watched the children play in the sweltering heat. With the well-manicured lawns and lush green bushes, this place looked entirely different than how it had been on New Year's Eve half a year ago. That night, the courtyard was empty and silent. The grounds were frozen and the trees were bare. It must have been bitterly cold, but all she remembered was the fuzzy warmth inside her as Anthony led her away to some place unknown. Excited, she had followed him, leaving behind them a trail of their own footsteps on the light layer of snow on the ground.

While they walked, he had turned to her and flashed her a bright smile. She loved his smile. How she longed to see him with that smile again.

"Excuse me," she said and got up from her seat. The guests nodded in acknowledgment and returned to their conversations. She left the table and went inside the Caldwells' house.

Had it only been six months since the Fur Ball? It felt to her as if a much longer time had passed. That evening was now a distant memory.

She went to the window facing the courtyard by which she had stood that night, contemplating taking a walk outside. This was the very spot where her life took an irreversible change of course, where her destiny revealed itself. Her destiny. He had been right in front of her all along. Only she hadn't known it for the longest time.

"Want to get out of here?"
"And go where? Home?"
"I know of a better place."
"All right."
"Go get our coats. I'll tell Mother and Father we're leaving.

A bittersweet sadness crept up her heart.

"You miss him very much, don't you?" someone said behind her. She turned around. It was Katherine.

Katherine came up next to her and pushed the curtain further open, exposing fully the beautiful sunlit view outside. The room immediately brightened. Tessa turned back toward the window. Quietly, they gazed out.

"We miss him too," Katherine said. "The week after he left, Father was beside himself. Uncle William had to come to calm him down, can you believe that?"

Tessa did not answer but kept her gaze out the window.

"I hope he'll come back soon and you two will be together again."

Tessa gave her a doubtful look. That Katherine cared the least bit about her involvement with Anthony never occurred to her. If anything, she thought Katherine would rather Anthony be with one of the girls who were well known within Chicago high society.

As if she had guessed what Tessa was thinking, Katherine tilted her head and looked Tessa in the eye. Embarrassed by her own presumptuous thoughts, Tessa looked away.

Katherine smiled. "In the end, only someone as extraordinary as you could have captured his heart anyway. When I saw you two together, I realized that you two were always meant for each other."

Not expecting such words from Katherine, Tessa didn't know how to respond, but Katherine disregarded Tessa's silence and continued. "You should've seen the look on Lilith Reinhardt's face that night when Anthony left with you in full view of everyone." She narrowed her eyes with a playful smile as if they were sharing a secret. Tessa couldn't help but smile back.

"When Anthony left for the war, I finally realized how silly and frivolous I'd always been," Katherine said, her tone now serious. "The war's been going on for years. The whole world has turned into a mess. Men are dying every day and people are suffering everywhere. Me? I was oblivious, living in my sheltered world, tête-à-têtes with girls as mindless as I was, all of us dreaming of marrying the perfect guy who would come and sweep us off our feet." She gripped the curtain and snickered at herself. "But we forgot one thing. All those perfect guys are kind of preoccupied at the moment, you know what I mean? They are a little busy trying to outrun gunfire and escape bombshells."

Tessa didn't know what to say. She had never heard Katherine talk this way.

"I thought the war would never touch me," Katherine said. "Then Anthony was drafted, and it all hit home. Everything I used to care about felt stupid." She let go of the curtain. "I worry about him too. We all love him. The only thing that matters now is that he comes back safe. As long as he's away in the army, I won't be able to go on like I used to as if whatever happens to the world would not affect me."

Tessa reached out and touched Katherine on the arm. Even if they had nothing else in common, they both cared about Anthony. What happened to Anthony impacted all of their lives.

"You always knew better," Katherine said to her. "You were way ahead of us. You became a cadet nurse even before Anthony was drafted."

"You did well too, Katherine," Tessa said, feeling awkward. Just a moment ago, she was doubting Katherine, still holding her old prejudices against her, while here, Katherine was giving her praise and support. "St. Mary's is a first-rate academy. Graduating from there is no small feat." She meant this too. It was not a hollow compliment.

Katherine waved her hand in dismissal and gazed out the window again. They stood side-by-side, each carrying their own heavy thoughts.

"I'm heading off to Wellesley in the fall." Katherine broke the silence.

"You are? That's wonderful news! Congratulations." Tessa was truly happy for her. "Uncle Leon and Aunt Anna are willing to let you go to Massachusetts alone?"

Katherine nodded. "Before Anthony left, I thought I would go to a women's college nearby, be close to home and establish myself in Chicago society. I thought I'd pass the time in school until I found myself a husband and got married. I don't want to do that anymore. I don't even want to think about marriage for a long, long time." A spark of soul appeared in her once vapid eyes.

"What do you want to do instead?" Tessa asked, curious.

"I want to become a journalist. I want to know what's going on in the world, and I want to help inform everyone about what I find out," Katherine said, her voice full of conviction. "We can't afford to live in a protective bubble and be ignorant of what's going on around us anymore."

Were these the words of Leon Caldwell's daughter? Leon Caldwell, the most outspoken isolationist in Chicago before Pearl Harbor? Tessa could not believe what she had heard. "That's very ambitious. Anthony will be so proud of you when he hears about this. He will!"

"I hope so," Katherine said.

"I'm surprised Uncle Leon is okay with your decision though."

"It took Father a few days to get used to the idea of me going off, but I've decided this is what I want. He's come to terms with it. He's already contacted his old Harvard Business School friends in Boston to set me up with an internship with the *Boston Daily News*. I know I'm still privileged, but I will make the most of my opportunities."

"I have no doubt you'll do well," Tessa said.

"Don't doubt yourself either," Katherine said in return. "Don't give up hope. We'll win this war, and Anthony will come back. And then, you, me, Anthony, Alexander, we can do anything. The world is ours."

Katherine held up her head and Tessa followed her gaze. The clear blue sky outside looked limitless. At that moment, even though the world was as uncertain as ever, everything did seem possible.

A yellow Labrador ran up to Katherine, barking and wagging its tail. Katherine bent to pet it and it poked its nose into her hand. "Coco, good dog." She stroked its head. The dog jumped up on its hind legs and tried to hug her. "Whoa! Calm down, girl. Down!" Katherine laughed.

Alexander came into the room. "Tessa, do you want to see the new puppies?"

"Coco had puppies?"

"You've been so out of touch these days. We never see you anymore. Coco had new puppies last month. Come take a look." Speaking with excitement, his voice cracked. He made a face and walked out toward the back of the house. Tessa followed him. He must have grown at least two inches taller since the last time she saw him.

Yes. She had been out of touch.

Alexander led them out to the veranda where the puppies were cuddling in a large dog bed. Coco hopped over and sniffed the litter, then circled excitedly around Alexander. The puppies that were awake crawled over each other, disturbing the ones that were trying to sleep.

"They're so cute!" Tessa came close and played with each one.

Katherine kneeled down next to her. "Do you want one?"

Tessa looked at the litter. One of the pups had the most adorable droopy eyes she had ever seen. When she petted it, it raised its tiny paw and brushed its own face. "With my schedule? I don't have time to take care of a dog," she said, but she already knew the perfect person who did. "Would you save this adorable little fella for me? I want to give it to a friend of mine."

"Sure."

Tessa picked up the puppy and held it up to her face. "We're going to find you a very nice home, you cute little snowball."

CHAPTER EIGHTEEN

June 30, 1943

Dear Mother, Father, and Tessa,

I have completed my training at the OCS and am now officially a second lieutenant. I've been assigned to the Third Infantry Division of the Sixth Army Corps. I had hoped that I could come home for a brief visit before being shipped overseas, but unfortunately, it is not to be. As I write, I am awaiting deployment at the military base at Newport News, Virginia. I won't know where I'll be sent until I arrive at my destination. Even if I knew, the military rules forbid disclosure of our locations. I can only promise you that I will write as often as I can.

I hope you are all well. Please give my regards to Uncle Leon and everyone else.

— Love, Anthony

TREMBLING, Aunt Sophia held onto the letter, trying not to cry. Uncle William put his arms around her and tried to comfort her while he gazed at the family photos lined up above the mantle of the fireplace. The photos displayed a collage of images of

Anthony growing up, from when he was a small child visiting Santa Claus, to when he was a teenager camping with his father, and his graduation from high school. Nothing in the photos gave a hint that this boy would one day become a soldier.

Seeing how worried Uncle William and Aunt Sophia looked, Tessa wished she could do something. In all the time since she had lived here, she had ever seen Uncle William look so fazed and helpless.

Noticing Tessa's stare, Uncle William turned to her. She was at a loss for words. She didn't know how to console him. When their eyes met, she thought she understood what was going through his mind besides his worries for Anthony's safety. Once Anthony was deployed, his life would change. The boy in those photos would embark on a life different from the one they had planned for him. What would happen after that, no one knew. The secure world they had built for him had crumbled.

For herself though, Anthony's letter delivered the first concrete piece of information she could grasp.

The Third Infantry Division of the Sixth Army Corps. Finally, she had what she needed to begin her quest.

And what a lucky coincidence. The Sixth Corps. Ellie had been assigned to the Sixth Corps. How wonderful it would be if she could join up with Ellie! She wondered if Ellie might be able to help her find a way to get assigned to the same hospital unit.

Yes. There was hope. She had a target to go after now.

"Tessa, the military doesn't work that way," Dr. Donovan tried to explain to her. "Your overseas assignment is not a vacation. You don't get to choose where you go. You go where you're needed. That's why it's called an assignment."

"But I really, really want to be with the Sixth Army Corps," Tessa said. "Surely the medical units supporting them can use one more nurse. You're ranked as a colonel. Isn't there something you can do? Don't you have any say in where your trainees are assigned?"

"Tessa, have you not heard a word I said?" Donovan leaned forward at his desk, exasperated. They had been talking in circles like this for almost half an hour. "I don't want to discourage you from service. Your enthusiasm is much appreciated, but you are asking the impossible," he said. "Why do you want so much to join the Sixth Corps anyway? Is it because of Ellie Swanson?"

Ellie? Certainly, she would love to join up with Ellie, although that was not the reason why she was here today making her request. But if that was what Dr. Donovan thought, and if his misunderstanding could help...

"Yes," she said. "Ellie has been so supportive to me since I became a cadet nurse. I made it this far only because of her." She saw a look of sympathy in Donovan's eyes. "The idea of going to war... it is frightening." She tried to sound as scared as possible. "I want to serve but now it has struck me that I'll be going far away from home to the war zone. I would feel so much better if Ellie were with me."

"Tessa, I want to help, but what you're asking is beyond my power. I'm just a small unit in a much, much larger machine that operates entirely by its own rules, and so are you."

A large machine that operates entirely by its own rules. Tessa frowned. She didn't care. She wanted to shove those rules away and impose her own rules. This was her life.

"You're a good nurse. You've done well here. I have absolute confidence you will do fine on your own without Ellie. Wherever you'll be assigned, there will be other doctors and nurses there to support you."

Frustrated, Tessa thanked him and left. She closed the office door behind her and tried to think of what she could do next. What she wanted felt so daunting.

In the hospital library, Tessa stared at the open book on the table, trying to read but could not absorb anything. There had to be a way to get what she wanted. She couldn't give up only because Dr. Donovan said it was impossible. She had to keep trying.

Deep in her own thoughts, she didn't notice when Sarah Brinkman came up to her. "You looked so focused, I didn't want to disturb you." Sarah put her books on the table and sat down. "But then I saw you're sitting here this whole time and haven't turned your page at all, so I figured you probably aren't reading." She pulled her chair closer. "How did it go with Dr. Donovan? Will he help you get the assignment you want?"

"How did you know?" Tessa asked, surprised. She hadn't told Sarah anything about her plans.

"All right, don't be mad, but Ellie told me."

Ellie told her? But Ellie had promised not to tell anyone.

"I know. She promised you she would keep this a secret," Sarah said. "Don't be angry with her. I'm the only one she told. She was worried about you. She wanted to make sure someone would be here for you in case things don't work out. I swear I haven't said a thing to a single soul." Sarah held her hand up as if making an oath.

Skeptical, Tessa asked, "You seriously haven't told anybody?" Sarah was not one to hold back when it came to talking and blabbering.

"Cross my heart." Sarah made a cross gesture over her chest. "I know this is important to you. I wouldn't even be asking you about it if I didn't see you looking so distraught all day after talking to Dr. Donovan this morning."

Tessa still had reservations. Ellie had been gone for two months now, but this was the first time Sarah had brought up the subject with her. How was Sarah able to stay quiet for so long? Could she trust Sarah with a secret?

"So what did Dr. Donovan say?"

"He said it's beyond his power to help."

"I'm sorry," Sarah said. "Don't lose hope yet."

"You don't think it's a crazy idea? Me trying to get assigned to a specific unit?"

"So what if it is? That shouldn't stop you from trying if that's what you really want."

Tessa felt her guard falling. She didn't realize how much she needed to hear that someone understood and supported her.

"Have you thought of anyone else you can ask for help?" Sarah asked.

Touched by Sarah's encouragement, Tessa decided to tell Sarah, "As coincidence would have it, Ellie is with the medical unit serving the same army division as Anthony."

"How about that? Write to her. Ask her if some senior officer in her medical unit can request for you to be assigned to them."

Tessa had thought of that already. What she hadn't thought of was that Sarah cared about her. She had never considered Sarah as a close friend or confidant. To her, Sarah was a co-worker, initially convenient to have around to save her from mindless small talk with others at work, and later on, someone she preferred to work with simply because she got used to her. She had no idea Sarah was looking out for her and knew she had talked to Dr. Donovan this morning or that Sarah was concerned that she was distressed. Sarah was not usually an observant person, and she would not have guessed Sarah would notice these things. Besides, it must have taken a chatterbox like Sarah a huge amount of self-restraint to keep a secret.

"What about you?" she asked Sarah in return. "Are you ready for deployment?"

"Absolutely! My brothers will be so proud. I have you to thank for it too. If it weren't for you, I would never have thought of transferring to the Nurses Specialized Training Program. I wouldn't have had the confidence to go for it. You're an inspiration to me, Tessa."

"Don't say that. You know now why I did it. You're the one who wishes to go overseas to serve. You are the real inspiration."

Sarah shook her head. "I admire you, Tessa. When you want

something, you just grab the reins and do it. You don't let rules and conventions stop you. You made me realize everything is possible."

Uncomfortable with such a direct compliment, Tessa gave her an uneasy smile.

"So don't give up. Keep trying," Sarah said.

Tessa nodded. It was good to hear someone say that what she wanted to do was not impossible.

PART VI
BAPTISM OF BLOOD

CHAPTER NINETEEN

THE SHIP MOVED CLOSER and closer to the port of Licata on the southern coast of Sicily, sailing through the strong but balmy August wind of the Mediterranean Sea. From afar, Anthony could see the reddish-brown hills covered by deep green vegetation. Below the hills, the city appeared intact with white and yellow stone buildings lining the coastline. Only after he disembarked and walked through the city did he realize the ruin that the war had made of this place.

In July, the Allied forces had succeeded in driving the Axis troops back up north and secured both Sicily and Palermo as Allied bases. In the wake of their defeat, the Nazis had demolished all the cities they had occupied. All infrastructure was destroyed by bombs and aerial attacks to stall the Allies and deprive them of roads, bridges, water, and other resources. Licata was among the ruins on their trail of retreat. Along the streets, rubble piled up two to three stories high all over the grounds. Countless buildings were obliterated in parts, leaving some with only one or two walls still standing.

Passing by the weary local civilians cleaning up the wreckage, Anthony saw for the first time the gravity of the devastation afflicting this part of the world. How fortunate the Americans had been to be so far removed from all these calamities. In their own comfort and safety, how easy had it been to turn a blind eye to the miseries that the people here were suffering? He wished he could do something to help. It all seemed so senseless.

He followed his instructions and came to the command post of one Colonel Callahan to report for duty. The Colonel was not there when he arrived. One of the two staff sergeants at work volunteered to look up his unit assignment records. While he waited, a familiar voice from behind greeted him. "Ardley. I heard an Anthony Ardley was coming. I was hoping it's the same Anthony Ardley I knew."

Anthony turned around. Behind him was his old college friend, Warren Hendricks. They had met in phys. ed. class back at the University.

"Warren!" Anthony couldn't believe his eyes. "No way! You're here too?"

"I sure am."

Immediately, Anthony noticed the two silver stripes on Warren's uniform. "You're a captain?!" Not only that, Warren looked well and in shape, nothing like the feeble classmate he had helped train.

The staff sergeant had by now located Anthony's records. "You're to report to Captain Gene Harding, sir." The sergeant handed him a stack of notes and papers with information about his unit, instructions as to his accommodation, and arrival procedures.

"Captain Harding," Warren said. "You're with Company M. Come on, I'll take you to him." He led Anthony out the door.

"I can't believe you're a captain. That's incredible." Anthony couldn't get over the surprise of finding Warren here. It had been almost two years since the last time they had seen each other. They had so much to catch up on. "What happened to you after you enlisted?"

"I went through basic training like everybody else. After that, I qualified for the OCS. I finished that and the army assigned me to the intelligence unit, probably because they didn't trust me to outrun your average infantry soldier. Suits me fine." He laughed. "I don't trust me either. I did okay with the physical training, all thanks to you, but you know me. I wouldn't rely on me for face-to-face combat." He was joking, but Anthony didn't believe it. Warren was being modest. He must have done exceptionally well to reach the rank of captain in such a short time.

"So how's this for coincidence? I'm the intelligence officer assigned to work with the 3rd Division."

"We're in the same Division?"

"Yep," Warren glanced at their division unit's blue-and-white striped insignia on Anthony's sleeves. "We're the Rock of Marne."

"We'll be working together!"

"That's right. I've been coming by Colonel Callahan's outpost all day waiting for you to arrive. What took you so long? I thought you would have enlisted long ago."

"Nah, I got held up." Anthony took the small photo of Tessa out of his uniform pocket and showed it to Warren.

"Cute! I wouldn't have wanted to come either if I were you."

Anthony put the photo back in his pocket. "What about you? You got anyone waiting for you back home?"

"In fact, there is a very special girl, but not the way you think," Warren took a black-and-white photo from his own pocket and showed it to Anthony. The picture showed Warren with a girl about twelve years old. "My little sister, Bessie. She has a heart condition and she's prone to getting sick a lot. The hardest thing for me when I enlisted was having to leave her. I worry about her a lot."

"I'm sorry to hear that."

"She's a sweetheart. I miss her."

They came to Warren's jeep and his driver, a staff sergeant, drove them to a place that looked like it had once been a three-storey office building. "Central Command," Warren told him and got out of the vehicle. Anthony picked up his duffle bag and followed him. As they entered, a young officer with a silver stripe insignia on his shoulders exited the front entrance. "Captain," the young officer raised his hand and saluted Warren. His uniform could not conceal his well-toned physique.

"Lieutenant." Warren saluted back and Anthony did the same. "Good timing. If I could have a minute," Warren said to the young officer, "this is Second Lieutenant Anthony Ardley. He arrived earlier today. He's the new replacement for your company." Warren then turned to Anthony. "Lieutenant, this is First Lieutenant Wesley Sharpe."

Wesley looked at Anthony. His eyes reminded Anthony of those of an eagle. Although Warren was the ranking officer, Wesley carried more of an air of authority.

"Lieutenant," Wesley said in acknowledgment and went on his way again. Anthony couldn't help taking a second look at Wesley. Of all the people he had met since joining the army, Wesley was the only one who gave him the impression of a real combat soldier.

"He's a helluva first lieutenant," Warren told Anthony as they stepped into the building.

Inside, they found Captain Harding at his desk reviewing a set of maps. When they entered, Harding rose from his seat. He looked to be in his late twenties and much less intimidating than Wesley.

"Captain," Warren said. "I brought you your replacement for second lieutenant."

Harding turned his attention to Anthony. Without hesitation, Anthony stepped up. He wanted to make a good first impression. "Second Lieutenant Anthony Ardley reporting for duty, sir."

"At ease," Harding said. He seemed friendly enough. "You arrived just in time. Our afternoon training session begins in two hours. You can join us today."

"Yes, sir."

"I'm glad you're here. We've got a lot of work ahead."

"Yes, Captain," Anthony answered. Everything was off to a good start. The Captain and Wesley both gave him a good feeling.

Now, he must prove himself worthy to join their rank. He had worked hard to prepare himself back at the OCS. He was ready. He would do the best he could to serve their unit. He would not disappoint them, or himself.

"Walk with me." Captain Harding personally invited Anthony to join him on the way to training before leaving the command headquarters. Eager, Anthony grabbed his rifle and backpack and followed Harding to meet up with the unit. "You've come at a good time," Harding continued. "Our unit's on reserve. You'll have a chance to get used to things and get to know everyone before we go on our next mission."

"Yes, Captain," Anthony said. Harding seemed to be a reasonable man.

They came to the edge of the woods. Wesley Sharpe and most of the men from their company had already arrived.

"All right, listen up," Harding called out to the men. "This is Second Lieutenant Ardley. He'll be in command from now on when I say so." The troop listened. No one seemed overly enthused one way or another. Only Wesley showed interest. He fixed his eyes on Anthony, observing him. Unsure of Wesley's intent, Anthony kept his face straight and pretended not to notice.

Harding then introduced Anthony individually to the noncom officers. "Sergeant Beck, he's our first sergeant. He's been with us since Africa." Beck, a stocky man with thick lips, stomped over and saluted. His biceps bulged when he bent his arms. "Sergeant Jones and Sergeant Oliver." The two sergeants saluted. After the initial introductions, Harding proceeded to lead the unit into the woods for a simulation exercise of camouflage in the forest, following a plan to combat an enemy unit set up by another company. "Beck, you're with me. Oliver, you go with Lieutenant Sharpe. Jones, you're with Lieutenant Ardley."

Divided into three groups, the troops headed in separate

directions into the woods. Wesley's group went off first to the right. Harding and his men took the dirt path diverging to the left. Still taking in his surroundings and assessing the way his unit operated, Anthony surveyed the terrain ahead, paying no particular attention to those who were not following him until Beck passed by him. "Ninety-day wonder," Beck mumbled within earshot.

Anthony stopped. Unapologetic, Beck looked right back at him before turning away.

"Don't mind him," Sergeant Jones came up to him. "Beck's an old warhorse. He thinks he's better than everybody. Frankly, if you ask me, he's got nothing on anybody. He's dumb as a rock."

Mindful not to speak ill of his officers, even one who had just insulted him, Anthony did not reply but walked on.

"Don't you worry, though," Jones said, "I got your back if you need it."

"Thanks, Sergeant Jones."

"Jonesy," the sergeant corrected him. "Everybody calls me Jonesy." He walked alongside Anthony. A short man, about five-foot-six with a slim body, he didn't have the stature that commanded authority like Wesley Sharpe or Beck, but he carried himself with ease and it was clear he was very familiar with the ways of the army. "I've been with the company for a year. Ollie, that's Sergeant Oliver by the way, we're from the same hometown, La Porte, Indiana. Ollie and I joined the army together. He's not doing too well right now. That poor guy just got a Dear John letter yesterday. Turns out, his girlfriend's been running around back home with his old boss. Talk about a stab in the back."

"We're here, Lieutenant, Sergeant," said the young private who had been tracking their route. They had reached the spot where their simulation exercise would begin.

"What's your name?" Anthony asked the private.

"Fox, sir. My name's Zachary Fox." Fox looked no more than seventeen, but appeared smart and self-confident for his age.

"Fox is our company's best sniper," Jonesy said. "You can't go wrong with him around. Right, kid?"

Fox smiled but did not deny it. The rest of the platoon now stood at attention, waiting for directions. Anthony stepped up. He was ready to start when his mind jerked back to Beck. Ninety-day wonder.

The men stood waiting for his order. He looked at them. A trace of uncertainty slipped in. These men had fought real battles. In comparison, the training he received at the OCS felt like child's play. If he had to lead these men into battle tomorrow, would they listen to him? Would they trust him?

More importantly, would he trust himself to lead them to victory and safety?

He led them through the simulation exercise as best he could, doing his best to appear in control even as he battled his doubts.

Ninety-day wonder. Beck's words followed him all the way back to the city after they finished their training.

CHAPTER TWENTY

STANDING by the window in Jack's office, Tessa looked out onto the streets. The sky outside had darkened, but she was not ready to go home. She was not ready to be alone with her own thoughts and fears.

Her efforts to gain an assignment to a medical unit attached to the Army Sixth Corps had gotten her nowhere. Dr. Donovan could do no more than to give her a letter of recommendation. Her letters to the heads of the field hospital and evacuation hospitals serving the Sixth Corps had all gone unanswered. The army officials at different personnel divisions she had written to had given her no response. She felt like she was calling out to the wilderness and no one could hear her.

She worried about Anthony too. In his last letter, he said he had arrived overseas. The fact of his deployment to war had finally sunk in. She hadn't slept well since.

"What was it like being on the front line?" she asked Jack, still staring out the window.

From behind his desk, Jack asked her, "What is it you want to hear? I can lie and tell you not to worry, just like I tell all the other girls whose boyfriends and husbands have gone off to war. I can tell you the Americans have the greatest army in the world and we will crush the enemy. I can say to you, everything will be all right, but I know you didn't come to hear that."

Tessa braced herself. Jack was right. She had come here because she wanted to know what Anthony was facing. She needed to talk to someone who had been there, someone she could trust.

"I won't sweeten the truth for you," Jack said. "If I do, you'll know it anyway. The truth is, bullets and grenades don't discriminate when you're out there."

She knew this already, but she had to hear it. She needed to know. Too many people at home didn't want to hear what was happening to their soldiers. Unlike them, she wanted to know.

"But you shouldn't think of only the worst-case scenarios. We don't know where he is. He could have been sent to London or Australia. A lot of troops are stationed in these places for a long time without being called to combat. Or the army might find another use for him and reassign him to the staff. Everything is random in the military. It felt that way to me anyway. You never know."

Could Anthony be so lucky? She wondered. If only it wasn't so impossible to find someone who could help her get assigned to his division. There had to be a way. She wanted to be there for him, to be there with him. "I wish I could do something."

"Here's what I would do if I were you." Jack pulled out a bottle of whiskey and two shot glasses from his desk drawer. "Pray, then have a drink and hope for the best." He poured one for himself and one for her. "Have one."

"This is your advice? Have a drink?"

"It's the only thing you can do." He raised his shot glass. "To Anthony's safe return."

No. This couldn't be the only thing she could do. Nonetheless, she picked up the glass. Right now, she could use a drink. She took the entire shot in a single swallow. The liquor burned down her throat, to her heart and into her stomach and it felt good. The cutting heat of the alcohol fueled her, burning away from her heart the faintest thought of giving up.

She put the emptied glass on the desk and sat down across from Jack.

"How's your leg?" she asked him.

"Much better, thanks. The doctor said if I continue improving at this rate, I should be off the crutches in a few months. I may be able to get around with a cane." He looked down at his leg. She saw no bitterness on his face, but she still felt for him for what had happened. She would never forget how he had once dominated the dance floor. This war destroyed Jack in body and Ron in spirit, and what they suffered left her scarred too.

"I have a patient," she said. "He has these..." She tapped her finger against her temple. "He has these imaginary back pains. We've tried everything but there's no way to treat him because his pains aren't real. Dr. Donovan said he feels a lot of pain and guilt for his friends who died in the war and the imaginary pains are a way for him to punish himself. Did you see anything like that when you were in the army?"

Jack looked at her. "No. Not exactly. I'll say this though. I saw men losing their minds in different ways. It was traumatizing to see so many people being shot and blown up day after day. Some found ways to cope. Others had a tougher time. I think we Catholics handled it better than most of the others."

"The Catholics?" He must be joking. "Why? Because God favors the Catholics?"

"No. But like I said, everything that happens at war is random. When you can't make sense of anything, it helps to think there's a higher authority in control."

"What are you suggesting? That I go find God to help my patient?" She could hardly take this seriously.

"You can try." He was not joking. "Or maybe you can help him find a way of spiritual release. You said it's all in his head, right?"

He poured himself another shot of whiskey. "Want another one?"

She pushed her glass toward him and he filled it up. She turned the shot glass around and around on the desk, thinking over what he had said.

Ask God for help. Why not? Everyone else who could help her was out of reach and unattainable. She might as well add God to the list.

Sitting on his bed in a neatly pressed shirt and trousers, Ron waited anxiously for Tessa to come for her morning break visit. Yesterday, she had told him they would be going out for an excursion this morning. She had kept it a surprise where they were going and only told him he needed to dress properly. Not wanting to disappoint her, he took special care to shave, comb his hair, and tidy himself up. He was all ready to go.

"Hello, Ron," Tessa greeted him with a bright smile when she arrived. "Look at you! You look so handsome, I almost can't recognize you."

"Thanks," he answered.

"He's been waiting for you to come by for more than half an hour," Tommy said in the next bed. "He tried to read but all he did was check the clock on the wall and count the minutes."

"That's great, because I am looking forward to taking him out," Tessa said. "How are you feeling today?" she asked Ron.

"It feels good to be out of the hospital robe," he said. Earlier, when he looked in the mirror and saw his own reflection, he saw his old self, Ron Castile before he had gone off to war. He hadn't seen that self in a long time. He had almost forgotten what he looked like in civilian clothing.

"Good. Let's go," she said.

Outside on the street, Ron watched for people's reactions to him. He felt nervous. His back muscles were tightening up again. His legs stiffened and he started to drag. The passersby, though, were not gawking at him. While Tessa hailed a taxi, a woman in a fashionable suit dress and a pillbox hat walked by holding a little girl by the hand. The woman did not notice him, but the little girl turned to him and smiled. He didn't know what to do. The girl had the most angelic smile he had ever seen. How could such a sweet little angel smile at him? He felt ashamed, but touched.

"Come on," the woman said to the girl and urged her to keep walking. The girl waved goodbye to him. He smiled and gave her a timid wave back.

While he watched the girl and her mother walk away, a boy about thirteen or fourteen years old came up to him and asked, "Newspaper, sir?" The boy held out a folded newspaper and showed him the headline. "Italy Quits! Unconditional Surrender and Ordered to Resist the Nazis."

He looked at the newspaper, then at the boy. He couldn't think about the war anymore. He shook his head. The boy shrugged, then walked away.

"Let's go, Ron," Tessa said. A taxi pulled up and they got inside. On the way, he looked out the window, watching everything that was happening on the streets.

"That used to be one of my favorite restaurants." He pointed to a restaurant with the name "Charley" in large letters on the red awning over the front door.

"Maybe I can invite my friends and we can go there sometime when you are all better," Tessa said.

The taxi dropped them off in front of a church not too far from the Ardley's house. "We're going to church?" Ron asked.

"Yes. My Aunt Sophia and Uncle William go to this church." Tessa opened the taxi door. "I, on the other hand, don't come nearly often enough." She made a guilty face.

Hesitant, Ron got out of the car. At the church's entrance, he paused.

Tessa took him by the arm. "We'll say a prayer together for your fallen friends and comrades."

He had no choice but to follow her. Inside, the chapel was empty. Tessa led him to the first row of pews and they sat down.

"Is there anyone in particular you want us to pray for?" she asked. He shook his head.

"Okay. We'll pray for all of them then. Mind you, I am not very good at this." She held her hands together, closed her eyes, and bowed her head in prayer. "Dear Father, we pray for all the soldiers who served with Ron who are now in your heavenly kingdom. May they all rest in peace as you take them into your loving arms..."

Tessa continued, but "all the soldiers who served with Ron" were the only words he heard. Visions of the times when he and Pete Whitfield went on patrols together when they were still Marine privates appeared before his eyes. Memories of bodies of men he once knew lying dead on the ground at Guadalcanal swamped his mind. He looked up at the sculpture of Jesus above the altar. The crucified body of Christ reminded him of something grotesque. Once, he had seen the head of a dead Japanese soldier hanging on a stick on top of a Sherman tank. It hung and rotted there for days.

He felt nauseous.

Unable to stand the sight of the sculpture any longer, he looked away from the altar and gazed at the stained-glass windows on the side of the chapel. Each window depicted a scene from the Bible. Next to the one of the Sermon on the Mount, a plaque proclaimed the Ten Commandments.

"Thou Shall Not Kill." He stared at the first line on the plaque. A sour lump rose in the back of his throat.

A priest entered, walking toward the confessional. Ron got up and walked toward him. Startled, Tessa stopped praying. "Ron?"

Not hearing her, Ron approached the priest and grabbed him by the sleeve. The priest looked at him, surprised.

"Father," Ron cried. "Can you forgive me?"

The priest's eyes softened. "What did you do?"

"I killed so many people," Ron said. "At first, I only did it for our own protection. It was either them or us. We only killed when we had to. After a while, we cared less and less whether we had to kill or not. Our troop, we even had a contest going to see how many kills we each had. Sometimes, we shot them off even when they could've been captured. It didn't matter. We did it because we could." He lost his grip on the priest. His entire body was shaking. "But now, I see their dead faces around me all the time. I see them in my sleep. I see them when I'm awake. They won't leave me alone. I want to tell them I'm sorry. I want to ask them to forgive me but there's no way." He grabbed the priest's arm again. "You're a priest. You have the power to forgive me, right? Father, can you forgive me? Tell me, please. Am I forgiven?" Ron broke down and sobbed.

The priest watched him, then looked up. His eyes and Tessa's met for a moment. The priest then looked further to the back of the church. Tessa looked to the same spot and found Frank Castile sitting in the last pew. Castile nodded to acknowledge the priest, then got up and walked out.

The priest returned his attention to Ron, laying his hand on him and speaking quietly into his ear. Tessa took one look at Ron and the priest, then rushed out after the general.

Outside, Tessa shouted, "General Castile! General Castile! Wait!"

The general stopped.

"How did you know we were here?" she asked.

"Dr. Donovan told me."

That was news to her. Dr. Donovan hadn't told her anything about the general coming.

"Despite what you might think, Graham, I do care about my son. I call the hospital regularly to check on his progress. Dr. Donovan told me you would be taking Ron to church. I came to see how he's doing."

Worried that the general might think their treatments were ineffective after Ron's breakdown just now, Tessa tried to explain, "He's getting better. What you saw in there...we were praying for his fallen friends and he was overwhelmed thinking of them. That's all. He's not like that on most days anymore. I swear!"

Castile held up his hand. "I know. You don't have to explain. I've entrusted him to Dr. Donovan and all of you."

She hoped so. She didn't want all their efforts to be for naught if the general changed his mind.

"I heard you've been a great help to him," Castile said.

Tessa did not admit this nor did she care to take credit. Her immediate concern was Ron. Against her better judgment, she asked, "Would you come in and join us in prayers?"

"No. I don't know if he's ready to see me yet. Dr. Donovan warned me not to provoke him or agitate him. I'll see him when you all decide it's time."

Tessa felt both relieved and disappointed at his refusal.

"I do hope he'll be well enough to come home soon. His mother and I miss him."

Ron's mother. Tessa had not thought of her before. It was good to know Ron had someone who loved him waiting for him at home. It was good to hear Castile speak about Ron like a father rather than a general.

"Good day, Graham."

Tessa watched him walk away. When his car had driven away, she went back into the church. The priest was still talking to Ron. They were now seated in a pew and Ron had calmed down. By the time they returned to the hospital that afternoon, Ron was in much better spirits.

There was only one more thing. Every morning, she had taken away the dinner knife he had hidden under his pillow. In the evening, he would sneak another one off his tray and keep it with him overnight. It was time for that to stop.

While he was not looking, Tessa replaced the knife under his pillow with a wooden cross.

The next day, when she came for her morning visit, Ron held up the cross he had found under his pillow to show her. He gave her a playful smile like they were keeping a secret between them.

This was the liveliest he had ever been since coming to this hospital. "My back," he said, "it doesn't hurt anymore."

This was more than she ever expected from their little trip yesterday.

"I think I'm ready to go home," he said. "I'm ready to start over."

CHAPTER TWENTY-ONE

WALKING DOWN THE STREET, Anthony was amazed once again to see how quickly the city of Licata was being rebuilt. Everywhere he looked, ordinary life had returned. As the days passed, the gigantic piles of rubble he saw when he first arrived grew smaller and smaller until they disappeared altogether. Food shortages remained, but with the help of supplies from the Allies, some cafes and restaurants had reopened. A group of laughing children chased by a small dog ran past a poster on a restaurant's front window announcing in large, bold letters, "Sicilian Pasta Eating Contest for Allied Soldiers. 8 p.m. - Tonight."

Trade activities had resumed with locals lining up pull carts filled with olives, fruit, and vegetables. He had never seen tomatoes so big and oranges so orange. The Sicilian fruits and produce were big and lush. He stopped at one of the carts, bought a persimmon and took a bite before continuing on his way.

Life had not been too tough since he had come to Italy. Aside from training, he was free to do what he wanted. Some evenings, he and Warren would catch a movie shown by the army. Other nights, they would go listen to the army band perform. One Sunday, he went to see the Valley of the Temples, an archeological park where seven spectacular Greek temples were built between the sixth and the fifth centuries B.C. If it weren't for the remains of the bombing destructions and the presence of the Allied armies, he would almost feel like a tourist. He had even learned to speak a few Italian phrases in order to get around.

He had no complaints about his accommodations either. The army had assigned him to quarter with an elderly Sicilian couple, and the couple had put him up in a small room in their little house. Despite its small size, they kept their home clean and tidy. After months of living in barracks, it was a nice change to stay in a real home. Communication was difficult, as he did not speak much Italian and they did not speak English. Still, somehow, they got by. Everyday, he would give the old lady his food ration and she would make simple meals for him. What she made tasted ten times better than the food the army had fed him at camp all year. One night, the old man offered him a glass of grappa. That was a very generous act of welcome considering the city was still suffering from a shortage of supplies. Alcohol, especially, was scarce. The old man must have been saving the bottle like a hidden treasure.

Today, he went to the army post office to pick up his mail and packages. Jim Darnell, a lance corporal in his company, was there too. Darnell was in his thirties. That made him one of the oldest men in their company. Some of the boys jokingly called him "Grandpa."

"Good afternoon, Lieutenant." Looking happy and forgetting army protocol, Darnell greeted him like an old friend.

Anthony didn't mind. He was barely getting used to commanding someone almost a decade older than him. "What do you have there?" He pointed to the bags Darnell was putting into a paper box.

"A few gifts for my children," he said. "Some dolls, toys, blankets. A necklace for my wife."

"How old are your kids?" Anthony asked him.

"My daughter Janet is the oldest. She's seven. Jimmy is five. And the twins, Samuel and Samantha, they've just turned three.

You want to see their picture?" He took a photo out of his pocket and showed it to Anthony. In the photo, his wife was sitting on a chair in the center, holding one baby in each arm, presumably the twins. Darnell stood behind her with his older kids beside him, one on each side. He wore a pink and yellow hat and a uniform of the same colors with an apron. Behind them were several small tables with chairs and an ice cream counter.

"This was taken before you were deployed?" Anthony asked. Darnell nodded. "You worked in an ice cream shop?"

"I own it!" A proud smile came on his face. "It was a dream for my wife and I to have all the little kids in the neighborhood come every day after school. Those little ones are so adorable. They're always so eager to find out the surprise topping of the day."

From the way Darnell smiled, Anthony could almost see him behind the ice cream counter, scooping ice cream into cones to serve to neighborhood kids while indulging them with extra toppings and his hearty kindness. The image of Darnell, in a pink and yellow outfit in his ice cream shop full of children, was not one he could easily reconcile with the Jim Darnell in full army uniform, carrying guns and military gear and charged to kill.

After picking up his mail, Anthony went to the USO canteen. Although it was mid-afternoon and the canteen was half empty, he nonetheless chose an inconspicuous table in the corner so he could be alone to enjoy his coffee and to read one of the new books his parents had sent him. Small pleasures such as a quiet afternoon reading by himself were something he had learned to appreciate after months of army life. He was about to finish the first chapter when someone interrupted him.

"Is that *The Lady or the Tiger*?"

Anthony put down his book. A young man with raven dark hair stood before him. They looked about the same age. He, too, wore the gold stripe of a second lieutenant, except he also wore a white band with a red cross around the sleeve.

"Yes," Anthony said. "My parents sent it."

"You like folk tales?" Uninvited, the medic took a seat.

"I do." Anthony flipped the book over. The cover showed a conflicted young man standing before two doors in an ancient Roman arena. Behind one door was a maiden selected to be his bride. Behind the other, a fierce, hungry tiger awaited. As punishment for falling in love with the daughter of a barbaric king, the young man must choose which door to open. His fate depended on the princess, the beautiful girl shown above the arena whose finger pointed to the right. Would the princess send him into the arms of another woman or to his death?

"I do like folk tales," Anthony said. "Mythologies too."

The medic picked up the book and thumbed through the pages. "You know what the problem is when people read this story? They read it from the lover's perspective. It poses the question like he had a choice, but all he really had was a game of chance. Maybe the princess was a lovesick idiot or maybe she was a jealous viper. Whatever. In the end, his situation remained the same. His decision wouldn't change what was behind either door, so whether he believed the princess or not, his chances were still fifty-fifty." He put the book down. "It's a boring story when you read it that way, like watching someone roll dice."

"What's your take then?" Anthony asked, curious. It had been months since anyone had engaged him in a stimulating conversation about literature. Not since he left Chicago.

"My take? I'd rather approach it from the princess's perspective."

"The princess?"

"Yes. See, hers was not a game of chance. She could be the mastermind behind the scene. She held her lover's life in her hand. She held all the cards and she could decide the outcome. What do you think went through her mind when she was presented with her choices?"

"If I had to guess? She pointed him to the door with the tiger. The story implied she was consumed by jealousy."

The medic shook his head. "Too easy. What fun is there if she was nothing but a stereotypical jealous girl?"

"All right. What would you do then if you were the princess?"

"Me? I'd send him to the door with the maiden, of course."

"Because you love him?"

"Hell no!" The medic looked at Anthony as if it was the most ridiculous thing he had heard. "I don't do anything for love." He paused to make the point, then relaxed again. "But that would be a smarter choice than feeding her lover to the tiger."

"Why's that?"

"Because I'd arrange to kill the maiden when their wedding was over. The maiden would be dead before her wedding night began. She was the princess, right? Then she could easily arrange that."

"Kill the maiden? But the maiden was innocent!"

"Life's not fair, is it?" The medic answered without a beat. Anthony couldn't be sure if he was joking or not. Someone who could talk so freely about killing was a medic?

"So you see, the princess could have it both ways," the medic concluded. "Why kill her lover when she could kill the maiden? She could keep her lover alive without sending him to the maiden's marital bed. She could one-up everybody, including her father the king."

"Shrewd," Anthony said, "but you're wrong."

"I am?" The medic looked puzzled. "How so?"

"In your scenario, the princess assumed her lover would open the door she chose. What if he didn't?"

"You think he wouldn't trust her?"

"That could be. Or he really loved her. He might choose to die rather than be with another woman to prove his love to her."

The medic laughed in disbelief. "You got to be kidding!"

"Maybe. I'm still right and your scenario's flawed. The princess didn't hold all the cards. You have to factor in what her lover would do as part of the equation."

"Okay, you got me there," the medic conceded, then held out his hand. "Jesse Garland. I'm with the medical unit attached to your division."

Anthony shook his hand. "Anthony Ardley."

"I know. You're M Company's new second lieutenant. From Chicago, I hear."

"Yes," Anthony said. "Where are you from?"

"New York," Jesse said. "Gotham, if you like." He took out a pack of cigarettes and offered it to Anthony. Anthony declined. Jesse lit one for himself and inhaled. Anthony watched him in wonder. Unlike the army grunts and boors, Jesse had a very smooth way about him when he smoked. He took his time to light the cigarette. When he blew the smoke, he looked more like a movie star in a posh lounge than a serviceman in a military canteen.

"What were you doing before the army?" Anthony asked.

"Me?" Jesse said with a playful but dubious smile. "I was a professional fraud. I con people."

"You can't be serious."

"Ah! But that's just it. I am serious." Jesse said. "Sometimes the biggest lie you can tell is the truth. When the truth is so outrageous, no one would believe you. They would believe the exact opposite." He took another drag. "Enough about me. What did you do? Were you in school?"

"Close to graduation from university," Anthony admitted. "How'd you guess?"

"I'm good at reading people." Jesse glanced at Anthony's books on the table. "I haven't been in school since I was fifteen."

That surprised Anthony. With his polished manners and the sophisticated way he spoke, Jesse Garland did not look anything like a high school dropout. He could have easily fit in with the rest of the students at UC.

"What were you planning to do after you finished school?" Jesse asked. "I mean, if you weren't here."

"My parents wanted me to go into the family business."

"Really? What kind of business?"

"Real estate, trade, financial investments."

"Phew!" Jesse whistled. "I'm gonna have to hang around you

more." His cigarette now finished, he put it out and got up. "Good meeting you, Ardley. I'll see you around."

Anthony watched him walk away. He would like a friend like Jesse Garland, someone with whom he could have discussions like the one they just had.

No sooner than Jesse was gone, Warren came up to him with a coffee in his hand. "I see you've met Jesse Garland."

"Yes. Interesting guy."

"He's interesting all right," Warren said.

Anthony caught a note of caution in his voice. "What do you mean by that?"

"He joined our division right before Sicily. When he came he was a sergeant on the field. Next thing I know, the powers on high made him a lieutenant. It's very unusual for a medic to be promoted to officer rank. You know why they did it? They found out he could get things. To make sure they could get things from him without violating the anti-fraternization rules, they made him one of us."

"Get things? What kind of things?"

"Innocent things like socks, blankets, extra rations, food. And some not-so-benign things like booze, cigarettes, censored photos and magazines. Who knows? Whatever anyone needs."

"You mean Garland deals in the black market? Isn't that against the rules?"

"There's the rub. Garland doesn't take money for anything." Warren lowered his voice. "He trades favors, but never any favor for himself that would break any code. No one could ever get anything on him."

How intriguing. Anthony had never met anyone like that.

"I'd watch out if I were you," Warren joked. "If he's hitting you up, I betcha you got something he wants."

"What could he possibly want from me?"

"I don't know. I'm just saying." Warren finished his coffee. "You never know."

CHAPTER TWENTY-TWO

THE CEREMONY TO honor the nurse trainees who completed the Nurses Specialized Training Program was a low-key affair. The event included a few speeches and an official recognition of each of the trainees. All that suited Tessa fine. It saved her from having to explain to anyone why no one from her family attended. She still hadn't told anyone outside of the hospital she was on course to accept an assignment overseas. She was not ready to break the news to the Ardleys or her parents.

She still had not found any way to get assigned to the 3rd Division. She felt so silly now to have thought she could make this happen by sheer force of will.

Sitting alone on a bench in the hospital courtyard, she watched her fellow trainees and their families celebrate and roam about. It was now too late to back out. If she couldn't get the assignment she wanted, she would still have to deploy. But at least, her service overseas would be her own choice. She would be dealing with the war on her own terms. If she could not be with Anthony, she would still be doing the same thing he was doing.

That was all she could think of to console herself.

"Tessa," Sarah came over with her parents and a photographer in tow. "Won't you take a photo with me and my parents?"

Tessa smiled in agreement and the photographer took a snapshot.

"I'll tell the photographer to make a copy for you," Sarah said and insisted that Tessa join her and her parents at the luncheon reception that followed. On their way to the reception, Sarah pulled her aside. "Any response from anyone about your assignment?"

Tessa shook her head.

Sarah put her arm around Tessa's arm. "I've been thinking, why don't you try asking General Castile to help you?"

"You want me to ask General Castile?" That was preposterous. "That mean, full of himself, pompous..."

"He may be all that." Sarah didn't let her finish. "But you practically saved his son. Who knows what would have happened to Ron if it weren't for you? If you ask me, the general owes you a big favor."

"I don't know." Castile was the last person from whom Tessa wanted to plead for a favor. "I haven't exactly been respectful to him. I don't like him, and I don't think he likes me very much."

"He's still a general," Sarah said. "He can probably make things happen where others can't."

Tessa raised her head and looked ahead. Castile? Would she really have to go to Castile?

She lost all appetite for the luncheon reception.

CHAPTER TWENTY-THREE

THE ALLIED FORCES were moving north.

For Anthony, the inevitable moment had arrived. Following Operation Avalanche, the joint mission by the British and the American forces in September in which the Allies overtook Salerno, Italy, the 3rd Infantry Division had been called to move north toward Naples to reinforce the British troops. Ready or not, the time had come for him to assume the role he was trained to perform.

Their convoy traveled up the rocky roads toward the village of Acerno, passing piles after piles of stones and rock fragments left by shell explosions and grenades. Abandoned military trucks were lined up on the side of the road, some knocked out by bombers, others still intact but out of gas. Rifles, helmets, and gear were scattered everywhere. All were remnants that reminded him of the brutal battles that had gone on before they arrived and the reality that awaited him ahead.

At the unit's mobile base that evening, Captain Harding convened the officers to plan for the takedown of a German command outpost fifteen miles north.

Standing among the officers in his company, the gold stripe on Anthony's shoulders felt to him more like a mockery of his inexperience than a symbol of his higher rank. Beck made no effort to hide his contempt for him. While Beck would not openly contradict him, his eye rolls and yawns whenever Anthony spoke to the soldiers in the unit disrupted his attempts to assert his authority. He could reprimand Beck, but fussing over an experienced noncom's indirect slights would only make him look insecure. He would be better off being above it. Besides, they had real enemies ahead. The company needed Beck and his expertise. He did not want to create animosity between him and the company's first sergeant.

It wasn't only Beck. Jonesy and Ollie were nice enough. They always deferred to him and showed him the respect owed to a ranking officer. Still, he could not feel truly in command. The noncoms knew he was green. When they showed him deference, it felt like they were humoring him. They were all putting up a show pretending that he knew better. Their respect was not real. The order of command was unfair. Even he felt it.

If he could not convince the people below him, he had an even tougher time convincing the person above him. Wesley had been observing his every move. The first lieutenant's constant watchful eye added a load of extra pressure on him not to make any mistake.

Only Harding seemed unconcerned whether he had what it took to lead their men. The captain was the only one who didn't make him feel like an outsider.

"How do you see this play out, Lieutenant?" Captain Harding asked Wesley.

Sharpe studied the aerial photos of the enemy's outpost. "I say we surround them. Send one platoon to the front entrance, attack and draw them out. When their defense is preoccupied, a second platoon goes around to the back. Split up. Two squads go to block the Germans from escaping from the back while another squad goes for their stockpile of weapons here." He pointed to a shack next to the outpost.

"All right," said the captain. "You and Beck will take a platoon to the back of the outpost. Ardley, you'll take a platoon to their front entrance for the direct attack."

Lead the front attack? Anthony looked up. The captain wanted him to take the riskiest and most important part of the mission?

"It's your time to shine." The captain said. He showed not a trace of doubt.

"Captain," Wesley said, "may I suggest either Sergeant Beck or I be the one to lead the attack to secure the front?"

Anthony threw Wesley a glance. The captain was giving him an opportunity to prove himself. He did not want Wesley to take it away.

Wesley ignored him. "The front platoon will be exposed. They can use more back up."

Anthony couldn't contradict him, but he did not need back up.

"No need." Harding looked at Anthony. "Lieutenant Ardley will do fine. Won't you, Lieutenant?"

"I will, sir," Anthony said. He did not want the captain to doubt him.

Noting Wesley's unease, Harding asked the sergeants. "Any of you want to back up Lieutenant Ardley?"

The sergeants eyed each other. "I will," Jonesy volunteered.

"Good. Sergeant Oliver will stay behind with the reserve unit." The captain gathered the intelligence reports on the table in front of him. "That'll be all, gentlemen. Get a good night's rest. You'll need it."

As they left, Anthony felt Wesley watching him again. The first lieutenant did not like the captain's arrangement. That was clear to him, but he wasn't happy with Wesley implying in front of everyone that he wasn't up to the job either. He didn't need a babysitter.

He could not fail tomorrow. He must show Wesley he was capable of this. He would not let their unit down. He would change Wesley's mind about him.

· · ·

At 0400 hours, their company convoy set off for the German outpost. As they got closer, Anthony could feel his body tensing up. He reminded himself to keep calm. He must stay calm and in control.

The vehicles stopped half a mile away from their destination. Keeping quiet, the company of men set out on foot toward their barely visible target under the still-dark sky.

"Showtime." Jonesy jumped out of the vehicle.

"Lieutenant," Beck said to Anthony. "Get ready for your baptism of blood." He smirked as Anthony watched him pass by and went ahead.

They came to the line where the enemy's outpost was within their view. Wesley stopped the unit and directed the officers to lead their troops into position. "Beck, take the men around that way to the back. Jonesy, go with him."

"What?" Jonesy asked.

"You heard me. Go."

Jonesy paused, then glanced at Anthony and walked away. Wesley pointed to Anthony. "Ardley, you're with me."

Confused, Anthony said, "But the captain said…"

"The captain's not here. Situation's changed. New rules." He stepped up and signaled their men to go forward. "Follow me," he said to Anthony.

Frustrated but having no choice, Anthony did as Wesley ordered. He could not understand. Wesley Sharpe had just sabotaged him.

They hopped down into a ditch canal and stepped over the body of a dead British soldier lying face down. What was he doing here? Anthony wondered. Was he on a reconnaissance mission? There was no way to know. A small notebook lay next to his body. The notebook's pages had been shredded by bullets, but the photo that had fallen out of it was still intact and he could see a woman holding a child. He turned away. Subconsciously, he touched his own pocket where he kept the photo of Tessa, the one he had asked her to send to him.

They moved closer until they reached a spot before where they must run through open land to the outpost's front door. A sliver of morning sunlight had broken over the horizon. Above them, pieces of human limbs hanging on the trees and body parts strewn across the field became visible. Feeling nauseous, Anthony winced and looked away.

The war was real now.

He glanced at Wesley. It no longer mattered who was leading the mission.

"Try to not get yourself killed in the next two hours," Wesley said to him. "If you can stay alive through this, chances are you'll live for the long haul."

Swallowing hard, Anthony tugged the cross hanging around his neck, more glad than ever that Tessa had sent it to him.

"Be careful when you run across," Wesley said. "There might be mines."

Right. The mines. He knew that. He had learned about this in training. But regardless, he was glad Wesley reminded him.

"We go ahead on my signal," Wesley told them.

In the next minute, everything turned into chaos. "Move! Move!" Anthony heard men shouting all around him. Gunfire rained down from every direction. Where were the shots coming from? When did the Germans realize they were here? A bullet flew past his temple. Just missed. Another barrage of bullets came. Machine gun bullets. The bullets showered down on them like a rapid hailstorm. He ran. Ran as fast as he could and ran for his life. Shells hit the ground around him, splashing up dirt that pelted against his leg. It hurt. Sweat drenched his back and his chest. His heart pounded and he was running out of breath. Needed to run faster. Needed to get to the wall of the outpost building where he could take cover.

A shell exploded somewhere to his left side, followed by screams. Some of his men running alongside him got hit. Maybe they all got hit. He couldn't tell. The stench of burnt hair and human flesh made him gag. He wrinkled his nose to fend off the smell. Behind him, someone howled. He turned his head. A medic ran toward a soldier lying on the ground. He continued running and stepped on a detached hand. His mind couldn't process the ghastly sight.

When he reached the side of the building, Wesley had already gone inside. Others followed and he hurried in with them.

Gunshots fired off inside the enemy outpost. He could hear Wesley shouting upstairs. The men who came in with him charged into room after room, searching out their enemies. In the midst of the confusion, Anthony saw the stairs leading to the basement. He went down with his rifle aiming ahead, ready to shoot.

He had just reached the bottom of the stairs when a German soldier jumped out from hiding. For a brief moment, maybe as short as a split second, they came face to face and their eyes met, their guns aimed pointedly at each other.

By instinct, Anthony pulled the trigger.

The bullet hit the German soldier in the chest. The force of the gunshot propelled his body backward and he slammed against the wall. Anthony pulled the trigger again. Again. And again. In fright, he kept firing just in case the man might still be alive. The German soldier's body slumped motionless on the floor. He didn't know how many times he had shot the man. When he stopped shooting, he took several deep breaths and tried to think.

He almost died.

The man lying motionless on the floor had meant to kill him.

He walked up to the dead body. Blood gushed out from bullet wounds and the stain spread on the soldier's uniform. He pushed the man's shoulder to make sure he was dead. The soft flesh of the dead man beneath his fingers surprised him. He almost forgot the body belonged to a human. What happened?

He just killed someone.

The thought made him sick. He turned away. He took one sweeping look of the empty basement and returned upstairs.

Above on the second floor, Wesley Sharpe had subdued the

enemies stationed at the outpost. Jonesy had secured the back and led the squad in.

"Round them up and take them outside," Wesley told Jonesy and headed back downstairs. In German, Jonesy ordered the captured men to walk outside.

"Jonesy speaks German?" Anthony asked Fox, who had caught up with Wesley while Anthony was down in the basement.

"Sergeant Jones's mother was a German immigrant," Fox said. "Crazy, isn't it? He's fighting his mother's native land." He looked at the four dead German soldiers on the floor. "Sergeant Jones didn't do this though. Lieutenant Sharpe did. He took down these men by himself."

Anthony dropped his shoulders. He could not have done this. He could hardly get over killing one enemy soldier in the basement.

"He caught those five Krauts who Sergeant Jones is marching out too." Fox swung his rifle across his shoulder. "One of them's a German major. The captain's going to be pleased. Command will have an intel party tonight."

Before leaving with Fox, Anthony took one more look at the dead German men. No. He could not have done this. Wesley made the correct call to take over.

Outside, Beck and Jonesy had rounded up more German soldiers by the shack where the Germans kept their stockpile of arms. Beck was giving Wesley an update and Anthony was about to join them when he noticed one of their own men lying in the weeds. He ran over to him. The injured soldier had been shot in the chest.

"Medic! Medic!" he shouted and kneeled down next to the soldier. The soldier made no sound and his body was convulsing. Anthony pressed his hands on top of the soldier's wound to try to stop the bleeding.

"He's in shock," Jesse said. He had heard Anthony's call for help. "Give him some water!" He told Anthony as he tore open the soldier's uniform and spattered sulfa on his wound. "I said give him water!" Jesse shouted, jerking Anthony out of his stupor. Anthony opened his canteen and put it next to the soldier's lips. The soldier swallowed the water, gasping between gulps.

"You'll be all right." Jesse said to the soldier while he patched him up as best as he could. "Stay with me, okay? Stay with me." He inserted a needle in the soldier's arm and gave him plasma. "Get a truck here," he said to Anthony. "We have to get him to the hospital."

Anthony got up and ran to call for help.

Back at the base, Anthony sat alone and watched the sun climb the high noon sky. The trees and fields looked normal like it was any other day. Everything was clear and illuminated, but his own mind was a blur. He could not remember what happened before he got into the vehicle after their mission was over. He remembered telling a communications sergeant to call for a vehicle for Jesse and the injured soldier. He recalled riding back in the military vehicle and the unit breaking into an impromptu celebration for a mission accomplished. Liquor found at the German outpost was passed around and everyone toasted to everything both worthy and ridiculous. Other than that, he couldn't remember what else had happened. He felt numb.

Wesley came over and sat down next to him. "Do you know why Harding sent you to lead the platoon to initiate the attack?"

Anthony didn't answer. He had no idea. After what he saw today, he didn't know why the captain would task him with leading the assault. Someone with more experience should have led the mission.

"You see all those men over there?" Wesley glanced at the men in their company still drinking and celebrating. "They're all battle-tested. Jones, Ollie, even Fox. Some of them, like Beck, they've been fighting this war for more than two years. They've got experience. The captain wouldn't risk losing them if he didn't have to."

Anthony frowned. What was Wesley saying?

"Better to send the least valuable ones out to take the first hits. The ones with no experience have the least to contribute. That was why half the platoon he sent to attack the front was made up of replacements. You included. Didn't you notice?"

Anthony's heart sank.

"The replacements," Wesley looked at him, "they make good human shields."

A human shield. He felt ill.

"Don't take it personally," Wesley said. "It's purely a strategic decision. Every other captain is doing the same thing. Besides, most rookies like it that way, trying to prove they're tough and to fit in."

Scowling, Anthony stared straight ahead.

"There was always a chance you would make it out okay."

Perhaps. Probably not. "Thank you then, for changing the plan and looking out for me." He felt completely used.

"Don't thank me. I wasn't trying to save you. I might've done the same thing if I were the captain and I had a more favorable set of circumstances to work with."

Anthony didn't know what he meant.

"The men in this company need people who will look out for them. If something should happen to me, someone else will need to take charge and do what needs to be done, or a lot of them are going to die. We've lost three second lieutenants this year already. All of them wasted. All of them KIA." He looked Anthony in the eyes. "We don't have the luxury to keep filling the position with inexperienced junior officers, especially not when someone who can excel at the job comes along."

Did Wesley just say he could excel at the job? Wesley valued him but the captain didn't? He felt all confused. "What about the captain? Isn't he in charge?"

Before Wesley could answer, a jeep pulled up the road. A major and his lieutenant got out and Harding went to greet them. Their unit had won another fight and both the major and the captain could bask in the glory of having their mission accomplished.

"The captain has his own agenda," Wesley said. "Whatever he has in mind, it's now up to you and me to get everyone through this. For that reason alone, I've got your back. In the meantime, you need to step up your game and figure out how this outfit really works and do it fast. Figure out how to get our men behind you. You can't command them if they don't trust you."

With that said, Wesley got up and walked away. Anthony lowered his head. His hands were still covered with the dried blood of the injured soldier earlier. The bloodstains had smeared all over his uniform.

He opened his bloodstained hands. It could easily have been his own blood.

The baptism of blood.

PART VII
GOODBYE CHICAGO

CHAPTER TWENTY-FOUR

ON THE DAY of Ron Castile's discharge from the hospital, Alexander brought along the puppy with the droopy eyes. "This is Snowball." Tessa took the leash from Alexander and handed it to Ron. "Snowball will keep you company when I'm not there."

Ron broke into a smile as he bent down to pet the puppy. Wagging its tail, the puppy licked his face. "Thank you, Tessa," Ron said. "Thank you for everything."

"Don't mention it," Tessa said. "Come on, let's get you home." She waved goodbye to Alexander and walked Ron from the courtyard to the exit for the patients' loading zone. There, his parents stood waiting by their car.

"Ronnie," Mrs. Castile cried out and embraced him the minute she saw him.

"Mother," Ron put his arms around her. Wary, he said to Frank Castile, "Father."

Frank Castile put his thick arms around his son. "Welcome home, son."

Ron smiled, obviously relieved. Before they left, Mrs. Castile turned to Tessa. "Miss Graham. You must be the nurse I've heard so much about." She took Tessa's hand. "Thank you for helping Ronnie."

"It was my duty, Ma'am. We are all very happy for his recovery."

"Would you come to our house for dinner tonight?" Mrs. Castile asked, still holding Tessa's hand. "We're having a special dinner to celebrate Ron's homecoming, and I won't take no for an answer."

Tessa looked at Frank Castile. For once, he actually smiled.

"Please come, Tessa," Ron said. "I'd love to be able to thank you for everything you've done."

Ron looked so hopeful, she didn't want to disappoint him. "Thank you, Mrs. Castile. I'll be there."

The Castiles took their son away. Heading back into the hospital, Tessa wondered how she would survive dinner with Frank Castile. What could she possibly talk to him about?

On the other hand, in the back of her mind, she couldn't stop thinking about what Sarah had said.

He's still a general. He can probably make things happen where others can't.

Could she ask Frank Castile for help? Or would he scold her? Would such a request backfire and invite his scorn for asking for special treatment?

Dinner at the Castiles was more relaxed than Tessa had expected. Surprisingly, the Castiles had a younger son, Allen, who was not in the military but was attending school at Loyola University. Tessa wondered how Frank Castile could have allowed one of his sons to not be in the service.

At the table, Mrs. Castile and Allen carried the conversations, updating Ron on things that had happened and news about their friends and relatives while Ron had been away. Ron looked happy to be home. In between the family news, Mrs. Castile asked Tessa about her work and her family. No one mentioned anything about the war or Ron's time in the marines. Tessa guessed they didn't want to remind Ron in case that might upset him.

Frank Castile didn't say much and he rarely cracked a smile. Yet, his steely exterior had softened. His eyes glowed with affection whenever he looked at his wife. His normally wooden face seemed milder and his posture less stiff and overbearing.

"Frank," Mrs. Castile said while passing a plate of vegetables. "Aunt Estelle wants to come over tomorrow. Would you pick her up and drive her over for lunch?"

"Dear, can she come after I leave?" he asked, a bit exasperated. "I'm heading back to Washington the day after tomorrow."

"Frank!" Mrs. Castile said, seemingly oblivious to the effect Frank Castile had on other people. "She wants to see Ronnie. We shouldn't make her wait."

"All that woman does is whine and gossip."

"Now you be nice. She's an old lady. We must show her proper respect."

"I can't sit through lunch with her."

"You can and you will."

Tessa held her smile. How could it be? This lovely, petite woman was giving the fearsome General Castile orders.

"You can pick her up at her house at eleven-thirty tomorrow," Mrs. Castile said. "We'll have a nice family lunch together. All of us."

"All right, dear. If that's what you want."

Tessa couldn't believe what she heard, but the general wasn't taking an order. This was his way of indulging his wife. From the doting way he looked at Mrs. Castile, he clearly adored her. Tessa never would have thought Frank Castile had this softer side to him.

Could she really approach him for help?

At this point, what had she got to lose? When dinner was over, she asked to speak privately to him and he invited her to his study.

Frank Castile's office was like an extension of the man. From the dark wood colors and the rich, brown carpet, the room felt heavy and serious. No clutter could be seen anywhere. All the furniture was arranged in practical order with every personal item neatly organized and displayed. Only the soft lighting emanating from the lamps saved the room from feeling cold and sterile.

"My sons." Frank Castile picked up a photo displayed on his desk and showed Tessa. In it, three boys had come off the basketball court. Tessa recognized the one in the middle as Ron and the one on the left to be Allen Castile. Ron was still a teenager in the photo.

Frank Castile took a seat at his desk and motioned to her to sit down. "You know Ron. You've met Allen. The other one is Patrick. He's the oldest."

Tessa sat down across from him and put the photo back on the desk. Castile looked at the photo. His eyes beamed with pride. "We're a military family. I served in the Great War. Patrick is in the Air Force. He's based in the Pacific now. Allen has acute asthma and is disqualified from joining. Most people would be glad to have any excuse to get out of the draft, but not Allen. There is no one he looks up to more than his two older brothers. It hasn't been easy for him not being able to follow in their footsteps."

Tessa listened. She had always thought she irritated the general as much as he annoyed her. She didn't expect him to talk to her about his own family.

He picked up the photo again. "Of the three, Ron is the strongest and smartest. Only the toughest men can make it through to the Marines. Ron passed all the requirements with flying colors. My wife and I always expected him to do great things. We knew he would face risks and dangers at war, but the worst we ever expected was that he would die a hero." He put down the photo and looked at Tessa. "So you can see how heartbreaking this whole experience has been for me and my wife. When I saw the film you showed me, it was devastating to see what had become of him."

"He's much better now, sir," Tessa said. "He's still a tough and intelligent man. That's why he is recovering so fast. And I find him to be very kind. He'll continue to get better."

"You deserve a lot of credit, Graham. Not just for your work in treating him, but in going above and beyond to fight for him and stand up for him. You've shown a lot of courage. I like that. If you were a man, I would recruit you to join the army in an instant. If I had a daughter, I would want her to be like you."

His compliment surprised her. She had no idea he thought so positively of her.

"What is it you want to talk to me about?" he asked. "Is it something about Ron?"

"No, sir. It's something about me." He waited for her to explain. She felt awkward and unsure how to start. "I completed my nurses' training two weeks ago."

"Congratulations. Well done."

"I've chosen to volunteer for service overseas."

"I'm glad to hear that." His response was just as she expected.

"There is just one thing." She mustered all her nerves. "I want to be assigned to a medical unit attached to the Sixth Army Corps. I want to ask you to arrange and authorize my assignment."

"That's an odd request," Castile said. "What is your reason for asking?"

Too embarrassed to tell him the truth, she thought of the time when she made this same request to Dr. Donovan several months ago. "My friend Ellie Swanson is with the 33rd Field Hospital attached to the Sixth Army Corps. I worked with her when she was a nurse trainee. I want to work with her again."

Castile sat stone-faced. His piercing stare made her exceedingly uncomfortable and she felt compelled to explain herself further. "I have a family member serving in the Sixth Army Corps."

The general remained disturbingly quiet. The look of disapproval on his face did not bode well. She wondered if this was a mistake after all. Maybe she never should have broached the subject with him. Nervous, she locked her fingers on her lap.

Castile crossed his arms. "Are you aware I once used to interrogate prisoners of war?" he asked. "You're a very good liar, Graham, but I can always tell when people are lying."

Her body froze. She wished that there were some place in the room where she could hide.

"Tell me the real reason why you're asking for this," Castile said.

Unable to look him in the eye, she looked sideways and tried to think of what to say. Telling the general about her love life was the last thing on earth she wanted. She considered withdrawing her request and leaving the room. But if she did that, she would lose any chance of finding her way to Anthony. It was now or never. She tightened her grip of her hands. "My boyfriend is in the Army Sixth Corps and I want to be with him."

Castile stared at her. He showed no hint of what he was thinking. But now that the truth was out, Tessa felt no fear or embarrassment anymore. She dared to face him and waited to hear what he would say.

"I admire your devotion to your boyfriend, Graham, but I don't like distractions within the army," Castile said. "Your presence in the same division as your boyfriend could be a distraction for both of you. And if you think he could protect you because you two are working at the same place, then you're sorely mistaken."

"I won't be a distraction!" Tessa said. "I am a responsible nurse. I am good at what I do. You can see that in my records. If I go, I will do my job, and I will make sure to let him do his. I'm not afraid of being on the front lines either. I don't need him or anyone to protect me."

Castile seemed unmoved. She felt her chance slipping away. "I don't have any illusion it would be a honeymoon if I am assigned to the same unit with him," she said. "I want to choose my own role in this war. I want to be by his side when he fights. Whatever he has to face, I want to face the same. That is why I intend to serve overseas even if you refuse my request. But if you would grant me this one favor, I would cherish the chance to be near him, in case…" *In case he doesn't make it.* But she could not bring herself to say that.

"Who is this young man you're so intent on joining?" Castile asked.

Thoroughly embarrassed, she said, "His name is Anthony Ardley. He's a junior officer with the 3rd Infantry Division." Her voice nearly faded to a whisper.

An odd smile came across Frank Castile's face when he heard Anthony's name. Unsure why Castile found this so amusing, Tessa started to feel irritated. Did he think everything she said was a joke? That was enough. She couldn't stand this. She would not stay and be interrogated and mocked any longer. She should cut this meeting short before she lost control of herself and said something to him that she might regret. "Sir, I will take my leave now if you won't help me. Please forget I asked." She got up from the chair.

"Sit down," he said. His voice was not harsh but still commanding. Tessa sat back down in the chair.

"If I grant you your request, would you give me your word you will put your duties as your number one priority at all times? And I mean at all times."

"Of course, sir," Tessa said. He didn't have to ask. It never crossed her mind to do anything less.

"And would you promise me you will not be a distraction to him in any manner whatsoever?"

"No, sir, I promise I will not. I'll do everything I can to make sure of that. I'll make sure he promises the same." She would do anything she could to convince Castile.

"I don't welcome distractions. But then again, the army can always use a morale boost. Perhaps an honorable young lieutenant would be motivated to fight harder if he knew his girlfriend was fully committed to the cause of his mission and fighting alongside with him."

Tessa sat up in her seat. Was Castile saying what she thought he meant? Would he give her the assignment she wanted?

"I might be making a terrible mistake," Castile said, "but I will grant your request, on the condition that you will always remember your promise to me."

Tessa couldn't believe it. This was happening. After all this time, after running into one stonewall after another until she had almost given up hope and the entire prospect seemed more and more ridiculous, unrealistic, and far-fetched, she would get what she wanted. She wanted to jump out of her seat. "I will, sir. You have my word. I promise."

Castile nodded. "This is not a request I would have ordinarily granted. I'm agreeing on the account that you've proven yourself to be dedicated to your work. Don't break my trust."

"I won't." She couldn't hold her smile in anymore.

"Thank you for what you've done for my son," Castile added.

"It was always my wish to see him recover too." She sincerely meant that.

"I will send word to notify the officer in charge of administration at the Sixth Corps. When you get to your destination, go see Colonel Callahan. Tell him that I sent you. He'll put you in touch with Lieutenant Ardley."

"Yes, sir." This was beyond what she had hoped for.

But just as joy overtook her, a new realization came to her. The general's consent meant she would soon have to say goodbye to all the people she loved here.

And her parents. What would they think when they found out?

CHAPTER TWENTY-FIVE

ON A BENCH by the Buckingham Fountain in Grant Park, Tessa and Ruby watched the water shoot high into the air. It was a beautiful spectacle. Tessa was sure she would miss it when she left.

"I'll miss you so much," Ruby said. "I can't believe that you're really leaving."

"I'll miss you too," Tessa said. "You're my best friend here, and you're the only one I trust to help me. No one else knows I'm leaving except for the people I work with at the hospital." She took two envelopes out of her bag. "This letter is for my parents. You can mail it. And this letter is for Uncle William and Aunt Sophia. I'll tell them I need to stay at the hospital for a weekend shift. When you give this letter to them on Monday, I'll be well on my way to deployment."

"Are you sure you don't want to tell them in person? They'll be so upset when they find out."

"I know, but I don't want them to try to stop me."

Ruby took the letters. "You're so brave to do this. You did it all on your own too. I wouldn't have dared."

For a while, they sat in silence. Tessa looked out to the lake.

She still had a few days left in Chicago, but her mind had already sailed off far away.

"Do you know where you'll be going?"

"No. We're not supposed to know until we arrive. Troop movements are military secrets. All I know is, I'm supposed to join the people in my unit leaving from Chicago at the train station Saturday morning."

"Anthony will be so surprised when he sees you," Ruby said. "You love him very much, don't you?"

Hearing his name made Tessa smile. "I didn't even think much of him at first. We argued with each other from the day we met. And then, it was as if he had always been there, waiting for me. The best thing to ever happen to me was right there in front of me, and it took me so long to see it."

Ruby listened with dreamy eyes. This was the first time Tessa had spoken openly about her feelings for Anthony.

"Will you tell Jack and Henry I'm sorry for not saying goodbye before I go?" Tessa asked. "I know they'd be worried, and I don't want to alarm anyone before I leave. Tell them I'll write to them as soon as I can."

"I'll do that," Ruby said. Tessa could hear the sadness in her voice. She thought of the old days before Jack left for the war, when the four of them would cruise around in Jack's old car on Saturday afternoons or play Monopoly and card games together. Those days that passed would never return.

She took out several packs of bubble gum and a box of chocolates.

"Where did you get these?" Ruby asked, surprised. With the sugar ration, candies were not easy to come by these days.

"The black market." Tessa unwrapped a pack of gum and offered it to Ruby. "I paid good prices for these." They each took a piece and started to out-do each other blowing bubbles. When Ruby blew a large one that covered half her face, Tessa poked it. The gum flattened on Ruby's lips and Tessa laughed.

"Hey! No fair," Ruby said, but she laughed too.

Behind their laughter, Tessa felt a shadow of loss. This would be the last time she and Ruby would have fun together this way. She did not know when or if they would ever see each other again. All the good times they had together like this one would soon be a thing of the past. If they did see each other again in the future, they would no longer be schoolgirls talking about boys and playing silly games. Their girlhood was over.

What lay ahead? She could not tell from looking into the vast horizon before her.

Tessa boarded the vessel with a large red cross painted on the sides of its hull. On the deck, she stopped and turned around to look once more at the American shore. Three years had passed since she first arrived here at the port of Boston with Uncle William. Today, this port would once again set her onto the path of her new life.

For a long time, all she had dreamt of was the day when she would board a ship to leave, but this was not how she had envisioned she would depart. No one was here to bid her farewell like she had imagined. No suitcases filled with gifts for her parents and her friends in London would come with her. In her fatigues with her hair tied up, the only things she carried were her uniforms, mess kit, gas mask, and a few other government-issued items. Other military medical personnel walked past and hustled her along.

Her desired return destination had always been London. But now, her destination was unknown.

No regrets, she told herself. And no, her destination was not unknown. Her destination was Anthony. With that thought, she smiled to herself and stepped ahead.

She made her way to her cabin. A cheerful young woman with a sweet, heart-shaped face greeted her. "Hi. You must be Tessa Graham. I'm Gracie Hall. We're cabin mates. We're both assigned to the 33rd Field Hospital." The young woman warmly introduced herself.

Tessa gave her a reserved but courteous smile, then dropped off the duffle bag and excused herself to go back up to the deck. The ship had begun its journey. She could feel the floor swaying beneath her feet.

On the deck, the large American flag flew in the ocean wind. She looked at the views all about. The land behind was shrinking farther and farther away. Two other ships had joined them, one on each side of the vessel she was on. More ships followed and moved toward them. Soon they formed a full naval convoy.

Above her, the booms of jet engines thundered from the skies. She looked up. A squadron of destroyers flew directly above, escorting the ships to shield them from submarine attacks.

She had entered Anthony's world.

I'm right behind you, Anthony. She sent her thoughts out to the sea. *Right behind you.*

CHAPTER TWENTY-SIX

October 20, 1943

Dear Mother and Father,

When you receive this letter, I will be far from Chicago. You will probably have heard from Uncle William and Aunt Sophia already. Please don't fault them for what I have done. They had no idea. I kept my plans secret from them and I am the only one to blame. They have been nothing but kind, loving, and generous to me these last three years. I love them dearly like my own family. I know that they must feel terrible and they must be thinking that they failed you. They did not. I made the choice all on my own.

I am on my way to wherever Anthony is. I will be an army nurse for the U.S. Army's 33rd Field Hospital. It is one of the military medical units attached to Anthony's division.

I know that no amount of apology from me will make up for taking off this way. You sent me away three years ago to protect me, and now I am defying your wish by heading straight to the war. Please understand that I can no longer hide every time people I love are placed in danger. Not anymore.

Please forgive me. I am in love with Anthony. I know he is in love with me too. I can't bear to be away from him. I want to be near him and face whatever dangers that he must face, together with him and alongside him. If anything were to happen to him and I were not there, I would regret it forever. My life would be hollow without him.

But when I think of boarding the ship to head to where he is, when I think of seeing him again, my heart flares. Every part of me feels this is the right thing to do. I feel like I can soar high into the sky.

So I made up my mind to find my way to him. I decided to follow his path. After he was drafted, I transferred to a special programme at the hospital for training military nurses for assignments overseas. That enabled me to complete my training this year. I did everything I could to obtain an assignment that would allow me to be with him. For a long time, it seemed like a futile effort. But with luck on my side, or perhaps it was fate, I finally succeeded. When you get this letter, I will hopefully have reunited with him already.

It is hard for me to admit my feelings so openly, even to you, but I want you to understand why I have done this. Please don't worry about me. I am no longer the little girl you knew when I left London. I am not afraid of what will come. I promise I will take care of myself.

I hope that wherever I am going will be in the European theatre. Then I will at least be closer to you. Maybe where I am heading is England and this will bring me closer to home. If that happens, I might even be able to see you again. I miss you both immensely.

I will write to you as soon as I can, once I find Anthony.

— With all my love, Tessa

October 20, 1943

Dear Uncle William and Aunt Sophia,

Please accept my deepest apology for leaving so suddenly without saying goodbye, for concealing my plans from you for such a long time, and for leaving you in this difficult position as my guardians. I am sorry for all the agony and troubles that I may have caused you.

As of last Thursday, I have left Chicago for deployment overseas as an army nurse. By the time you receive this letter, I may have already left the country. I have been planning this for a very long time. After Anthony left last January, I transferred to a special program for training military nurses for overseas assignments, which enabled me to finish my training in September. Since we learned of Anthony's unit assignment, I have done all I could to get assigned to a medical unit attached to his division. I succeeded. I will be joining the U.S. Army's 33rd Field Hospital and am now on my way to where Anthony is.

I have not told Anthony about this. I didn't want him to tell you or my parents, and I didn't want him to try to talk me out of it. I didn't want any of you to try to stop me.

Please forgive me for not having told you any of this until now. I love Anthony. I want to be by his side. I cannot wait to see him.

Thank you for taking care of me these last three years and welcoming me into your home. I am blessed to have you both as part of my family, and also Uncle Leon and his family. Although it pained me to be apart from my parents, I am so glad that I have had the chance to get to know all of you.

I have already written to my parents to break the news to them. I asked them not to blame you for what I have done. If they do, then please accept my apology. One day, I will make it up to you.

On July 4th, at Uncle Leon's party, Katherine and I had a talk. From that talk, I realised I must take my future into my own hands. The world now belongs to Anthony and me, to Katherine, to Alexander, and to everyone in our generation. It is only right that we should be the ones to fight for it. Please don't worry about me. I am not afraid at all. I am so happy to know that I will be by Anthony's side, and both of us will be doing all that we can to make our world and our future a better one.

Ruby has the army postal address where you can write to me. I will write to you again when I arrive at my destination. Maybe Anthony and I will write to you together.

— Love, Tessa

October 27, 1943

Dear Tessa,

What happened?! We received a telegram from William today telling us that you have left Chicago to become a military nurse overseas? His telegram said he and Sophia were unaware you had left until your friend Ruby delivered a letter to them, and that you have sent a letter to us too? Are you all right? Where are you?

How could this have happened? We don't understand. I have so many questions! Your father and I are waiting anxiously for your letter and more information from William, but I cannot wait any longer to write to you. I wish I could have jumped onto a ship to America to talk some sense into you before you left. I want to go and find you. How could you do something like this without telling us? I am worried sick and so is your father.

I hope this letter reaches you soon. When you get this letter, please contact us at once! Send a telegram if you can. Let us know where you are and whether you are safe.

Please write to us immediately!

— We love you, Mother and Father

P.S.: Your father is too distraught to write to you at this moment. He has cancelled all his performances until we hear from you.

October 27, 1943

Dear Tessa,

I am at a loss for words! I don't know how to begin writing this letter. I don't know when this letter will finally reach you. You left us nothing but a military postal address. I hope the army will forward this letter to you as soon as possible after you arrive, wherever you are.

First, I want you to know that I am praying every day for your safety. I pray that no harm will ever come to you. Your Uncle William and I love you and we miss you very, very much.

Now, I am very, very upset at what you have done. I am pained that you, too, are now drawn into this tide of events beyond our control. Although I am not your mother, I have loved you as my own daughter ever since you have come to live with us. I feel no less pain at your deployment than I felt when Anthony left. I fear for both of you. I wish you were back here with us, safe and away from danger. Speaking as Anthony's mother, I know he would not have wanted you to take on this kind of risk.

Leon too is very upset. It breaks his heart to know that yet another family member has gone to war. As soon as he heard what happened, he called every politician, government official and military person he knew, trying to move heaven and earth to find out where you are. No one could help him. He was told that the locations of army personnel are classified. He is very sad and concerned.

You must write to us the minute you arrive. You must let us know that you are all right. If you don't, I will not forgive you. Please write to your parents too. I can't imagine how worried they must be.

Do you have enough money? Do you need us to send you anything? Whatever you need, whatever we can do for you, let us know. I am waiting anxiously to hear from you.

— Love and prayers, Sophia

October 27, 1943

Dear Tessa,

When Ruby delivered your letter to us, I telegraphed your parents right away. Your departure was a big shock to us all. I am of course extremely worried, as is Sophie.

I have always believed in giving children a wide latitude of freedom and allowing them the privacy and independence to make their own choices in life. But this time, I blame myself. I should have discovered what you had been doing at the hospital much, much sooner. You may not have liked my interference, but yes, I would have tried to stop you. As your guardian, your safety is my first priority. In that respect, I have failed. I truly regret that. Your parents will have every right to blame me if anything should happen to you.

There is no turning back. I can only hope that Sophie and I have done enough in the last few years to give you the right kind of guidance, and the confidence and wisdom you will need to face what is ahead. Your life will not be easy from now on, but I believe in you. I have faith that you will overcome all the difficulties you will now face. What you did took months of planning and a lot of effort, so I know you did not make a hasty decision. I trust that you have thought this through long and hard, and this is what you really want. As what is done cannot be undone, the next best thing I can do is to be firmly behind you. Please know that you have my full support.

And what can I say as a father, that you hold so much love for my son? You love him so much that you would risk your own life for him. As Anthony's father, I can only thank you. He is very fortunate to have you in his life and all your love. It is my most sincere wish that you two will have a very long and bright future together ahead. I hope you and Anthony will find each other, and both of you make it out of this war safe and sound, and we will all be reunited as a family once again.

After discussing this with your Aunt Sophia, we decided not to tell Anthony about this for now. We will let you find your way to him. If you are meant to reunite with him, then you will. Otherwise, there is no use in alarming him. I hope that you will agree with our decision. My guess is that if you had wanted him to know, you would have written to him about it yourself.

Don't worry about your mother, your father, your Aunt Sophia, and

Uncle Leon. It is unavoidable for everyone to be shocked and upset. I am sure your parents will be angry. Don't worry if your parents blame me and Sophie. Everyone will eventually find a way to accept your decision. What concerns me most now is not them, but you. You have a very tough road ahead. Do not take on extra burden by feeling guilty and worrying about us. Let me worry about everyone else. Just take good care of yourself.

I hope this letter reaches you soon. You and Anthony are always in my thoughts.

— My best wishes and always, William

WESTERN UNION
Telegram to Mr. and Mrs. Dean Graham

October 28, 1943

Spoke to Chicago Veterans Hospital Superintendent. Am sending you letter today with further information regarding Tessa. Our children are in precarious situations. They will face many hardships and carry much burden. They need our love and support. Please do not be harsh on her. My fault and oversight. I take full responsibility for what happened. — William

---

November 12, 1943

Dear Tessa,

Your letter (the one that you entrusted Ruby to send to us) finally arrived. For more than two weeks, your father and I have been worried

sick, not knowing where you are and whether you are all right. We still have so many questions and we are still waiting to hear from you. I hope you have arrived safely, wherever you were headed. But at least now I know the reasons for your decision.

I am filled with so many mixed emotions after reading your letter. As your mother, I want to shout as loudly as I can at the top of my voice to tell you that you should wait for Anthony to come back. There is no need to put yourself at risk too. I cannot help but want to ask you, are you sure that Anthony is the one for you? So sure that you would make this drastic decision to follow him to war? Are you sure that there might not be someone else out there for you? Yes, I want to ask these questions even if the person you claim to love is William's son. I cannot do anything about Anthony being drafted, but I want so very much to find a reason to convince you to not put yourself in danger.

But if you truly love him as much as you said, then I also know that if I were in your place, I would've done the exact same thing. I would chase and follow your father to the end of this earth. I think of the time when I left Chicago with your father. I felt no fear then either, only sadness at leaving behind the people I loved.

After my initial shock, anger, and fear, I am slowly coming to terms with your decision. I will be praying constantly for your and Anthony's safe return. We are all here for you. You have all of our love. Whatever we can do for you, let me know. Write to us as often as you can. Please promise me that.

Despite everything, I am very proud of you. I know you will do your best to help all the soldiers injured in the war.

Your father is beyond distraught. He is having a hard time coping with what happened. He is also not very happy with anyone named Anthony right now, but I'm sure that he will come around soon.

— Missing you dearly and love you very much, Mother

November 4, 1943

Dear Tessa,

I hope everything is well. Why haven't I heard from you in weeks? Yesterday I got my mail. I received four letters from my parents, two from Uncle Leon and one each from Katherine and Alexander, but nothing from you. Is everything alright? Are you ill? Please don't tell me you've met another guy and have forgotten about me. (Just kidding — but actually, it happens. A sergeant I know named Ollie got a Dear John letter from his girlfriend back home recently. Ok, come to think of it, maybe it's better I don't hear from you if you are going to send me a Dear John letter…)

The British troops relieved us from the front this week, thankfully. We will have several days of rest back at the army headquarters in the city. I'm glad to get a break from K rations too. I plan to hit some restaurants and eateries while I'm in the city. The last few days before we came back, all my fellow officers and I could talk about was steak. Which cuts we like best. How we like it cooked. I never thought it was possible to have such an extended and in-depth discussion about a piece of steak. It was terrible though because the more we talked, the hungrier we got, and there was not much we could do to satiate our craving. Every few hours we would all agree for our own sanity to stop talking about steak, only for the topic to come back, over and over again!

Speaking of restaurants, where I'm at, the locals' lives are slowly returning to normal and it is such a good thing to see. Restaurants have reopened and are making good money serving the GIs. The downside is that food distribution for the locals is still in short supply. There seems to be an unevenness in how basic necessities and food are being distributed. I think it will take some time before everything is back in full operation again. One thing I'm thankful for is that my old college friend Warren Hendricks is with me. Back at school, I was the one who encouraged him and pushed him along. Now, he's the one giving me advice and looking out for me. He has really come out of his shell since he joined the army and is an excellent officer. He has a very keen mind in assessing data. His analysis of military intelligence is always spot on. When we have time off, we spend a lot of time together.

I made a new friend from New York City with whom I get along quite well. His name is Jesse Garland. He's not like anyone I've ever met but maybe that's what makes him so interesting. We have similar interests in books, art, and music. He's the only one here I can have a good conversation with about these things. Being in the army can be very boring. A lot of times we sit around waiting for the next mission, or waiting to go to the enemy, or waiting for the enemy to come to us. We would get all geared up and hustle somewhere only to wait for hours. Jesse and I have had some great conversations talking about the books we've read, lives of authors and artists, and things of that sort during our many hours of waiting around. A traveling opera troupe is performing "Pagliacci" at the city theater tonight. Jesse and I plan to go see it.

Take care now. Write me soon! I miss you.

— Love, Anthony

PART VIII
NAPLES

CHAPTER TWENTY-SEVEN

"Holy cow! Look at that motherfucking mountain!" Jonesy cried out as their company's convoy rode into Naples. The Allied forces had reached the Volturno River north of Naples on October 6th. With Naples now secured, the British and American troops were moving in.

"That's not a mountain, you moron. That's Mt. Vesuvius. It's a volcano," Ollie replied.

"It's a mountain. If it's not a mountain then why would they call it Mount Vesuvius?"

"It's a volcano!"

Behind them, the jeep Anthony and Warren were riding in suddenly came to a halt. The sergeant who was driving the vehicle turned off the ignition, then turned it on and off again several times.

"What's the matter?" Warren asked.

"Don't know, sir. The car wasn't driving right so I stopped it but now the engine won't start."

"Are we out of gas?" Anthony asked.

"No. We still got a quarter tank. I'll take a look." He got out of the car to check on the engine while the rest of the troops and convoy drove on past them.

Jim Darnell stopped and came over. "Need some help? I'm pretty good with cars."

Warren motioned him to the engine. The driver moved aside and Darnell took a look. He said something to the driver, shook his head, and came back to Anthony and Warren. "The engine's dead. You'll have to catch another ride."

But the convoy had already moved on. It was too late to hitch a ride.

"We're not that far from the checkpoint. Shall we walk?" Warren got out of the vehicle. Anthony picked up his pack and followed.

As they walked, a large group of small children dressed in rags surrounded them. Their heads were too big for their bodies and their eyes too large for their faces. None of them smiled. Further behind them, a group of adults, all too thin with sunken cheeks, stood and watched. The group grew bigger and bigger. All were looking at them but too scared to come forward.

"What's going on?" Anthony asked. "What's wrong with them?"

"Starvation," Warren said. "These people haven't had much to eat in a very long time. It's part of the Krauts' scorched-earth tactics. Cut off the city's food supplies. Demolish the roads, the bridges, and everything else to slow us down now that we're here."

Merciless tactics, Anthony thought. Twice on their way here, they had been halted because the Germans had blown up the roads or the bridges. Their battalion engineers had to rebuild new crossings for them to go forward. Heaps of bricks and piles of rubble in the middle of the road kept blocking their way. The Germans had put them there. Even in their defeat, the Germans had to destroy everything to the ground. The resulting damage to Naples was devastating.

"Here, take these." Darnell took several cans of SPAM out of his pack and gave them to the hungry children. "Take this home," he gave a can of corned beef to a little boy, who grabbed it and ran off while holding the can tight to his chest to keep the other kids from taking it away from him. Darnell gave out the rest of his canned food and crackers until he had no more left. Anthony, Warren, and their driver followed suit, passing out canned meat, crackers, chocolates, even leftover K rations and whatever else they could dig up. But after giving away everything they had, there was still not enough.

"Come on, let's go," Warren said.

They walked away from the starving children. The children stood behind like living ghosts and watched them leave.

"I don't know what I'd do if my kids were hungry like that," Darnell said.

Anthony thought of the time when Darnell had shown him the picture of his four children and how happy Darnell was when he talked about the neighborhood kids coming to his ice cream parlor. It must be difficult for Darnell to see children suffer.

"Those kids back there should be going to ice cream shops and candy stores after school. Not begging for food. Not like this." Darnell mumbled to himself.

Anthony threw him a glance. Once again, Anthony thought, this man didn't belong here.

More crowds entered the streets on the outskirts of Naples. Large crowds. Small crowds. All staring at them with their sunken eyes and hollow cheeks, but they had no more food left to give them.

"The Allied humanitarian aid will come," Warren said, although neither he nor Anthony were comforted by knowing this as these hungry people stared at them.

They arrived at their checkpoint where the rest of their company were already unloading and settling into their temporary quarters. Jonesy, looking fresh and clean, saw them and excitedly came down the street, waving and hollering, "Look, Lieutenant, Captain. I'm a new man. Hot shower, fresh clean laundry. Sweet! They got our mobile shower set up back there…" Before he could finish, a bucket of dirty water splashed all over his pants. A woman with her hair tied up and covered with an old, faded pink scarf had dumped another bucket of used dirty water onto the street.

"What the fuck!" Jonesy screamed. "I just showered! Aw, shit! This water stinks! Hey, bitch! What the fuck was that?"

Behind him, Ollie bent over laughing. The woman merely glanced at him. Her face looked tired and weary. Without an apology, she went back inside her house.

"The Krauts blew up all the plumbing and the water pipes before they retreated," Warren said. "These people have no other way to get rid of their used water."

Ollie, still laughing, tried to contain himself to give Anthony a message. "The captain said to tell you to meet him at the common room over at that building in three hours."

They parted ways with Darnell and the driver and went to the officers' quarters. After a quick lunch, Anthony went to clean himself up. In the shower, he closed his eyes and let the water cascade down from the top of his head down the rest of his body. It occurred to him that he hadn't gone swimming in a very long time. He could really go for a good swim.

How did they all end up in this living hell? He wished the shower water could wash away all the misery around him.

Three hours later at the command post, Captain Harding told him they had a new mission.

"We're only staying here for two nights. The Krauts have left Naples but they're holding on up north just outside the city. They're still running air raids and dropping bombs everywhere." Harding pointed out a range of area on a map. "Here are the latest reports on the locations of their communications outposts, airfields, and ammunitions dumps. We'll clear all of these areas north of the city."

Anthony studied the information given to him.

"I want you to organize the platoons and take out the outpost in the village right here." Harding circled a spot on the map. "Think you're up for the job?"

"Sure. Of course, sir." He wondered if Harding was offering him up as a sacrificial lamb again, or if Harding really thought he could lead the attack.

Afterward, he wandered into the bar near his quarters. He needed time to think.

The bartender gave him a beer. Deep in thought, he held it without drinking it.

Harding wanted him to lead a mission. He was a lieutenant. Leading a mission was part of his duties.

Think you're up for the job?

Nothing showed the captain to be anything but a leader giving a junior officer a chance to shine.

Do you know why Harding sent you to lead the platoon to initiate the attack?

Wesley's warning came back to him.

Better to send the least valuable ones out to take the first hits…The replacements…they make good human shields.

Was Harding leaving him out to sink or swim on his own to protect those whom he deemed more important?

Could Wesley be wrong?

But Wesley saved him. He might not even be alive right now if it weren't for Wesley.

He's a helluva first lieutenant.

Warren had nothing but high praise for Wesley. If nothing else, he could trust Warren.

"Two shots of scotch, please," someone said to the server, breaking his train of thought.

Anthony looked up. It was Jesse Garland, the medic.

"I saw you walk in." Jesse sat down next to him. "I fleeced those suckers over there." He looked over at a table of officers playing cards. "Want to help me get rid of this chump change tonight?" He took a stash of bills and coins out of his pocket and put them on the bar. "We can go see that traveling stand-up comedian perform, hit a few bars afterward? Make it a night on the town."

Anthony wasn't up for it. He had too much on his mind. "Maybe another time. I got some things to sort out."

"What kind of things?"

Anthony gripped his beer. "I don't know if I'm doing my job right."

Jesse looked amused.

"What's so funny?" Anthony asked.

"You're over-thinking things." Jesse took the shots the bartender placed on the bar and put one in front of Anthony. "There's no right way to do what we're here to do. Only one thing matters."

"What's that?"

"Stay alive. You and I didn't choose to be here. We're not here to earn medals. We're not here to prove we're warriors. All that matters is we stay alive, because if we're dead, then nothing else matters. Stay alive, and try to keep everyone else alive. That's all you need to worry about. Good job, bad job. What does it matter?" He held up his shot of scotch. "To staying alive." He downed his scotch. Anthony picked up his shot and did the same.

"You need to get your mind off everything else," Jesse said. "I know just the thing to do."

"On yeah?"

"After dinner, you're coming with me to pick up a couple of Red Cross donut girls. We'll all go watch the comedian together and have some fun. How about that?"

"No," Anthony said. "I'll go see the comedian but I'm not picking up any girls. I've told you before, I have a girlfriend."

"Who said anything about you?" Jesse signaled the bartender for more. "I am picking up both of the donut girls for me. I'm not planning on sharing. I only said you're coming with me. But feel free to tell them all about your girlfriend and how faithful you are to her. Girls swoon over that kind of stuff." With a conspiratorial smile, he gave Anthony his second shot. "You'll make me look good. I'm with you so they'll think I'm just like you."

Anthony laughed. Garland. The guy was outrageous.

But, was Garland right? Was he overthinking things? Was staying alive the only thing that mattered?

He thought of the ruins he had seen since he came to Italy. Cities, obliterated and turned to dust from Licata to Acerno and beyond. Naples, with its people starving and children begging for food from Darnell. Darnell, the mild man who loved children, the father of four kids who was better suited to selling ice cream than to fighting a war.

No. Staying alive could not be the only thing that mattered.

But Garland did say, stay alive, and try to keep everyone else alive. Wesley said the same thing. Wesley said it was now up to the two of them to look out for their men.

That was it. Keep everyone alive. He drank his second shot.

Yes. That was what he must do. Innocent civilians, fellow soldiers, the men in his unit. Especially the men in his unit. Keeping his men alive would be his own priority, no matter what Harding's plans and motives might be. He must do whatever it took to make sure of that.

CHAPTER TWENTY-EIGHT

WHEN THE VESSEL docked at the port of Naples, the only thing on Tessa's mind was to go straight to the administrative office to find Colonel Callahan. All newly arrived personnel must report to Callahan's office to obtain their registration instructions, but she could not care less about all that. What she wanted was to find out where Anthony was and to go see him.

Behind her, Gracie Hall, her cabin mate on the ship who was also assigned to the 33rd Field Hospital, walked as fast as she could trying to keep pace with her. The trip had been grueling for Gracie. She had lived in Wisconsin all her life and had never been on an ocean liner. While at sea, a storm raged for three days, bringing horrifying waves. So seasick, she kept telling Tessa she was going to die. It was a total relief for them both when they at last landed.

But now that they had landed, they were practically sprinting to the registration office instead of taking it easy as Gracie had hoped. "Tessa! Slow down. Wait for me. What's the hurry?"

"You can go at your own pace," Tessa said.

"I'm afraid I'll get lost. I've never been to a foreign country before. I've never even been to another state until I was deployed."

"Then hurry." Tessa continued on at an even faster speed.

They reached Colonel Callahan's office with Gracie completely out of breath. Tessa pushed the office door open and went straight to the staff sergeant on duty. "Hello," she said, her voice full of anticipation. "We're nurses arriving for duty with the 33rd Field Hospital. We're here to register."

"Lieutenants," the staff sergeant said. "May I have your names please?"

"I'm Tessa Graham."

"I'm Gracie Hall," Gracie said from behind Tessa.

"Just a moment please." The staff sergeant pulled two folders of documents from the file cabinet and handed one to each of them. "This is a map of the area. Follow this street, make a left turn two blocks from the post office here, go another three blocks and you'll find the General Hospital. The nurses of the 33rd Field Hospital are stationed there. Here are your registration papers and passes. Keep them safe with you at all times."

"Thank you." Tessa took the information. "Is Colonel Callahan here? May I please speak with him?"

"May I ask what your business is with the colonel?"

"General Frank Castile sent me. He told me to speak to the colonel directly."

"I see. Please wait." The staff sergeant went to an office upstairs.

While they waited, Gracie asked, "You want to see the colonel?"

"Yes," Tess said. "My boyfriend is here. The Colonel can help me locate him."

Realization dawned on Gracie. "That's why you were in such a hurry."

The staff sergeant returned with an older man who wore a full bird on his army uniform. "Lieutenant Graham," he said to Tessa. "You've arrived. I've been expecting you. General Castile sent me a message about you."

"Colonel," Tessa said. "General Castile told me to come see you when I got here. He said you'd be able to help me locate Lieutenant Anthony Ardley. He's a second lieutenant with the Third Infantry Division."

"Yes, of course. Bad timing though. The Third Infantry left for a mission yesterday. They're due to be relieved in two weeks. I'll be sure to arrange for you to meet up with him when his unit returns."

Tessa's heart sank. Two weeks. She made it all the way here and still she had to wait another two weeks.

It's all right, she told herself. *Just two more weeks.*

Following the staff sergeant's road directions, Tessa and Gracie came to the army General Hospital at Naples. From the outside, the hospital's exterior was unremarkable, having been previously a local hospital which the Allies had taken over after their arrival. Inside, though, was a massive scene of organized chaos unlike any hospital Tessa had ever seen. Too many people were in transit and too many things were happening all at once. All the operating systems seemed to be a patchwork. Make-shift surgical wards, stacks of cartons and metal boxes used as chairs and tables, the place was held together with ingenious but temporary and desperate solutions thought up by someone to make up for the lack of one thing or another.

And so many people. Everywhere, cots and beds filled with wounded soldiers resting or asleep from exhaustion lay all around in no particular order. By the hospital entrance, nearly a hundred men, all immobilized by war injuries, spread across the floor. Their litters were up against each other with no place in between. They lay waiting to be carried to a medical vessel to return home, if and when a ship arrived. There was no telling when. Strangely, they looked to be in good spirits. Perhaps they felt relief because for them, the war was over.

With Gracie behind her, Tessa went up to the second floor and made her way to the hospital's administrative offices. There, she found a familiar figure at a table reviewing patient files with another nurse.

"Ellie!"

Ellie Swanson looked up. "Tessa?" She dropped the files and gave Tessa a welcoming hug. "You arrived! I've been looking forward to seeing you since I got your letter telling me you're coming. This is unbelievable. You did it. You're here!"

"Hi there," Gracie said from behind Tessa, "I'm Gracie Hall. I'm assigned to the 33rd Field Hospital too."

"Hello Gracie," Ellie said.

"Don't forget me," said the other nurse in the office. "I'm Irene."

"Tessa, you and Irene will have much to talk about," Ellie said. "Irene's sister is an actress in New York." She turned to Irene. "Tessa's father is an actor in London."

"We'll have to trade stories," Irene said to Tessa. "Ellie, why don't you help them get oriented? I can finish up here."

"Yes," Ellie said to Tessa and Gracie. "Let me take you to our quarters."

After settling in, Ellie took them on a tour of the hospital, guiding them through the different parts of the building and introducing them to the hospital staff. "Our unit is on reserve right now because the army has just secured Naples last month," Ellie said. "Some troops are still on the front north of here holding the line. For a while, it looked like we would follow them and continue up north, but last week, the army command changed course and pulled everyone back, so for now we are on hold. Many of us in 33rd are helping out here until we get instructions for our next mission. There's a minor epidemic of malaria going on so we're all very busy.'"

The door swung open when they passed a surgical unit. A middle-aged doctor came out looking exhausted from having finished another surgical procedure, but as soon as he saw Ellie, energy returned to his face.

"Ellie," the doctor said.

"Dr. Haley," Ellie said, reflexively running her hand down her hair and pushing it behind her ear. She sounded almost shy. Tessa had never heard her speak like this to a doctor before. "Doctor, this is Tessa Graham and Gracie Hall. They just arrived. They're joining our hospital unit," Ellie turned to Tessa and Gracie. "This is Colonel Aaron Haley, Chief Surgeon and Superintendent of the 33rd Field Hospital."

"Pleasure to meet you both," the doctor said, extending his hand for a handshake. It was an unexpected gesture by a superior ranking officer.

Tessa shook his hand. The doctor, perhaps in his mid-forties, looked relatively handsome despite being tired. His handshake felt steady and reliable. When he smiled, the gentle kindness in his eyes disarmed her. She felt at ease with him right away. "Pleased to meet you too, Colonel."

"Same here, sir." Gracie shook his hand.

"I'd really prefer it if you all call me doctor instead of colonel or sir." He looked at his watch. "It's almost lunch time. I'm hungry. Should we all go and have lunch?" He asked them all but was looking only at Ellie. Ellie did not answer but looked down at the floor. A blush of pink passed on her cheeks.

Seeing Ellie's reaction, Tessa said, "Thank you, Doctor Haley. We would definitely like that."

"Let's go then," he said. Ellie was about to say something when a harsh voice interrupted her.

"Swanson! I thought I told you to organize the X-ray files. What are you doing loitering around here?"

Tessa looked past Ellie to see where the harsh voice came from. An older nurse, possibly in her forties, approached. Her glasses obscured her eyes. A bitter hardness hung on the corners of her lips. Her hair, pulled back tightly into a bun, looked dry, brittle, and uncared for even for military nurses too busy to tend to vanity grooming. She held her head high, as if she wanted to show off her low-maintenance appearance as a symbol of superiority.

"I'm sorry, Captain," Ellie said. "This is Tessa Graham and Gracie Hall. They're our new replacements for 33rd. They arrived this morning. I'm showing them around the hospital." She turned to Tessa and Gracie. "Captain Fran Milton is the 33rd's Chief Nurse. We all report to her."

Milton eyed Tessa and Gracie up and down once. Without addressing them, she said to Ellie, "Finish your tour and take them to Lieutenant Sanford. Get them assigned to work immediately. Then I want you to finish organizing those X-ray files today. Your inefficiency is trying my patience, Lieutenant."

Tessa could not believe Milton's harsh tone toward Ellie. Ellie was so nice and sweet to everybody. How could anyone talk to Ellie this way? Inefficient? Ellie? Everyone knew Ellie was an excellent nurse. What was this woman talking about?

"Captain," Dr. Haley said. "These young ladies just arrived. Why not give them a break? I'm about to take them to the canteen for lunch."

"Colonel, if you don't mind me saying, someone of your rank and file should know better than to fraternize with young nurses of lower rank."

"You know I'm not big on military etiquette. We're not soldiers. We are medical professionals." He gave the three young nurses a reassuring smile. "Anyway, it's lunch time and we're all hungry."

"We're not here to socialize, Colonel. We have a lot of work to do." Milton held the files she was holding up to her chest. "Swanson, finish your tour and show the new nurses where to get K rations from the kitchen. Then take them to Sanford as I said and get them assigned to shifts to start work right away."

"Yes, ma'am," Ellie said.

Milton wasn't finished. "Colonel, since you are on your way to the canteen, then it's a perfect time for you and I to have a working lunch to go over our management procedures for our next mission, as well as our plans for repatriating patients."

Tessa glanced at Ellie, whose disappointment was obvious.

"Well, Lieutenant?" Milton said to Ellie. "Go."

"Yes, ma'am," Ellie answered and signaled Tessa and Gracie to follow her. Tessa wanted to say goodbye to Dr. Haley, but his gaze followed only Ellie while Ellie walked away. Tessa decided to leave him be.

CHAPTER TWENTY-NINE

FOR DAYS, the rain would not let up. The dreary cold and wetness tested Tessa to her limit. The climate of the approaching winter here was even worse than England. Things would be better if they had heat and electricity, but the Germans had destroyed the city's utility lines and cables. Relief from the weather would come only if the systems were fixed, but the constant rain kept hampering the repair progress itself. There was no relief from the weather because of the broken heating system, and the broken heating system could not be fixed because of the weather. It was all one dreadful, vicious cycle.

Whenever she thought that she could not tolerate it anymore, she thought of Anthony. He had it worse, she reminded herself. How miserable it must be to be outside all the time and sleeping in pup tents and foxholes in this weather. She would not let herself complain. As long as she could see him, everything else she could endure. She focused on her work and did her best to help the patients. That, too, was challenging because of equipment shortages and lack of supplies, and overcapacity of patients continued to be a problem.

No matter, she thought. Each hour that passed brought her closer to the day when she and Anthony would be together again.

When the rain eventually stopped, the day was brightened not only by the rare sun, but also the word that she had been waiting for from Colonel Callahan's office. Anthony's division had returned. An armored jeep had come to take her to his base camp in Naples. On Colonel Callahan's order, she was to be relieved from duty for the afternoon.

Nervous anticipation filled her heart during the ride. She had looked forward to this moment for so long. Now that she was about to see him, she felt overwhelmed. How should she greet him? What should she say to him? He would be so shocked, for sure, but would he be happy to see her? They had not seen each other for almost a year. Would everything still feel the same? Emotions whirled in her heart like waves.

The vehicle stopped at a roundabout surrounding a water fountain. In the center of the fountain was the statue of the Roman goddess Iris carrying a water pitcher and pouring water onto the ground. No water flowed from the pitcher though since the water pipes were broken, but at least, the statue remained intact and unharmed. A remnant of the city's beauty was preserved.

A full convoy of military vehicles was parked on the cobblestone streets. Her driver pointed to a building beyond the crowd of returning soldiers. "Check with the administrative outpost over there," he said. "They'll be able to help you."

But she didn't need their help. She already saw him. He was right before her eyes, standing by an armored truck talking to three other men while soldiers unloaded packs of guns and equipment from the vehicle.

"I'll pick you up back here in two hours," the driver said. Barely listening, she thanked him as he drove away.

Hesitant, she walked toward him, but stopped. She couldn't just walk up to him, could she? Would her unexpected appearance cause a scene? There were other soldiers with him. This was too embarrassing. All she could do was look at him.

He looked so good in his uniform. Just seeing him like this made her heart melt.

She stood there, watching him, wondering what she should do. At first, he did not notice her. Deep in conversation with the other three soldiers, he glanced briefly in her direction, pointed at something behind her, and looked away.

And then, as if something turned in his mind, he looked in her direction again. This time, he froze. He stopped talking and stared at her, his face in complete shock.

"Lieutenant?" Jonesy asked. "Lieutenant, what's the matter?"

Anthony did not answer. The others with whom he was talking all turned in the direction he was looking. Stunned, Anthony walked toward her.

"Lieutenant?" Jonesy called out to him.

Anthony ignored him and continued walking as if he did not hear him. He came up to Tessa and grabbed her shoulders. Although he couldn't utter a word, she could see a thousand questions on his face.

"Yes," she said. "Yes, it's really me."

Without saying anything, he wrapped her tightly in his arms and kissed her. His kiss was so voracious and deep, it almost suffocated her. Laughing, she put her own arms around him. At last, she could feel him. He was really there, tangibly there in her arms again.

Behind him, the three men he was talking to watched in wild disbelief.

"Yowser!" Jonesy shouted. "Holy Mother of Christ! Am I really seeing what I'm seeing?"

Embarrassed, she pulled back. She did not mean to be so indiscreet, but for a moment, she had forgotten all the people around them. The instant her and Anthony's eyes met, she felt as if only the two of them existed.

She glanced over at the three men. One of them, the one with raven dark hair, caught her eye. She could not help noticing his extraordinary good looks. Having grown up in the theater community with her father, she had seen her share of good-looking people. Rarely could anyone impress her with their looks.

But this young man was so exceptionally attractive, even she noticed. He, too, was looking at her. His intense, dark eyes drew her attention like an enigma.

"All right boys," Warren said. "Move along. Nothing to see here." He ordered the other two to walk away with him.

The soldier with raven dark hair was still watching her as he walked away.

"But how? What…How is this possible?" Anthony asked after they left.

"I got myself assigned to the 33rd Field Hospital. It's all I ever wanted to do since you were drafted. To follow you."

"But you've got at least another year of training!"

"No. I switched to a special program right after you left home. I wanted to finish as quickly as I could. As soon as I found out you were assigned to the Sixth Corps, I wrote to everyone I could think of and asked to be assigned to the same division. And now, I'm here. I've been here for two weeks. I've been waiting for you to come back from the front."

"Dear God! Tessa!" He pulled her into his arms again. "So stupid! You're so stupid." He said over and over again while kissing her face and her head. "You're so stupid. What have you done? You shouldn't have come here. So stupid."

Tessa was now laughing and crying at the same time.

"Oh Jeezes!" he pushed her away. "I'm so dirty! I haven't showered in two weeks. I stink! Argh! How can you have me see you like this?" He caressed her face and ran his fingers through the locks of her hair that had fallen out of her ponytail, touching her lightly as if he was afraid he might damage her. "I got you all dirty."

"No, you didn't. Anyway, I don't care." She threw her arms around him again and put her face against his chest. How she had craved to feel his warmth and his heartbeat.

"Come here!" He took her hand and led her to the front steps of an abandoned building where they could sit down and talk away from the crowd.

"How did you talk Mother and Father into letting you come?" he asked.

"I didn't tell them."

"You didn't tell them?"

"No. I told them I had a weekend shift at the hospital and I wrote them a letter telling them where I had gone. Ruby gave it to them after I left."

"My God. They must have had heart attacks."

"Probably. I'm sorry."

"What am I going to do about you? Is there any way I can send you back? It's not safe here."

"It's not safe here but you're here. I can't send you back either." She took his hand. "I don't want to go back. I want to be with you. We'll face this war together."

He put his arm around her and pulled her close against him.

"Those soldiers back there, are they your friends?"

He didn't answer but just looked at her and smiled.

"What?" she asked him.

"I was just thinking, your British accent is so cute."

Tessa punched him lightly and he gave her a soft kiss on her cheek.

"They cut your hair." She ran her hand over the side of his head.

"Does it look bad?"

"No. Not at all." She touched his arm. No. He didn't look bad, but he looked different. Less boyish and rougher than how he used to be. His entire body manifested strength. A primitive kind of strength that made her want to touch him. "I'm so glad to see you."

"I wish you hadn't come to this hell, but I'm glad to see you too." He kissed her again. "I missed you so much."

It's all worth it, she thought to herself. Everything she did to get here was worth it. If she had to climb mountains and cross the oceans to get here, it would still be worth it. She would do it all over again.

PART IX
JESSE GARLAND

CHAPTER THIRTY

For Jesse Garland, life was all about survival. This was the case in his life before the army, and this was the case in his life in the army. By survival, he didn't mean surviving enemy attacks and escaping bombs and shells in battles. What he meant was survival of the thing called life. He didn't know what it meant to enjoy life. For him, life was a series of circumstances which he must necessarily deal with for the sole reason that he was alive, and dealing with it meant figuring out how to navigate life to his own best advantages. Sometimes, it could get tiresome, but it was never beyond him to figure out what situation he was in, the chips with which he had to bargain, and the best way to game the system.

He had never questioned his life before or how he lived it. He never knew anything different. This was how life had always been. Life was about getting through the day, day after day. Where it ended and how it would get there, he never had any reason or desire to give it a second thought. As for people? He never cared about anyone, and no one ever cared about him. And that was all right.

So why did the sudden appearance of that girl shake him up so much?

The instant he laid his eyes on her, he felt as if he saw a revelation, a monumental revelation that made him question what everything in life was all about.

Why was she causing a tsunami in his mind? She wasn't even his type. He preferred blondes. Full-figured, buxom blondes with long, shapely legs, dewy eyes, and sweet honey lips. This girl was a brunette, and she looked a bit too thin and willowy for his taste.

But she was so beautiful!

All of her was beautiful. In her nurse's uniform with her blue cape floating in the air, she was a white vision to the answer of life itself. And those eyes. He had never seen such clear and perceptive eyes. They mesmerized him. There was a moment, a quick, blinking moment, when their eyes met. The look she gave him arrested his heart. He felt like she could see through him into his soul.

No wonder Ardley was out of control when he saw her. She must be his girlfriend, the one whom he refused to stray from and who he said was a nurse. Where did he meet this girl? He never mentioned she was coming.

And yet, there was that moment when she looked right at him when he, Jonesy and Warren were walking away. Was he delusional to think she actually noticed him?

You're doomed, Jesse Garland, he laughed at himself. The joke was on him. He thought he had life all figured out. But now, everything had changed, changed into shapes and patterns he could no longer recognize. How to navigate this? He didn't have the faintest clue.

Returning to the company quarters, Anthony braced for the worst. Of all the men who had to be there when Tessa came, it had to be Jonesy. That big mouth. No doubt, everyone in the unit must have heard by now about his public display of affection like news hot off the press. This news would be talked about for days, maybe even weeks, passing along as hearsay upon hearsay, with new twists and details piling on until it morphed into something entirely unrecognizable. Never underestimate the imaginations of bored men stuck in the army with little to do. Their capability to gossip could put any village woman to shame.

Coming upon the abandoned villa where his company had set up their quarters, he took a deep breath before he entered. The property, a neo-classical residence that might have once been the home of an affluent Napoli family, now housed a troop of unruly soldiers ready to make him the target of their jokes.

He would never live this down for the rest of his army life.

Just as he expected, everyone gave him curious stares as soon as he walked in, smirks hanging on their faces. Needless to say, Jonesy had the biggest smirk of them all. Ignoring him, Anthony swept his eyes across the room. To his relief, Captain Harding and Wesley Sharpe were nowhere in sight. He headed straight to the stairs for his room. He had no desire to stick around here.

"Lieutenant Romeo," Jonesy said in a sing-song voice, just loud enough for him to hear but not so obvious that the comment was directed at him.

He ignored the loudmouthed sergeant and went upstairs. Best to admit nothing and deny nothing. It was the only way.

In the common area upstairs, Warren and the other officers threw him questioning looks too. Only Jesse, reclining in one of the sofa seats, behaved as usual. Immersed in reading a copy of the army weekly magazine "Yank," Jesse didn't even look up when Anthony entered.

"What?" Anthony said to Warren.

"Nothing." Warren held up his hand. "I didn't say anything."

"Want a beer?" Clayton, the officer from the signal company held up a beer bottle to Anthony.

"No thanks." Anthony had no interest in dishing out details to Clayton or anyone. His only interest was to get back to his room away from everyone and let the gossip die.

"Come on, Ardley. Have a beer with us." Clayton got up and

put his arm around his shoulder. Anthony hadn't realized they were now buddies. "Who was the girl? You sonofabitch. You just got here. How'd you hit up a nurse so quick?"

"I didn't hit up a nurse," Anthony said. "She's my girlfriend. My girlfriend from home."

"The same girl in that photo you carry around?" Warren pointed to Anthony's uniform pocket. Anthony couldn't help smiling.

"Your girlfriend was coming and you didn't say a thing?" Clayton asked.

"I didn't know she was coming. It was a surprise to me too."

"You didn't know? Right. We're supposed to believe you?"

"Believe whatever you want." He shook Clayton's arm off and started to leave.

"We should take her out," Jesse said without looking up.

"Come on, Garland. Not you too."

"I'm not being facetious." Jesse put down the magazine. "I'm completely sincere and serious. She just arrived, right? We should show her a good time. Make her feel welcomed." He leaned forward from his seat. "Let's take her to see the army band perform tomorrow night."

"Great idea, Garland," Clayton said. "You can get a few more nurses to join us and we'll make it a party."

"No," Anthony said. He needed to put a stop to this. He was not going to impose on Tessa to spend an evening with all these guys. "She has to work. She can't come out on a whim."

"I can get her off work," Jesse said. "I'll talk to Marcy Sanford, the nurse who works at the hospital's administrative office. She manages staffing. She'll do anything I ask. I can ask her to give your girlfriend and a couple of nurses I know the night off."

"Marcy Sanford!" Clayton said. "That old lady? My God, Jesse, is there anyone not off limits to you?"

"She's not old, she's thirty-five. Anyway, it's not like what you think. She's a widow. She gets lonely. All she needs is a compliment or two now and then. Besides, how do you think I get all those extra medicines and supplies the other units can't get their hands on? She doesn't get much attention from men. A little flattery goes a long way. She likes me. She'll give me anything I ask for." Casting the magazine aside, Jesse got up from the sofa. "I'll head over to the hospital now to talk to dear sweet Marcy, and we'll have ourselves the company of some fine young ladies tomorrow night." On his way out, he winked at Anthony, who could do nothing but watch everything fall further out of control.

"Thank you, Marcy," Jesse said as he took the extra bandages and sulfa she had secretly stocked away for him. She was having a bad hair day again. Every time it rained, her frizzy hair would puff like a balloon of weeds. The afternoon shower just now did not do her any favors.

"Don't mention it," she said. Then, lowering her voice, she handed him a bundle of small scissors and said, "Take these too." She shoved the bundle into his hand and closed his fist. "We're short of supplies. These just came in. I grabbed them for you. Last time you said your unit needed them."

"Marcy! You're a darling!" Jesse put the scissors away into his supplies pouch.

"Oh, and one more thing." She pulled out a radio from her desk drawer. "One of the GIs who went home left this behind. He was so excited to be discharged. He said he won't need this anymore. I thought one of your boys might want it."

"Thank you," Jesse accepted everything she gave him without question. "So, I'm going to ask you again. Are you sure you don't want to come dancing with us tomorrow night?" He asked even though he knew she would refuse. Marcy was too shy and too old. She wouldn't dare to go out with the boys, but he knew he could make her giddy by asking.

"Oh, no." She giggled and waved her hand. "Don't be silly.

Dancing's for you young folks. I wouldn't be able to keep up with you all."

"I'm crushed," he said. "I'm very disappointed." He would have said a few more things to flatter her, but Fran Milton was approaching. Milton was one of the few people here he wouldn't touch with a ten-foot pole. Not that he couldn't find a way to push her buttons if he wanted. That woman clearly had unfulfilled wishes and dreams, and he was in the business of selling dreams. A case like hers would be too easy for him, but no way. That woman was bad news. Her negativity seethed over like a stewing pot of a witch's brew. He could do without that.

He better leave now. When Milton came and discovered Marcy had given away precious extra supplies to him, poor Marcy would be in for it. He didn't want to be there when that happened. "I must get going now. Thanks again for giving the nurses the night off tomorrow."

"You're welcome," Marcy said, still not realizing Milton was coming.

Jesse put everything in his pack and walked away. Milton passed without noticing him. She was zeroing in on Marcy.

Behind him, he could hear Milton scold Marcy. "Sanford! Have we received the new delivery of medics' supplies yet? I've asked you twice to follow up on this. How many times do I have to tell you?"

"Sorry, Ma'am." Marcy shrunk in her seat. "I'll check on it right away."

Poor Marcy. She was in for it all right.

"…Why don't we ever have enough scissors for the medics? I'm tired of all the complaints…"

Smiling, Jesse adjusted the strap of his bag on his shoulder and continued walking.

With her mind still in the clouds after seeing Anthony earlier today, Tessa was glad that all she had to do for the rest of the night was to clean and sanitize surgical equipment. It was a simple enough task, not like helping to treat a patient, or worse, assisting with a surgical procedure. She didn't know how she could possibly concentrate.

Of course, she would force herself to focus if she must, but she would rather not have to do that at the moment. Right now, all she wanted to think about was Anthony and everything that happened when she saw him. She could give herself that little indulgence after all those months they had to endure away from each other. She wanted to relive every moment of their reunion in her mind.

Another reason she was glad was she knew she had a silly grin on her face. She must look like an idiot but she couldn't help it. She was bursting with happiness. Thank goodness she was in this room alone. She didn't want anyone to see her with this foolish grin.

Lost in her thoughts, she didn't notice the person leaning against the side of the doorway watching her. She moved here to there around the room, doing her work but with her mind somewhere far, far away. When she finally sensed she was being watched, she looked over at him. Standing by the door was the person she saw earlier when she went to look for Anthony. The one with raven dark hair, intense eyes, and extraordinary good looks. Wary, she stopped and stared back at him.

"Hi. You're Tessa Graham?" the person said. He wore a white band with a red cross on his arm. "I'm Jesse Garland. I work with Lieutenant Ardley. I came to give you a message from him."

Tessa relaxed. She noted his gold stripe rank insignia and gave him a reserved smile. "Lieutenant Garland."

"Please. Call me Jesse."

"Okay." She minded herself not to be rude to Anthony's friend. "Hello, Jesse. You said you have a message from Anthony?"

"Tomorrow night, eight o'clock. Be ready. He and the rest of us are coming to take you for a night out to see the army band perform."

"The rest of us?"

"Us. His friends in the division."

Tessa hesitated. Why would Anthony want them to be out with a group of people? They only just reunited and barely had any time together. Wouldn't he rather be alone with her if they could see each other? But then she remembered he had planned a special evening introducing Mary Winters to all his friends back when they were dating. Could he have planned something similar for her this time?

He must have. He wanted everyone to know she was his girlfriend. "I would love to go," she said, "but I have to work tomorrow night."

"Don't worry about that," Jesse said. "I talked to Lieutenant Sanford. She's given you the night off."

Just then, Irene entered. Irene was the nurse Tessa had met on the first day she arrived, the one whose sister was an actress in New York. "Hi Tessa," Irene said, barely acknowledging Tessa before turning her full attention away. "Hi, Jesse." Her voice changed when she spoke to him. Low, suggestive, and much more feminine.

"Hello, Irene," he said. He lowered his eyes to her. His voice, too, changed. Deeper and seductive.

Irene passed him, swinging her hips and tossing her hair as she walked. She opened the medicine cabinet and browsed around, looking for something. "What brought you here at this hour?"

"You."

"Don't lie."

"I'm not lying. You," he said, then threw a quick glance at Tessa. "And Miss Graham here. We boys are taking you both out to see the army band perform tomorrow night. Lieutenant Ardley's order. That's Lieutenant Ardley, Miss Graham's boyfriend. He wants us all to give Miss Graham a very special welcome."

"Really?!" Irene let go of the cabin door. "Have you talked to Sanford yet?"

"All taken care of. I invited Sanford too. I know she'd never come. She wouldn't dare do anything that might appear improper, but she was so flattered to be asked, she was never going to say no about you girls coming."

"Oh, Jesse, you're the best!"

"Tomorrow night. Eight o'clock. We'll pick you both up in front of the hospital."

Irene grabbed a random bottle of pills and, before leaving the room, walked up to Jesse and straightened his uniform collar. "I'll see you tomorrow night," she said, her voice breathier and even more titillating than before. Jesse ran his hand slowly down her waist and backside.

Awkward at being present, Tessa looked away and did not see Jesse watching her reaction as he ran his hand down Irene.

"Eight o'clock tomorrow night," Jesse said to Tessa and left with Irene.

Her high from seeing Anthony now subdued, Tessa continued cleaning the surgical equipment. She wondered why Irene never mentioned that her boyfriend was a medic here.

CHAPTER THIRTY-ONE

THE FOLLOWING EVENING, Tessa and Irene waited for the boys in front of the hospital when Alice, another nurse in their unit, showed up. An outgoing girl from Los Angeles who dabbled in a modeling career before becoming a military nurse, she had joined the 33rd the same time as Ellie and Irene.

"Hi, girls!" Alice rushed up to them, out of breath. "My God, I almost didn't make it. Milton went off on one of her tirades again when one of the patients' files went missing. It wasn't even my fault. My only mistake was being in the wrong place at the wrong time. I happened to be there when she discovered the error and she started yelling at everybody. She went on and on about how we were all a disgrace for being disorganized. I thought I'd never get out of there."

"I didn't know you were coming," Irene said.

"Of course I'm coming. Jesse invited me."

"He invited you too?" Irene pouted. Alice gave her a big smile.

"I thought Jesse was your boyfriend?" Tessa said to Irene.

Irene laughed. "Jesse? My boyfriend? Hardly. Although I wish. See? I thought I'll finally have him all to myself for one evening, and what do you know? Alice is here. Now I got all excited for nothing."

"Oh come on, Irene. Don't be selfish. Jesse's community property, okay? Is that fair?" Alice said. She too was laughing. Neither Alice nor Irene seemed to take the matter very seriously.

Seeing the perplexed look on Tessa's face, Irene explained to her, "Jesse Garland, unfortunately, is not the kind of man who would ever be tied down to any one woman."

"And yet you all like him?" Tessa asked.

"Sure. It's not like we're going to marry him. No harm having a little fun with our medical unit's very own Valentino, right, Alice?"

"Um hmm." Alice agreed and made a dreamy looking face that made Tessa laugh.

At eight o'clock, two army vehicles pulled up. From the first vehicle, Anthony called out to Tessa as soon as he saw her. "Tessa!"

She ran over to him and climbed into the jeep while he moved aside to make room for her. "Tessa, this is my friend Warren Hendricks. He's the classmate I told you about from UC."

She and Warren exchanged greetings. Anthony pointed out to her the other men in another jeep behind them. "The one in the front is Clayton. He can be a little brash. Don't mind him. The other one is Jesse Garland."

She recognized Jesse. "Yes. We've already met." Irene and Alice had now gotten into the other vehicle and each of them sat on one side of Jesse. It occurred to Tessa then that Jesse had invited the two prettiest nurses of the 33rd out tonight.

"Jesse's one of my better friends in the unit."

"Is he?"

"I wrote you about him, but maybe you didn't get my letter because you were already on your way here."

"Jesse said you ordered everyone to take me out tonight."

"What? He said that?! He was putting you on."

She felt slightly disappointed. She thought Anthony wanted to let all his friends know who she was, but he put his arm around her and pulled her close against him and that made her feel better again. "I would much rather be alone with you," he said in a low voice that only she could hear.

She would love to be alone with him too, although, for once, she didn't mind having people around. He had his arm around her the entire ride. He did want to openly show everyone she was his girl! She leaned closer to him.

After a short drive, they came to a restaurant that the army had converted into a club for entertaining G.I. servicemen. While they made their way to one of the remaining empty tables, Tessa took in the scene. Other than the attendees being mainly soldiers, the place was not unlike any other bar. What surprised her was the army band. The ensemble of eight men, all dressed in military uniforms, were rolling out tunes from the 1920s with different instruments. One of them even played the piano.

"Are the band members enlisted soldiers?" Tessa asked Anthony.

"They are. They're musicians recruited to play music for the combat troops, but these men do more than entertain. They get their hands dirty like the rest of us. I've even seen them take up arms in combat." The trumpet player blew a show-stopping solo segment and everyone applauded. "They're good, aren't they?"

"More than good. They are terrific!"

"Sometimes, they come to the front line to perform for us. I really like it when they come." A sorrowful look came across his face. By the hint of sadness in his voice, she could imagine how lonely and depressing it must be for him when he was out there. Wishing to comfort him, she put her hand on his. He looked at her. She could see in his eyes how much her affection meant to him.

The excitement heated up to another level when the band started to play Glenn Miller's swing jazz songs. The audience went wild and some of the soldiers took to the floor to swing dance with the local girls they had brought along. Anthony watched for her reaction and smiled.

"What?" She tried to deflect his look. He wouldn't say anything but continued smiling at her.

"No!" she said. "I'm not going to go out there to dance with these army boys. Look at them. They're not even good. They're just flinging the girls around." She wasn't exaggerating either. Watching them, she wondered if these boys might accidentally drop one of the girls on the floor and she would have to cut short her own evening to take the poor girl back to the hospital for treatment.

Overhearing what she said, Jesse turned to them and asked, "Do you two swing dance?"

"I can't," Anthony said, "but Tessa is really good."

"Is that so?" Jesse got up, walked over to her, and held out his hand. "May I?"

Taken aback by his invitation, Tessa hesitated. Jesse looked at Anthony. "Do you mind?"

"No, not at all," Anthony said. "Go on, Tessa. I know you like this. Go and have some fun."

Still unsure, Tessa took Jesse's hand and let him take her out to the floor. Anthony did say Jesse was his friend, so she didn't want to turn him down and be too standoffish. At least Jesse didn't seem like those other rough country boys who were tossing those poor girls around like they were sacks of potatoes.

As soon as they began, all her hesitation went by the wayside. Jesse was a fantastic dancer. With ease, he swung her every which way, pulling her in, then releasing. He pulled her forward and released her backward while leading them in circular turns, then lifted her and tossed her into the air. His steps were so quick, his hold of her was steady, and his movements were so fast.

He swing danced even better than Jack!

Tessa could not stop laughing the whole time. She hadn't let herself loose and had this kind of fun for a long, long time. When the music stopped and they were both trying to catch their breath, they found they were the only ones still dancing. She and Jesse were so good, all the other dancing couples had cleared the floor for them. Everybody in the room was clapping, hollering, and whistling in cheers. Tessa looked over at Anthony. He applauded along with everyone else, clearly wowed too while Clayton good-naturedly slapped him on the back.

Still holding on to her hand, Jesse asked, "Can you tango?"

"I can. My father taught me and he's the most amazing dancer. Although, I haven't done it in years."

He grabbed her waist and waltzed her over to the pianist. "Can we have some tango music please?"

Before she knew it, he had led her into the tango starting position. "I'll lead then."

She didn't expect this. She told him she could tango because it was true. She didn't mean she wanted to dance the tango with him right now. But she had no time to react. The high-pitch, wailing sound of the opening violin segment of "Tango Jalousie" began and he pulled her into a close embrace. The sudden closeness of their bodies took her by surprise.

The mournful and raging music continued as he circled around her, pivoting her movements into a front cross, side step, back cross, and side step until the rest of the band joined in with the next segment's diabolical tunes. All the while, he gazed at her, his eyes as intense as the first time she saw them. The wave of passion flowing from them overwhelmed her. Their bodies were close. Too close for her comfort. She looked away to see Anthony's reaction. Anthony was watching her with the rest of the crowd. He didn't appear to have noticed anything odd. He gave her a little smile. Touched, she smiled back.

"Hey, look at me," Jesse whispered into her ears, his voice sounding as duplicitous and seductive as the music being played. "You're dancing with me."

She nearly stumbled. "Ye…yes. Sorry." She faced him again and looked into his eyes. His eyes drew her like a magnet. It was hard to look away.

The tempo slowed down and the music changed from tunes of fiendish danger to doomed desire. He pulled her up against his chest, then stepped back and pulled her off her axis, forcing her to lean into him. When the first part of the song reached its fiery climax, he swept her up by the waist and led them into a series of small lifts, making their physical contacts unavoidable. When their bodies touched, their movements were neither flashy nor obvious. They happened so fast, only he and she knew. She could feel a latent, carnal undercurrent each time his body brushed against hers.

All this was too much. She could not dance so intimately with someone she had only just met. She was about to pull back away from him, but the music changed again. Going along with the romantic segment's smooth and lyrical beats, he switched to a normal embrace and led her with classic tango steps forward, sideways, and backward. Relieved, she continued. She could not help being impressed by the way he danced. His movements were so effortless and elegant, so crisp and controlled. He kept varying his steps, challenging her. His eyes were still on her, watching her every move and her every step to see if she would falter. Unfazed, she stared back at him and matched him step for step.

"You can keep up with me?" he said in wonder.

Of course she could. She wasn't a neophyte. She was Dean Graham's daughter. "You've seen nothing yet," she said. She wished she could show off more moves. If they weren't in front of so many soldiers, she would turn it up a notch and show him what she could really do. But as it was, she restrained herself and held back, mindful not to kick too high or make any exaggerated move that might invite the wrong kind of attention.

Perhaps sensing her reservation, he switched to a lighter move and led her to a side step to the left. But then without warning, in a quick change of momentum, he switched their weight to the right. The momentum caused her left leg to swing up behind her into a cute and eye-catching boleo kick. The sudden playful move made her laugh. He repeated this change of momentum several times. She stole a glance at him. He was trying to please her.

With her now more relaxed, he skillfully turned her around into a reverse embrace and led them into a set of forward steps. He then turned her around into another reverse embrace and they stepped toward the opposite direction. So smooth when he moved, she didn't notice how closely he was holding her in his arms.

He turned her back into a forward embrace and continued on, easily leading each circular step until the music came to an end. From their last movements, she expected they would end with the classic final pose in which she would lean backward away from him and extend out her arm. Instead, he pulled her body back up against him, grabbed her extending arm, and swung it around his neck while he slid his fingers slowly down her inner arm and down her back. They ended facing each other. Their faces were so close. If they were any closer, their lips would have touched. She could feel his warm breath on her face.

They came to a dead stop this way and the music ended on its last note. The room erupted into cheers and thunderous applause, loud whistles and howls.

Quickly, she pulled away from him. But if anything out of line had just happened, she seemed to be the only one to have noticed. She looked at Jesse, but he merely gave her a small bow while he mouthed the words, "Thank you." All traces of seduction he had shown earlier had disappeared. She looked over at Anthony. He gave her a thumb's up, his eyes beaming with pride.

"Excuse me," she said to Jesse and hurried back to Anthony. As soon as she sat down, she put her arm around his and held onto it like it was a lifesaver.

"You were awesome, Tessa!" Anthony said. "I didn't know you could tango that well. How come you never told me?"

Tessa gave him an awkward smile. "Did you see what Jesse did?"

"No." Anthony shook his head. "I'm sure he was great but I

wasn't watching him. I only had my eyes on you." He leaned close to her and whispered into her ear, "You look so amazingly sexy dancing like that. Makes me want to take you somewhere alone away from here."

His words, and what he was implying, sent a torrent of burning sensation straight up to her heart. She caressed her head against his arm, adoring the intimate sound of his voice.

"I might have to learn to tango so I can dance with you like that too."

"No," she said. "You don't have to do anything." She stroked his face. "Don't ever change."

Pleased, he gave her a small kiss on her forehead.

She took a sip of her wine and glanced in Jesse's direction. Jesse was still on the dance floor, surrounded by Alice and Irene, each demanding him to dance with them.

"Look at them. Is he always such a flirt?" Tessa asked Anthony.

"I don't know. I always thought it was the women who wouldn't leave him alone."

Jesse, Alice, and Irene were now making a minor spectacle of themselves with the two girls both vying for his attention. He put one arm around each girl and walked them away to the side while other couples returned to the floor and danced. He whispered to Irene, then to Alice. Whatever he said to them must have pleased them. Other men in the room could only watch in envy. And yet, Tessa had a gut feeling Jesse didn't enjoy any of it. A glimpse of boredom fleeted past his face even as he sweet-talked the girls and drew their admiring eyes. Everything he did looked like an act to her.

But whatever he was doing, it was none of her business. "Come on." She tugged Anthony. "Let's go outside and take a walk."

"Okay." He took her hand and together they left the club.

Once outside, he pulled her into a secluded side street, took her into his arms, and kissed her hard. His embrace was so tight, but she wanted more. She held him as close as she could and kissed him back. How she had longed to feel his arms around her again, to be able to touch him and to feel his touch. She laid her face against his neck and inhaled. She wanted to soak in his scent. She kissed his lips, his face, his chest where the top of his shirt was left unbuttoned. She wanted to taste every part of him. She couldn't get enough of him.

CHAPTER THIRTY-TWO

JESSE WATCHED Tessa and Anthony as they left their table and headed out of the bar. Irene and Alice were still to trying to outwit each other to get his attention, but he barely heard a word they said.

For the first time in his life, he found himself deeply drawn to another person. Tessa Graham. He could not get her out of his mind. Why was she immune to him? This had never happened before. Did she love Anthony Ardley that much?

So what if a girl was in love with someone else? Seducing a girl away from someone had never been a problem for him, and it wouldn't bother him one bit even if Ardley was the person from whom he would steal her away. But Tessa Graham was like an ice wall. He wasn't sure he could succeed with her. In any case, for reasons he couldn't quite understand, he felt unable to do what had always come so easily to him. In front of her, he didn't want to play his games, tell his lies, or talk his sweet talk. With her, he would feel ashamed if he tried any of that. She made him want, for the first time in his life, to be honest and decent to another person. He wanted her to know him for who he really was, not the facade built on tricks and lies, designed to serve an ulterior motive for the sheer purpose of survival.

There was only one problem. He had put on so many false identities over the years, he no longer knew who his true self was underneath all that.

Playing his act had become second nature to him. Here in the army, he had no need to use any of his arts. And yet, he couldn't help himself. Conning others into giving him things was a habit that he couldn't break. He had no need to be a womanizer here, and yet here he was, flirting with nurses like Alice and Irene and toying with their hearts even though it felt more like work than fun. And Ardley. Why did he befriend Ardley in the first place? Because Ardley was money. He could spot money from a hundred miles away. But what was the point? He was stuck on the front line with no end in sight. He had no need to go after money, but he couldn't resist. It was his instinct to orbit in the sphere of people who were moneyed.

As all his schemes were now only motions without motives, he and Ardley had actually become friends. Ardley was the first real friend he had had in a very long time. He almost started to value their friendship, until Tessa Graham came along. Part of him wished he had never met Ardley. Then he would never have met her. Thinking about her made him question everything about himself.

"You owe me two dances, Jesse. You danced two songs with Tessa," Alice said, half joking and half serious.

"No," Irene protested. "It's my turn. I asked first, Jesse. Earlier tonight, remember?"

"Ladies, ladies," Jesse said, "I'll dance with both of you. I promise. Just let me take a breather, okay? Come on. Let's have a drink." He led them both back to the table where Anthony and Tessa sat a while ago. He felt no inclination to dance with either Alice or Irene. Who were they kidding? No way they could dance as well as Tessa. He meant to stall and let the time pass until it was too late and they all had to leave.

Although come to think of it, he had never danced with such fire with anyone before either. Dance to impress women, yes.

Pretend to romance them, certainly. But when he danced the tango with Tessa, he felt an overwhelming desire to take her, to make her feel something for him. He didn't know what came over him.

Tessa's glass of wine was still on the table. She only finished half of it. Unable to take his eyes off it, he took the glass and drank the rest.

Alice and Irene were still talking to him. He pretended to listen, laughing occasionally with them, but his mind was elsewhere. He thought of yesterday when she came to their base camp. Ardley, stunned beyond words, forgot himself and took her into his arms, giving her a hell of a kiss right before everyone's eyes.

What would it feel like to be Ardley at that moment, to be able to do that, to give Tessa Graham a kiss she couldn't forget.

In that moment, she and Ardley looked like they took no notice of anyone or anything else in the rest of the world.

Maybe they were really in love. A cynical smile appeared on his face.

...There is no such thing as love, sweetheart, his mother said to him in her sultry voice. She was sitting at the dresser in front of the mirror, counting a stack of cash. Her pink silk robe covered her see-through peach satin slip, but neither could conceal her voluptuous curves. Her luscious black hair cascaded over her face and down her back. The smudges of make-up around her lips only accentuated her sensuality.

The client had left only moments ago. The smell of illicit sex hung like poison in the air.

His mother was no ordinary hooker. Her clients were rich and powerful men. Politicians, business tycoons, trust funders of the bluest of the blue-blooded elites of New York. There were famous actors, writers, and artists too. Men who the world deemed as movers and shakers. Men who considered themselves masters of the universe.

His home was no ordinary home. He and his mother lived in a spacious condominium on the highest floor in one of Madison Avenue's most coveted buildings. He never wanted for anything. He wore the finest clothes and ate the finest food at the finest restaurants. Every year, his mother took him on at least one extravagant vacation to Europe. With her, he lived a life of absolute excess.

He even had the best education. When he was nine, she tried to enroll him in that prestigious academy on Riverside Drive which all the rich kids in their building attended. Without explanation, the narrow-eyed woman with gray hair at the admissions office turned them down. He still remembered her cold reception and the haughty, condescending look on her face. His mother was furious.

"Fuck her. Snobby bitch. Who does she think she is? Just a stupid clerk. A dried-up hag with no money trying to rub a little shine off those who have. I'll show her," she said, grabbing his hand and dragging him out of the school building.

The following week, his mother hired all the best teachers from that academy as his private tutors, giving him weekly private lessons in French, Latin, math, music, and later on when he got older, history and literature too. All the teachers she approached accepted her offer. Teachers' salaries had their limits. The sum she offered was too good to resist. Money talked, and no questions were asked. Every day after regular classes at the local public school, he had another whole afternoon of more lessons, just so his mother could spite that bitch and prove her point.

His mother sent a limousine every day to pick up the teachers in front of the school. One time, she even came in person.

Wrapped in fur in the luxury vehicle, she rolled down the window and waited until that woman from the admissions office got off work and came outside. His mother stared straight at her, giving her a scornful eye and a saucy smile while his teacher got into the limo. The old hag, in her pathetic, old, and worn-out coat, with her dry, pruny skin and graying hair, averted her eyes and hurried away into the subway station.

Yes. By any standard, he grew up in a home that was a lap of luxury, except his home was also where his mother entertained her clients. When she was working, their home became his prison. He could not be seen. He could not make any noise. He could not leave his room until the clients were gone. He was not supposed to exist.

All those men sure love you, he said to his mother while he stood by her door watching her count the stash of cash. He was thirteen at the time.

There is no such thing as love, sweetheart.

Two years later, when he turned fifteen, he left, taking with him nothing of hers except her stunning good looks, which he had inherited from her.

If she bothered to look for him, he never knew of it. Maybe it was good riddance to her that he was gone. She was still beautiful. Having a grown-up son did nothing to help her business.

Garland was her last name. He didn't know his father. She never talked about him and he never asked.

Ironically, it was one of her associates who took him under his wing.

Quayle. He wasn't one of her clients. As unlikely as it was, she had a few confidants. They were people who came from the same gutter as she and somehow found ways to rise above, turning what would otherwise be businesses of filthy low-lives into profitable enterprises that generated cash from the super rich, and sometimes, the famous and powerful.

Quayle was even more than a confidant. Years ago, she and Quayle swindled the son of a politician together. She performed her tricks and then convinced the lad to trust Quayle. Quayle lured their prey deeper and deeper into debt with his half-baked business schemes. Together, she and Quayle stripped the boy clean. When his father discovered what had happened, the old man was in the middle of a fierce political campaign. A scandal with his son being conned by a hooker would have done him in. The old man paid them another hefty wad of cash to make everything go away. Quayle and his mother split the sum. The event launched their careers to a new level of clientele and they did not look back.

"You need to learn a trade to survive," Quayle told him. "Since you're a boy, there's nothing you can learn from your mother. But I can use a presentable pretty boy like you. What do you say if I take you as my apprentice? I'll teach you everything I know. We'll be in business together. A family business. Like father and son. What do you say?"

He moved into Quayle's home the day after his fifteenth birthday.

True to his word, Quayle taught him everything. They opened shell companies and set up false investment opportunities. The preyed on people with extra cash who were greedy for more and wanted to make another quick buck. They set up false charities, enticing people who felt guilty living their privileged lives in the face of those less fortunate, but who nonetheless would rather throw money at the problems than to commit any real time or efforts.

And then, there was the gambling. They brought the high rollers to the table and got a cut of every win by the house. They found the whales who couldn't help themselves, the ones who lived to chase that elusive high from the rush of taking reckless risks when the stakes were huge. Of course, the house always won in the end.

His education continued. Quayle saw to that. But gone were the math and Latin lessons. Quayle wanted him to learn all the finer things in life. Expensive aged wines, scotch, and brandy. Haute cuisine. Fine arts and classical literature. Ballroom dancing. Theaters and operas. Golf. All the things that would make him a refined man of taste who could mingle with men and women with money.

"To attract money, you have to look and act moneyed," Quayle said.

Not to mention attracting all the lonely wives and widows starving for attention, especially the attention of a handsome young man who wined and dined them, dazzled them with witty conversations, and danced with them under the star lights while whispering poetic adulations in their ears. Women in such dispositions were very eager to help a young man aspiring to start up various investment enterprises.

While he was at it, why not mix business with pleasure? So many beautiful women, wasted on men who had forgotten about them and neglected them at home.

As for Quayle? Quayle almost treated him like his own son.

Almost.

At first, Quayle treated him as the rookie. The way Quayle split their profits, Quayle would keep three-fourths and give him one-fourth of everything they had earned. That was okay in the beginning, but after a few years, the tide turned. With his handsome good looks and smooth finesse, he, not Quayle, became the one who brought in their biggest clients and a lion's share of their profits. He was a natural. Whether he claimed to be a young business manager, an heir to a wealthy clan, a European aristocrat, or simply a university student, people believed him. Quayle could never have pulled it off the way he could, but the most Quayle was willing to give him was one-third of what they earned.

He had already confronted Quayle several times about this. Quayle didn't want to talk about it, but things needed to change. It had to be a sixty-five/thirty-five split with him keeping the larger share, or he wanted out. His proposal was more than generous. He offered it only on account of Quayle having been the mentor who took him in and taught him everything he knew. He had long since surpassed Quayle at his own game. Quayle's games and tricks were old. The man was falling behind the times, losing his touch as well as his looks.

He didn't need Quayle anymore. He would do better on his own.

Despite his intention to be generous against his better judgment, he had a feeling Quayle wouldn't bite. He was ready to make that final break to venture out on his own. Then the draft letter came.

Just like that, all the drama came to a halt. He became the property of the United States government, and all that was left behind was a sordid life and a pointless existence.

CHAPTER THIRTY-THREE

FOR TESSA, the hardest thing about working at a military hospital was the lack of escape from people. The patients, bored and with nothing to do, were always observing everything she did. They all knew she liked dried fruits and walnuts. How they knew that, she had no idea. Neither were available here except on rare occasions when someone received a package from home. They knew when she had showered and washed her hair, and they somehow always knew when she saw Anthony. Afterward, they would never fail to ask her about it. They seemed to think that everything that she did was news for mass consumption. How could so many men be so nosy?

Then, there were her co-workers. There was no escape from them. The lack of privacy here was fifty times worse than back at the Chicago Veterans Hospital. Living in their tight, shared quarters, no one had any personal space. Working in the tense, high-pressured military hospital setting, everyone did everything together. Everyone knew everything about each other. There was no getting away and no peace.

Boring small talk and mindless gossip abounded. People needed ways to pass the time when they were all stuck in this claustrophobic environment at all hours of the day with no end in sight.

Occupational hazard, she thought. She wished Sarah were here, more than ever.

The hazard meter reached a fevered pitch in the hospital canteen at lunch the day after she went out with Anthony and the other officers to watch the army band perform.

"Ellie, you should've seen Tessa last night!" Alice fawned. "Did you know she's an amazing dancer?"

"No. I didn't."

Everyone turned their attention to Tessa. Tessa did not enjoy this. Not one bit.

"She and Jesse Garland brought the house down," Alice said. "That tango! I wish I could dance like that. I would have been so jealous and mad at you, Tessa, if you weren't already Lieutenant Ardley's girlfriend."

Tessa froze. Her chest tensed and she tightened her fingers around the handle of her fork. She didn't want them to talk about her and Anthony.

"Lieutenant Ardley. What a catch," Irene teased her. "A real front line soldier and an officer. Good looking too."

Tessa poked at her food. There was nothing in the world she wanted more at this moment than to have Sarah Brinkman to be right here, right now, right next to her. Now would be a very good time for Sarah to tell one of her endless tales about her four brothers or their many, many interests and hobbies, or give her soliloquy on how to bake the perfect pecan pie. Seeking rescue, she looked over at Ellie, but Ellie could only give her sympathetic eyes and a helpless smile.

Suddenly, Alice declared, "Jesse's mine."

Laughing, Irene countered, "Says who? I say he's mine!"

"Who's Jesse?" Gracie asked.

"You haven't met Jesse?" Alice asked. "Don't worry." She let out a deep sigh of desire. "You will. Every nurse..."

"... and woman..." Irene interrupted her.

"... and every woman here who isn't already married or attached will meet Jesse sooner or later," Alice said. "He's a real looker."

"He's a medic," Irene said. "A real sheik. Not like the rest of the men here. He's smart, classy, sophisticated. All the other men here are boorish brutes compared to him." As soon as she said this, she gasped, raised her hand to her mouth, and said to Tessa, "Except Lieutenant Ardley, of course."

Tessa tapped her fork on her mess kit and said nothing.

"What does he do in real life? This Jesse Garland," asked Gracie.

"He told me he's a scam artist," Alice said, laughing. Gracie widened her eyes, alarmed. "Oh, he was just kidding." Alice waved her hand. "When I pressed him, he told me he was an investment banker. He was so funny. He said investment bankers are glorified scam artists."

"All the younger nurses here are in love with him, Gracie," Irene said. "Wait until you meet him. You'll fall in love with him too."

Doubtful, Gracie gave Tessa a wary look.

"No," Alice said. "Not everyone. Ellie isn't in love with Jesse." It was now Ellie's turn to look uncomfortable.

"Ellie's got her eyes on Dr. Haley," Irene teased.

"That's right!" Alice chimed in. "Ellie's smarter than us. She likes someone more mature and serious, like Dr. Haley."

"What are you all talking about?" Ellie denied. "That's not true!" Her face flushed deep red. Tessa had never seen her look so flustered.

"Oh, Ellie, don't be shy. We all know Dr. Haley likes you too."

"Stop it. All of you." Ellie put her hands down on the table. "Dr. Haley is a very nice and kind man. You all shouldn't joke about him this way. It's not nice."

"Why, Ellie! We're not saying anything insulting about him. You're a beautiful young woman. Dr. Haley would be lucky to have you if you were to become his wife."

"Enough." Ellie stood up from her seat. "This is absurd. I'm leaving." She took her mess kit and walked away.

After she was gone, Gracie asked, "Is she angry?"

"Nah!" Alice said. "She's just embarrassed. She's too shy to admit it but I know she's head over heels in love with Dr. Haley."

"Isn't he's a bit old for her?" Irene asked.

Alice shrugged. "Maybe. I don't know. What is he? Forty-three? Forty-five? He's still an attractive man. Mature, accomplished, respectable. The two of them go well together."

While Alice and Irene talked, Tessa saw Dr. Haley coming into the mess hall. Good thing Ellie had left. She would be embarrassed to death to see him after what the girls had just said about her and Dr. Haley.

"Not so easy for Ellie though as long as the Fanny is watching," Irene said.

"The Fanny?" Tessa nearly choked on her food.

"You know, Captain Fran Milton," Irene said, making a sour face. "That woman is a total ass."

Tessa swallowed a large gulp of water. If only the American nurses knew that fanny was the vilest term used to insult a woman back in England.

"She was an army nurse during the Great War, so she thinks she knows everything," Alice said. "She's always bossing people around. She even bosses Dr. Haley around."

"So what?" Tessa asked. "What does Captain Milton have to do with Ellie and Dr. Haley?"

"The Captain's always interfering with them," said Irene.

"She interferes with everyone and everything," Alice said.

"Yes, but this is different. I think she's secretly in love with Dr. Haley," Irene whispered.

"No!" Alice exclaimed.

Irene nodded. "Yes. Just you watch closely. She's always finding one work excuse or another to be alone with him. And haven't you noticed? Only older, plain-looking nurses are ever assigned to work with him. I know Sanford is the one who manages assignments, but I suspect the Fanny has a hand in it. She's always in a crappy mood when Dr. Haley talks to the younger nurses, and she'd find this reason or that to pull the younger nurses away from him." Then, huddling closer to them and lowering her voice, she said, "Ellie gets it the worst. That bitch is always criticizing and embarrassing Ellie in front of Dr. Haley even when Ellie has done nothing wrong. I think it's because she knows that Dr. Haley likes Ellie too. The Fanny's jealous."

All this was news to Tessa. But now that she thought about it, the first time she met the Captain, the Captain had yelled at Ellie and humiliated her in front of everyone including Dr. Haley.

She watched Aaron Haley walk toward the food line. Along the way, he stopped every time he saw one of his patients eating and spoke to each one of them. What a nice man. Alice was right. Ellie and Dr. Haley would be good together.

Jesse leaned against the doorway once again, watching Tessa, waiting for her to notice him. Like last time, she was lost in her thoughts, unaware of his presence or how long he had been there. While she took inventory of the newly arrived medications and equipment in the make-shift medical supplies room, he watched her, transfixed by the beauty of the way she moved and the sound of her voice as she hummed the tune of the song "Moonlight and Roses."

When she finally noticed him, she looked surprised. "Jesse! Do you always stand around like that looking at people without saying anything?"

He smiled and didn't reply.

"It's unnerving. Why do you do that?"

Because I love looking at you.

"Because I don't want to interrupt you in the middle of whatever you're doing. Here." He handed her a piece of paper.

"It's a list of medical supplies I need. We're going off on another mission tomorrow."

She took the piece of paper and started to gather the items on the list.

"Did you have fun the other night?" he asked, referring to two nights ago when they had gone to the servicemen's club to watch the army band.

She put down the list, then looked directly at him. "As a matter of fact, I did. You're a very good dancer."

"Likewise, so are you."

"Although, you went a little overboard, don't you think?"

"Did I? How so?"

"You almost made me uncomfortable dancing with you."

He came closer to her, peeking at her face with a teasing smile as if searching for what she really thought. "Maybe I wasn't the problem. Maybe you felt uncomfortable because you found me irresistible."

He expected her to react with indignity, but she didn't. Without showing any emotion, she stared back at him. "Don't kid yourself. You're not the best looking man I've ever seen."

"Who is, then? Lieutenant Ardley?"

Tessa thought for a moment, then said, "My father."

"Your father! And you are your father's daughter. Isn't that an indirect way to say that you think you are very good looking yourself?" He cornered her against the table in the middle of the room, imposing himself on her but without touching her. "So what should two very good-looking people do when they find themselves alone with each other?"

"You shouldn't flirt with a girl who already has a boyfriend, especially when her boyfriend is your friend."

"Is that right? Okay, then now you know what a cad I really am."

Unimpressed, she pushed him lightly and moved away. "No you're not. You're only pretending to be one." She picked up the list and continued collecting medical supplies for him.

"Really? Why do you think that? Is it because you think there's a good guy underneath? Perhaps you'll uncover my good soul and change me into a better man?" He took a step closer to her again. "Would you like to try? I better warn you now, I'm a real cad. A cad of the worst kind."

Still unmoved, she said. "Don't you worry about me. I have no interest in making you a better man or a worse man. You're not my problem."

Indifference. He had wanted her to be sympathetic or outraged. He wanted to find evidence that he could elicit from her some kind of feelings for him, but all she was giving him was indifference. Her indifference stung like a sharp pinch. "Never said I was your problem." He retracted from her. His voice changed from playful to cold. "I don't care about anyone, so no one's ever cared about me. That's all right. I'm used to it."

"Fine," Tessa said. "If that's the way you want it. But you're still not a cad. You're only pretending to be one. I've seen a lot of actors, and I'm not fooled." She handed him a box filled with the supplies. "So why put on an act, Jesse Garland?" She stared at him. He felt like she was seeing right through him again.

Instead of answering her, he said, "Thanks for the supplies." He took the box and walked out.

What just happened? He thought as he walked away from the hospital. Always, he had been the one who held the upper hand and wreaked emotional rollercoasters on women. How did the tables get turned? What was her hold over him?

Why couldn't he stop thinking about her?

He did not like this situation. Not in the least.

Even after two years in Chicago, Thanksgiving's Day still felt like a foreign holiday to Tessa. But this time, she received something for which she was truly thankful, a letter from her father. It was the first time he had written to her since her deployment.

November 5, 1943

My dear daughter,

My heart felt like a rock—a boulder that had sunk into the sea when we received the telegram from William and Sophia telling us that you had left America to become an army nurse overseas. I felt like the ground I stood on had crumbled and I was falling into a deep abyss. I couldn't understand what happened. My immediate reaction was to blame everyone in sight. How could William have let this happen? We left you in his care. We trusted him. Who is this boy Anthony? What has he done to cloud your mind and lure you into this horrifyingly dangerous situation? I was even angry at your mother, wrongly transferring my anger onto her for having a family so utterly incompetent that a young girl could deceive them and get away from them. But mostly, I was angry at myself. How could I have sent you away from us for so long that I could no longer be by your side to protect you, to watch over you and to keep you safe?

Of all things, my family is what I cherish the most. I live in a world of constant make-believe. You and your mother are the two things that are real. My family is all that matters to me, and you are the most precious thing in my life. When you were born, I vowed that I would be a good father. Every day since, I have asked myself if I have succeeded. And now, I think I might have failed. Should I have sent you away? Your mother and I thought it was for the best for your safety. But did we—did I—make the right decision? If I had insisted on keeping you in London, could I have prevented setting into motion the chain of events that would ultimately lead you to the epicentre of danger? Perhaps everything would have been different had we made different choices.

Now, you have made your own choice to go after someone you say you love. As much as I wish I could have held you back, I could not help but think of the chances your mother and I took when we were young. Had she held on to a life of comfort and security under the protective sphere of the Ardleys, or had I held on to the promise of a flourishing career by remaining with that actress, you would not have been in my life today. The idea of not having you in my life is enough to drown me in an endless sea of regret. There is nothing in the world more important to me than you. Looking back, I am glad your mother and I followed our hearts and took our chances, for in doing so, we brought you into this world.

When I think of this, I realise that what I really want to tell you is this: If you are sure of the person you love, then do not let him go no matter what. Do not stand by and let happiness slip away from you.

My advice to you does not absolve me from failing at my responsibility as your father. I still wish I could have saved you from the dangerous path you have chosen. But with the situation being irreversible, I want you to know that I love you. I am always behind you in the decisions that you make.

Write to us. Your mother wants to hear from you, and so do I.

— Love, Father

P.S. I do not promise that I won't make mincemeat out of this Anthony boy if I ever see him.

She finished reading and folded the letter into her bag of belongings along with all the other letters she had received since she arrived in Italy. Of all the people back in London and Chicago, her father was the one she worried about the most. He had always been protective of her. It had been difficult for him when he sent her away. When he didn't write to her for weeks, she knew the news of her deployment must have caused him a world of anguish. Knowing her father had accepted the situation had put her mind at ease.

She wished she didn't have to leave everyone at home in such a state of worry. Nonetheless, being here now, she was more certain than ever she had made the right choice. She was needed here more than anywhere else. This was where she could answer soldiers' wailing cries to be saved and hospitals' desperate calls for help. Here, she had the satisfaction of laughing in the face of the war. She could put up a resistance against the war and wrestle back what it tried to take away. However insignificant her resistance was, the war no longer dictated her life. She could do something to fight back.

Most of all, she was with Anthony again. By his side was exactly where she belonged.

Thankfully, they were together.

She closed her bag and left her quarters to join the army's Thanksgiving dinner. Entering the mess hall, she searched for Anthony among the swarm of people. Even though the kitchen staff had expanded the dining areas and arranged the seating schedule to stagger the number of people arriving, the place was still packed with servicemen from every division, department, and unit, and she could barely squeeze past the entrance. No one followed the seating schedule. Everyone wanted to eat and join in the fun. Only the unfortunate souls stuck on missions up north outside of the city would miss this jubilant night.

"Tessa!" Anthony had spotted her before she could find him.

"Anthony!"

"Over here. We saved a seat for you." He grabbed her hand and led her to the food line. The spread of turkeys, mashed potatoes, cranberry sauce, green beans, and bread puddings put everyone in the best mood they had felt in months even though most of the food had come from cans. There were even pumpkin pies.

They filled their plates and joined Anthony's friends at the officers' table. She watched as he ate and laughed with the others, amused by how little it took to make him this happy.

How she loved him for it. If only their lives and the world could be this simple. She touched him on the shoulder. "How'd you like the food?"

"Best damn Thanksgiving dinner ever!" he said. Out of everyone's sight under the table, he put his hand on her knee and held it there while they ate.

She loved it. She loved the feeling when he touched her. Everything felt as sweet and tangy as the cranberry sauce.

"I got a V-Mail from Mother and Father this morning." He finished the last bite of his turkey. "They said they got your telegram about having found me."

"Oh good. I hope they've gotten over the shock of my leaving."

"Let's write them together after dinner."

"Okay," Tessa said. "We'll tell them all about the turkey from the can..."

"And the pre-dinner football game. Our boys won. We smoked the guys from Forty-Fifth."

"And we had pumpkin pies!"

"We can send a V-Mail together to your parents too if you want."

"About that..." She wondered, trying to envision her father's reaction. "Maybe if you start your letter writing campaign now, my father will stop being mad at you when the time comes for you to meet him."

"Meet your father? That sounds scary."

"Scarier than fighting the war?

"For sure!"

She touched his arm. As she looked into his eyes, she knew he had the same thoughts as she did. Tonight, they had so much to be thankful for. First, Anthony was not away on a mission and they could celebrate together. Even better, they were with each other again, not separated across the world. Most importantly, he was safe and alive. Tonight was a real Thanksgiving for both of them, with all the right food, the right atmosphere, and with each other.

PART X
JALOUSIE

CHAPTER THIRTY-FOUR

FRAN MILTON never thought she would serve in the military again after the Great War. Like last time, she signed up the instant America geared up for war. After all, someone had to step up and take responsibility. She was all about responsibility.

Unfortunately, responsibility was not a concept most people generally valued, or even understood. Take her family for instance. Her parents never valued anything that she did. She cooked the meals. She cleaned the house. When they couldn't pay the rent, she fended off the landlord until money came in. When her father got drunk, which happened often, she was the one to fetch him from the bars or the streets and take him home when he passed out in his drunken stupor. Did any of that matter? No. Her father was a drunk and her mother was a moron. All they cared about was Lizzie, her younger sister. It was always Lizzie this and Lizzie that. Everything that was worth anything went to Lizzie. Lizzie was so pretty. Lizzie was going to marry someone rich and save them all. Lizzie would make them all rich.

Lizzie herself was the worst. That wench. She thought she was God's gift to the earth.

Even after all these years, Fran still remembered the condescending way Lizzie looked at her.

"Pity," that wench said when Fran came into her room to bring her the new dress their mother had bought for her. "If you weren't such a bug-eyed Betty, you could find yourself a rich beau too."

Fran watched Lizzie's mouth move as she spoke. That vile red lipstick. The wench had no idea how nasty it made her look. What did that paramour of hers see in her? Men. They were all such fools. So easily deceived by the frivolous and superficial. Fran dumped the dress on Lizzie's bed and walked out.

They barely had enough money for food. This dress had cost a fortune. It was such a useless waste of money. That wench better deliver. If that fool she had her eye on didn't marry her in the end, they would lose all their investments on all those dresses and accessories she kept buying.

No matter. She had one thing over Lizzie. She was responsible. Unlike all of them, she knew how to be prepared and be responsible, even if these fools didn't know well enough to appreciate her for it. What use was Lizzie anyway? Lizzie was nothing but a pretty face. Lizzie didn't know how to do anything. If disaster ever struck, that dumb Dora would be nothing but a pathetic baggage. She, Fran, on the other hand, knew how to put things in order. She was saving these imbecile parents of hers every day and they didn't even know it.

It wasn't as if she had a choice anyway. Her mother, having no faith in her to find a rich husband for a meal ticket like Lizzie, started to fuss about her being a burden. Her mother only hinted at first, but soon enough, the hint became an outright question. How much longer would she remain living at home? Would she find somebody, anybody, to marry and get out of their house?

Marry she would not, but get out of the house she would. She looked around and took a job as a nurse. The pay wasn't high, but it sustained her. Besides, she was perfect for the job. Being a nurse was all about responsibility, and she was responsible.

A chance to show her true worth came when the Great War broke out and the military put out a call for volunteers to serve as military nurses. She jumped at the chance while her peers hesitated and refused. When the time came to do what must be done, she was the only one who stepped up to the plate. She alone did the honorable thing while the rest shirked their duties just when they were most needed.

Life in the military suited her fine. The order and discipline, she welcomed. The horror? No matter. She'd take looking at mangled bodies any day over that phony facade of the Lizzies of this world. When people are all maimed and torn, no one cared about her looks. They just wanted her to save them.

When the Great War ended, she returned to work in civilian hospitals. The years passed. Nothing changed. The hospital was the only place that made the most use of her commitment to responsibility. She had already accepted the fact that the hospital was where she would spend the rest of her life.

Then war broke out again in Europe and rumors ran rampant that the United States was mobilizing, and medical staff would be needed to go overseas again.

She answered the first call of duty a full two years before Pearl Harbor. The war would get worse. She expected it. She always planned for the worst so she could be prepared. It was necessary that she volunteer as early as possible. Mobilizing the medical units required extensive organization and preparation. She had done this before. She had a duty to put her experience to use when needed.

Everything had gone according to plan and exactly as she anticipated, except for Aaron Haley.

An exceptionally skilled surgeon, he was someone who took responsibility as seriously as she did. Just like her, he had dedicated his entire life to his medical career. The way she saw it, someone as gifted as Haley had a duty to society to maximize the use of his expertise. She suspected he knew that. Why else was he still unmarried? His contributions to the world would be greater if he focused on his career rather than his own personal life. They had both given their all and sacrificed for the greater good, unlike the leeches and Lizzies of this world.

In the two years they had worked together, she had grown fond of him. He was not like the other doctors. Before Aaron Haley, she had always had uneasy relationships with the doctors she worked with. No matter how professional she was and how well she did her job, they often underappreciated her. They let their biases and favoritisms get in the way. They praised the nurses they liked while they overlooked her. It was not that she wanted public recognition. She could care less. But when others got credit for things that she had done, that bothered her, and it happened a lot because on principle, she refused to play nice.

Aaron Haley was the exception. He respected her work. When others didn't notice all that she had done for the unit, he publicly credited her for it. He was never swayed by the pretty young things courting his favor. There were many such girls. They were shameless! But he gave credit where credit was due. On her part, she did her best to keep these troublemakers away from him so that they wouldn't interfere with his work.

Since she and Haley had met working together at the Army Medical Corps, they had settled into a good, cordial work routine. Barring emergencies, they would meet for breakfast every day to discuss the allocation of work to people under their management and to make sure they had the pulse of every part of their medical unit's operations. In the evening, when the workday was over, they would have their evening tea and go over any problems that had come up. They would figure out the solutions before the problems became disasters. Once a week, they would meet to discuss logistics and equipment deliveries.

She valued their relationship. It was one that she intended to maintain when this war was over. She wouldn't mind growing old this way. Two dedicated professionals, working as a united front for a common cause. Their lives could be fulfilled that way.

And if he ever decided he wanted more...

If he ever decided that he wanted more, how could it not be her? His work was the most important thing in the world to him. That was obvious. Who else had the skills, the experience, and the knowledge to help him further his work? They were both professionals in the science field, not creatures of emotions, or else they wouldn't have remained single for this long. She was the only one qualified to support him for the rest of his life's purpose. There was no question about it.

"Colonel, are you listening? You seem distracted," Fran asked Aaron. She had just given him a full rundown of the names of the patients on the list to be sent home. Arranging for transportation and coordinating with the navy to repatriate veterans had been a challenge lately. Something else in other divisions always took priority over the hospital's needs.

"Ah, yes, you were saying?" Aaron said, snapping back to attention. This meeting had dragged on for too long and he had tuned out for a bit. He had another project he was anxious to get to which was sitting in his desk drawer, but he knew it was important to Milton that they do their jobs properly and adhere to their work routine.

"I said we need to press the military transportation staff to move those patients out of the hospital more quickly. Those patients are ready to be sent home. We need to clear the hospital beds for new patients."

"Of course, Captain. You're right. I'll talk to the transportation staff sergeant again tomorrow. Why don't we break for the night? It's been a long day. We can both use some rest." He took a deep breath and rubbed his temple.

Before Fran could answer, someone knocked on the door.

"Come in," Aaron said.

Ellie Swanson entered. Aaron immediately sat up straight.

"I'm sorry to interrupt. Captain Milton, Colonel Callahan is here to see you," Ellie said. She lowered her voice in deference to Fran.

"What now?" Fran threw up her hand. "I've given him all the

records he wanted." She turned to Aaron. "I tell you, that man is incompetent. He needs someone to spoon-feed him. How he ever rose up the ranks, I'll never know." She took her files from Aaron's desk and started out the door. Out of the corner of her eye, she caught Ellie giving Aaron a shy smile.

"Lieutenant, come with me," she ordered Ellie.

"Yes, Ma'am."

Together, they left his office. Aaron finished his tea and opened the top right drawer of his desk. From the drawer, he took out a small wood-carved dove ornament he had been working on. This was what he had wanted to do the entire time when Fran Milton was droning on and on about relocating the patients. The relocation of patients was not an urgent issue. The winter weather had slowed the attacks and counter-attacks on the front. For the time being, shortage of hospital beds was not a concern. In any case, there wasn't much more he could do to sway the navy to accommodate their requests. There were only so many ships coming in. Every division needed them.

He picked up his small carving knife. It had been ages since he had made a wood-carved ornament. The urge to carve came back to him last week when a fellow doctor showed him a photo of his family with a Christmas tree. One of the ornaments hanging on the Christmas tree was a ceramic dove. It inspired him to return to his old hobby again. He used to be very good at carving wood ornaments and statues. In fact, he was good at anything that required a steady hand, patience, and attention to detail. In that respect, surgery and wood-carving were not all that different to him.

What he really wanted was to give Ellie Swanson a nice little Christmas present. The sight of Ellie Swanson just now gave him a second wind and a burst of fresh energy. He started carving out the details of the dove's wings. As he carved, he thought of her. She had made an impression on him ever since the first time he saw her. She, along with a group of new nurses, had arrived to join the 33rd in Africa back during the summer. They were all admirable young ladies, so brave to have come all this way to a strange foreign land in such dangerous conditions, wanting to help.

The battles in Sicily and Salerno brought in thousands of casualties. The soldiers' wounds were horrific. The pressure to care for so many trauma patients all at once stretched everyone's strength and abilities to the max. Yet, this young woman working beside him, who had never worked in a military field hospital before, who was so unassuming and modest on the outside, found the gumption to take in everything. She kept going as one patient after another rolled in. She never said a single word of complaint. Her gentle touch relieved the pains of the wounded in ways that morphine couldn't.

One night, in Salerno, he had collapsed in utter exhaustion and fell asleep on the beat-up couch in the room that served as his office in the abandoned school building where they had set up their mobile hospital. The chilly night air was blowing through the window, but he was too tired to get up to close it or put on his jacket. He'd been on his feet for twenty hours straight and hadn't slept in thirty-six hours. His feet and legs ached and he couldn't stand up, so he curled his body a little more and wished for the cold temperature to miraculously go away.

Half asleep, he felt a gentle hand stroking his forehead. Maybe he was dreaming. He couldn't tell. He was too tired to open his eyes. He felt someone putting a blanket over him. He forced his eyelids open and saw the shadow of the back of a young nurse at the door. Ellie Swanson. A cup of hot tea sat on the small wooden stand next to him by the couch. The wind had stopped and the window was closed.

It had been many years since anyone had done anything like this for him.

He continued carving, focusing on the beak. He left the beak slightly open so the bird appeared to be chirping. The bird looked happy this way. It would make her smile. It made him smile. Even in this broken city torn apart by war and destruction, the thought of Ellie Swanson cheered him up.

But then, he sighed. If only he weren't so old already. He was practically old enough to be her father.

He had waited all these years for the right person and that right feeling. He held onto the steadfast belief that given time, he would find that person. How unfortunate it was then that time itself had now become the impediment.

If he weren't so old already, he would not hesitate to go after her.

CHAPTER THIRTY-FIVE

It was an unusually cold December afternoon when Anthony finally had a chance to see Tessa again after Thanksgiving. When he was away on missions, he missed her, even more so now because he knew she would be here when he returned.

Despite being deployed in the same region, they were more often separated than not. Walking down the streets of Naples with her, he wished time would slow down. He cherished the little time they could have together, every minute of it.

On their way to the Palme Theater, he deliberately slowed down his pace. Today, the theater would be showing, "Thank Your Lucky Star." He didn't care if they missed part of it, he wasn't a fan of musicals. All he cared was that they were together. With her by his side, holding onto his arm, he could keep on walking.

"Look, Anthony! It's Kilroy!" She ran a few steps ahead of him to the side of a building where a graffiti of the cute little bald man with beady eyes and the long nose peeked over a wall. Next to the graffiti, someone had written, "KILROY WAS HERE."

He smiled.

She walked by a lamp post and swung around it, then pointed at the snow at the top of the mountains surrounding the city. "It snowed up there. Do you remember New Year's Eve last year? It was snowing that night."

Of course he remembered. That night, the temperature was freezing. Flurries of snowflakes drifted in the air when they walked across Uncle Leon's isolated courtyard, then across the Michigan Avenue Bridge on their way to the Allerton Hotel. He remembered how happy he was to be alone with her, just the two of them with no one else around except nameless passersby on the streets.

Just the two of them. Like now.

He watched her standing in the middle of the street, laughing and delighted with the snow on the mountain that reminded her of the night they first confessed their love to each other. She relished this moment of them together as much as he did. It was because of him that she found the snow to be a wonder, and it is because of her that he found these ruinous streets to nonetheless be a beautiful sight. Every place was beautiful as long as she was in it.

He wouldn't tell her that up on the mountains, the snow was not a wondrous amazement but an ordeal to suffer when he was sleeping outside night after night, especially if the sky was also pouring freezing rain. He didn't want her to know that two days ago, a bomb landed as close as fifty feet beside him as he dived into a foxhole, or that three days before that, a piece of metal from the enemy's shell hit the ground, ricocheted up, and nicked him in the thigh, or how on that same day, he saw two men walking ahead of him step on a mine and both of them had their legs blown off. He did not want to ruin the moment with these horrors. He wanted to have something wholesome to look forward to when he returned to her.

He thought back to that night on New Year's Eve. As long as she was in this world, then he still had something to fight for. As long as there would be winter days when they could walk side by side as the snowflakes fell, he would remember that he still had good things in this world to live for. As long as she was there for him, waiting for him to return to her, he would do whatever it took to stay alive.

For Christmas, he had only one wish. He wished this war would end. When it did, he would bring this girl home and start a new life with her. He could take it, whatever hardships and miseries, as long as she was there, and they had a future to look forward to.

He caught up to her and tugged her elbow to draw her attention back to him. She let him take her into his arms and buried her face against his chest. Yes. She was happy to be with him. He knew that. He was sure of it. He wanted to keep her in his arms, always, to protect her and keep her safe.

Outside the hospital, Tessa looked out to the Apennine Mountains beyond the city. Somewhere in those mountains, Anthony was with his men, holding onto the Allies' defensive lines.

Was he okay? She pulled her rose pendant out of her collar. Please let him be okay. Please let him be safe, she thought as she turned the pendant in her fingers.

He rarely told her what happened out there. Being his chivalrous self, he still wanted to protect her from the horrors he faced even though she was now here and could see much of it for herself. She understood his wishes and didn't ask. It was why she hadn't told him she was wearing the rose pendant. She didn't want him to know how much she missed him and worried about him. She didn't want him to feel the extra burden of her worries when he fought.

But how could she not know? She saw every day what happened to the soldiers brought to the hospital. She heard what they said when they talked. In the mountains, the Allies' advances north had come to a grinding halt. The Germans had taken full advantage of the geographical terrains to slow them down. Blizzards, snow, and poor visibility at the high altitudes hampered the Allied units from advancing on the ground. The weather conditions made it impossible for the American Air Force to capitalize on their superiority in full. The situation could not be sustained. Sooner or later, the Allied Command would have no choice but to change their strategy.

And change was coming.

In the weeks leading up to Christmas, Free French soldiers began to fill the streets. There were now as many of them as there were British and Americans in Naples. More and more American troops were returning to base and put on reserve. The French had replaced them in the fight.

What that meant for the Allies' strategy and the Sixth Army Corps, she did not know. For the moment, she was just glad that the American troops were coming back. The French arrival meant the Americans could spend Christmas at the base away from the front line. If Anthony's unit returned too, she and Anthony would be able to spend Christmas together. For this Christmas, that was what she wished for.

There were miracles on Christmas after all. Someone must have heard her prayers.

The day Anthony's unit returned, Jonesy and Ollie came to the hospital at once to invite the nurses to join their regiment's Christmas bash at the Villa of Count Zeffirelli.

Like all aristocrats, the Count had lost his entire fortune after the German occupation. His villa was all he had left. That and his dog, a little old terrier that was on its way to senility. It so happened, Jonesy and Ollie found it wandering around the streets one day, lost. Luckily, the poor dog wore a collar that bore the Count's family crest. They brought the dog back to the local nobleman, who had been crestfallen for days thinking it was lost forever. The two sergeants became friends with the count and somehow persuaded him to open up his once magnificent home to their battalion for a blowout Christmas party.

Not only that, they had convinced the command to let the officers and the grunts celebrate together. For one evening, all distinctions between officers and enlisted men would drop. The only thing the party needed was the company of ladies to make it a night. That, however, would pose no obstacle to the two sergeants determined on having fun after months of hard fighting. At the army hospital, Florence Nightingales of every hospital unit awaited. Problem solved.

Or so they thought until they tried to invite the nurses of the 33rd Field Hospital. They came around with their invitation while Tessa was reporting to Captain Milton.

"You all need to take your responsibilities much more seriously," Milton went off again on another one of her lectures when Tessa gave her a set of error-free patient reports. She could never acknowledge anyone for doing a good job. She could only focus on what she deemed wrong. "This is the problem with all you girls. You have no sense of what it means to be responsible. You all need to spend less time chitchatting with injured soldiers and more time doing your duties."

Tessa hardly needed this lecture. Of all people, she was the last to chitchat. Milton was straining to find something to complain about.

"We must all work as a team." Milton clasped her hands on her desk.

With great self-restraint, Tessa forced herself not to show any reaction. The truth was, Milton herself had the least team spirit of anyone.

"Being a team means we need to make sure everyone else is also doing their job. It's not enough that you are the one not wasting time. If your colleagues are wasting time cavorting with the soldiers, you have a duty to remind them there is work to be done. We are understaffed. When one person fails to do her share, others have to pick up the slack. That's why we must watch each other and make sure no one is shirking their—"

A loud knock on the door interrupted her. The door pushed open and Jonesy and Ollie came in without invitation.

"Lieutenant Graham!" Jonesy greeted Tessa with his jolly loud voice. Milton shot Tessa a suspicious look. Tessa did not care. She was glad for the interruption and gave Jonesy a quick smile.

"Captain! Dear, lovely Captain Milton! Like the Three Kings we've come and brought the Good News!! T'is the season when Christ is born…" Jonesy continued, oblivious to the aghast look on Fran Milton's face.

"…no, no, no, sorry that's not the good news…and there are only two of us here, not three." Ollie said. "But fear not, ladies. The real good news is, the officers and soldiers of the venerable Fifth Battalion cordially invite you…"

Jonesy didn't let him finish, "…the most outstanding, most beautiful, most compassionate nurses of the 33rd Field Hospital…"

"…to join us for our Christmas Eve party at the Villa de Count Zeffirelli," Ollie talked over him.

"We would be most honored by your presence," said Jonesy. "The nurses of the General Hospital unit, the 95th Evac Hospital, plus the 96th Evac have already accepted our invitation."

"And we would be most delighted if the nurses of the 33rd would join us as well," said Ollie. "Our battalion officers and enlisted men will all be there."

Tessa looked up. That meant Anthony would be there. They would be able to celebrate Christmas together.

"Absolutely not!" Milton said. Her harsh, final tone stunned all three of them. "A party. What nonsense! There are patients here in need of care. Who will take care of them if everyone leaves to go to a party?"

"Ma'am," Ollie said, "it'll only be a few hours for one evening."

"And we'll help you with whatever you need for the night," said Jonesy.

"I said no!" Milton adjusted her glasses and looked down at the papers on her desk. "In fact, if all the other hospital units have accepted your invitation, then we have all the more reason why the staff of 33rd must remain here to take care of the patients. At least some of us still remember that we have a job to do."

Offended, Jonesy lost his usual good humor. "How can you say that? What do you think we're all doing here?" Ollie tried to stop him but he continued. "Who's not doing their job? Where were you when our boys were out on the front line getting shot at and getting killed? It wouldn't kill you to do us a favor on Christmas Eve and let our boys have one night of fun after every kind of shit we've been through."

"Watch it, Sergeant!" Milton yelled back. "You're out of line. I order you both to leave here immediately!"

Just then, Aaron Haley walked in. "What's going on? What's all this commotion? I can hear you all out in the hallway."

Jonesy and Ollie both straightened up.

"Why all this shouting?" Aaron asked again.

"Colonel, we're having a holiday party on Christmas Eve," Jonesy said. "We've come to invite the nurses of the 33rd to join. The nurses of all the other hospital units have already accepted. They'll all be coming."

"A Christmas party? That sounds fun."

"Yes, sir. It will be. You are invited too, of course! You'll be our special guest of honor!"

Aaron smiled and waved his hand in dismissal.

"But Captain Milton here is refusing to let the nurses of 33rd come," said Ollie.

"Why?" Aaron asked Fran.

"Colonel, if everyone's gone, who will be left to take care of the patients?" Fran said.

Aaron didn't seem concerned. "It's one evening. The doctors on duty will still be here, and not all the nurses will want to go." He smiled at Jonesy and Ollie. "I'm sure we can work out a staffing arrangement to accommodate."

"Colonel," Fran stood up from her seat. "I strongly advise against this. What if an emergency comes up?"

"If an emergency comes up, you'll be here, and I'll be here."

You'll be here, and I'll be here...on Christmas Eve. Fran relented and loosened up behind the desk.

"I'm sure we can coordinate with the other hospital units and work out a schedule to cover everything for one night," Aaron said. It would be nice for the nurses to get a break and celebrate. It's Christmas after all."

Tessa, Jonesy, and Ollie looked to Fran. Surprisingly, she had dropped her hardline attitude. "If that's your decision, Colonel, then I have nothing more to say."

"Thank you, Colonel!" Ollie said.

"Yes. Thanks very much," said Jonesy. "We mean it, Doctor, you are invited too!"

Aaron only smiled. Ollie and Jonesy took their leave. On their way out, Jonesy said out loud to Tessa, "Goodbye, Lieutenant Graham. Lieutenant Ardley sends his love and kisses."

Tessa stared at him in horror. Milton and Aaron Haley both looked at her as her face turned crimson red.

CHAPTER THIRTY-SIX

"Dr. Haley? You wanted to see me?" Tessa knocked on Aaron's door and entered.

"Yes. Come on in please, and have a seat," he said, inviting her to take a seat across from him at his desk. He had meant to meet one-on-one with her and the rest of the new replacements for weeks. Some of them hadn't had a chance to work directly with him yet. He wanted to make sure they knew they could approach him.

"I'm sorry if I haven't done much to check on you and see how you've been doing," he said. "I try to get to know my staff individually whenever I can. It's difficult as we get very busy here. I have some free time today, so I thought I'd check in with you and the other new arrivals." He reclined back in his seat. "How are you doing? Are you handling the work okay?"

"I'm doing fine. Thank you for asking."

"I hope you're mentally prepared for much tougher situations." He looked out the window and sighed. "I don't know when it will happen, but when we're sent out into the fields again, things will get a lot tougher. It'll be intense. There'll be very long hours, a lot of pressure, and what you'll see will be much more traumatic."

"I will do my best when the time comes, Doctor."

"I have no doubt about that," he said. "I'm more concerned about you. Don't be afraid to ask for help. Remember, you can come and see me if you ever have any problem."

"Yes, Doctor," she answered politely. He didn't expect her to say more. From what he had seen, Tessa Graham tended to be quite reserved. She appeared ready to leave and he was about to dismiss her when she unexpectedly asked him, "Doctor, why did you decide to join the military? You don't seem to enjoy the army culture at all, and men can't be drafted to be doctors."

Her question caught him off guard. No one had ever asked him this before. In fact, for many years now, no one had asked him anything about himself. Being the head of the surgical department back in Boston, and now the superintendent of the field hospital, people came to him with their stories and their problems, not the other way around. No one thought someone as successful and esteemed as he would have problems they needed to ask about. If he had problems he couldn't resolve, then they wouldn't be able to solve it for him anyway.

"When the war started in Europe, there were a lot of rumors about potential American involvement," he told her. "Even four years ago, the American military had already begun mobilizing. The army started laying the groundwork for organizing military hospitals too. People at the hospital where I worked in Boston knew that. We talked a lot about it. Even back then, I knew the work here would be very important, especially if America went to war and our own troops were directly affected."

Tessa leaned forward in her seat. Her interest in his experience touched him.

"One day, I got a call from an old colleague of mine asking if I would like to help the army plan and set up military hospitals. The army needed a consultant to advise them on logistics. I did that for a while, part-time. Then Pearl Harbor happened, and overnight, the army needed a new pool of doctors to serve abroad. Doctors aren't like the enlisted soldiers or even commissioned officers. The enlisted men and officers are mostly young unmarried men. Doctors with proper qualifications are typically older and already married with children. It was difficult for them to leave their families behind. I don't have a family. I have a sister but she has her own family. I felt that, if I went, it'd be one less doctor with a family who would have to be here. So I came."

Tessa glanced at his ringless index finger. "If you don't mind me asking, why don't you have your own family?"

What a complicated question.

For years, everyone around him had told him it was time he should find himself a suitable wife and settle down with a family. More times than he could remember, people had tried to introduce him to women who would make good wives. How could an accomplished doctor be without a wife and a family?

Of course, he would love to have a family. But for him, that was not enough. He wanted more. He wanted more because life could offer more. He wanted that special feeling. That special feeling when he knew he had met the one.

It was not the kind of thing he could tell people. A man could not tell people such things without making a joke of himself. But he knew that feeling. He had felt it once long ago, when he was still a student studying medicine, still trying to make his way in the world.

She lived only two streets down from him in the little town in Michigan where they had both grown up. They were both so young then. They had so many dreams. When they fell in love, he knew he had found what he wanted in life. He thought that was what she wanted too.

Except it wasn't.

Papa thinks I should marry Vernon.

She wouldn't look him in the eye.

Forget what he thinks. What do you think?

When she finally gathered her nerves and faced him, he already knew the answer before she spoke. That magical feeling had disappeared. She was no longer the girl he knew.

You'll never be anything more than a country doctor. Vernon's going to do great things.

The day after that, he packed up the few belongings he had and left for Boston. He hadn't told her the hospital in Boston had offered him a full fellowship. He was ready to turn it down. For her, he would have stayed in their little town and lived a simple life with her with no regrets. Life was more than wealth, or status, or any such related things that people worshipped. Unfortunately, she too had fallen into that trap.

But he would not. He swore he would find that feeling again, and he would not settle for anything less.

For the next five years, he devoted his life to his work. In that time, he discovered another kind of love. He loved the work of a surgeon. If anything good had come out of that painful separation, it was that it gave him a chance to find out how good he could be. In the many years since, he had saved so many lives and healed so many people. That in itself had been a very rewarding experience.

As it was said, time healed all wounds. Five years later, even that break up began to feel like a distant event from another lifetime ago. Everyone had moved on. He had moved on.

Still, he never met anyone whom he felt had that special inner light that could light up his world. He saw no point in compromising and his work kept him plenty busy. He would not force himself into a relationship for the sake of meeting social expectation.

And then, time flew, and time was unforgiving. Once time left, it would not turn back. Before he knew it, he was no longer a young man. He had all but given up since he turned forty. He was settled and established, and he was comfortable with the idea of spending the rest of his life the way he now lived. It wasn't bad, really. He was highly regarded in his field. He had friends and supportive colleagues. His patients and their families appreciated him. He mourned when his mother passed away several years ago, but his sister and her family visited him once every summer, and his nieces and nephew were growing up to be fine young adults.

What he did not expect was that right here in this god-awful place that the army called the European theater, that special inner light had come to him again in the form of Ellie Swanson. He felt it the very first time he met her. The moment they shook hands, he thought they had both felt something.

The problem was, she was only in her early twenties. He was in his mid-forties already. How could he even think of pursuing her? While it was not unheard of for men to pursue women much younger than their age, he couldn't. He told himself to forget about it. She deserved someone her own age, someone who could share a full life and future with her, not someone who had already lived half his life like him.

"I could've had a family once. That was almost twenty years ago," he said to Tessa.

"Why didn't you?"

"She broke it off. And then, I guess time just went by and I didn't notice. I never met anyone else I wanted to pursue."

"Never?"

That wasn't true. "I'm too old."

"Nonsense. You look about the same age as my father, and I can tell you even now there are girls my age who would jump at the chance of meeting him."

"Your father?"

"My father's an actor. He's very popular and he's very handsome, although he is extremely devoted to my mother."

"I see." He couldn't imagine Ellie pining for him the way fans might swoon for an actor. "That's different then. I'm not an actor, and I'm probably nowhere near as handsome as your father."

"Actor or not, I don't think you're old. I don't think my father is old."

He smiled. "If there is someone, I would be too old for her." He didn't know why he was telling Tessa this.

She didn't say anything, but she gave him a knowing look and he knew right then she knew his secret.

How unbecoming of him, he chided himself. He was the chief superintendent. He should not have revealed such things about himself.

"Doctor, why don't you come to the Christmas party? I'm going, and Ellie's going." She made a point to stress the last part.

He hesitated.

"Just because you don't have a family doesn't mean you should be taken for granted. In fact, I think you of all people should not spend Christmas alone. Come to the party. You can meet my boyfriend. He's an army officer. I'm sure you'll like him. He's much nicer than I am. We can be your family for the night."

Her sincerity touched him. It had been a long time since he had celebrated the holidays. Being a single man, Christmas holidays came and went. It was all the same to him. When his mother was alive, she preferred to visit his sister and her family instead of him because his mother loved seeing her grandchildren. A few times he had gone to Michigan to spend the holidays with them, but usually, he volunteered to work through the holidays to relieve his colleagues who had families. It always felt like the right thing to do. The last two years in the army, he had worked through all the holidays too.

He glanced at his drawer. Last night, he had finished carving the dove.

"Join us, Doctor," Tessa said. "Ellie will be thrilled."

The way she said it gave him the push he needed. "All right. I think I will enjoy it."

"Wonderful! Ellie will be so happy."

Now he was worried again. "Tessa, please don't say anything to Lieutenant Swanson that I didn't mean. I mean, I don't want her to think that..." he stopped short and didn't know how to properly say what was on his mind.

"You don't want her to think what?" Tessa said with a mischievous smile.

"I don't...I...please don't make her feel uncomfortable around me. All I want is to go to the party and celebrate the holiday with all of you. All of you. Like a family."

"I won't say anything." Tessa got up, still with that mischievous smile on her face. "I'll be off now. You have a wonderful day, Doctor."

What had he done?

But, how wonderful! He could finally feel excited about the holiday.

He opened his drawer and took out the dove. It would be a nice little gift in the spirit of Christmas.

PART XI
THE CHRISTMAS BALL

CHAPTER THIRTY-SEVEN

CHRISTMAS EVE.

Against the gloom of war and the wounded, a festive mood prevailed among those stationed at the army base. The level of anticipation was perhaps even more so than normal as everyone sought a chance of escape from their brutal reality.

Convoys of armored vehicles arrived at the General Hospital to transport the nurses to the Italian Count's villa for the Christmas party. For one night, the women could wear evening dresses for a change. Some got to try on dresses sent to them from home but which they thought they would never have a chance to use. Others bought gowns from local dressmakers who made them in haste. The change of climate to cold weather could not deter their determination to look their best this evening.

Alone in her office, Fran Milton sat at her desk, reviewing patients' charts and graphs. All day long, she had to bear the noises of her staff's idle chatter about the Count's party. Nobody was concentrating on the work at hand. She would be glad when this foolishness was over and all the absurdities along with it would pass.

She checked the clock on her desk. Six o'clock. Time for her daily evening tea with Dr. Haley. She took the small raisin cake she had asked the kitchen to prepare for her today and headed to Aaron Haley's office. It was Christmas Eve after all. The cake would be a nice treat for both of them.

She arrived to find another doctor, Colonel Bernstein, at Aaron's desk.

"Captain Milton!" Dr. Bernstein said when she walked in.

"Why are you here? Where's Colonel Haley?" She demanded to know.

"Dr. Haley left half an hour ago. He's gone to Count Zeffirelli's Christmas bash. I told him I'll sub for him tonight." He smiled. "I don't celebrate Christmas anyway. I'm Jewish."

"He didn't tell me he was going."

"He didn't? Was he supposed to tell you?"

Unable to answer, Fran tensed her lips.

You'll be here, and I'll be here...

She tightened her hold on the plate of cake.

He said he'd be here. This was not right. This was not right.

Her hands shook.

He stood her up. This was humiliating.

"Thank you, Colonel Bernstein," she said in her usual cold voice and left. Heat flushed through her veins. Her body quivered. How could this be? Aaron Haley was not an irresponsible person. There was only one person to blame for this. She knew exactly who was at fault. He would not have neglected his duties and gone off like this on a night when the hospital was drastically understaffed if it weren't for that person. That person must be held responsible.

She walked down the corridor to the patients' ward. On her way, she dropped the raisin cake into a garbage disposal.

Before heading off to the Christmas party, Irene, Alice, Gracie, Ellie, and Tessa stopped by the patients' ward to say goodbye to those who were unfortunately not well enough to attend the holiday banquets and festivities of various army units and divisions. To cheer them up, they had promised to come in their evening dresses instead of their uniforms.

Although normally not one to put herself forth as the center of attention, Tessa agreed to go along with the nurses' promise. It was a small imposition to bring a lot of fun to the soldiers. When they entered the ward, the howls and whistles even made her laugh.

"Alice! Marry me?" a lieutenant with a broken leg asked.

"Skip the party," a corporal said. "Spend the evening with us instead."

In the midst of the excitement, Tessa went to a young soldier with bandages wrapped around his eyes. She sat down beside him and placed her hand on his. "Hello, Nicky, how are you doing?"

"Hi, Tessa. I'm fine." His voice was weak.

"So, Irene and Alice are both wearing black. Irene's gown has a gold belt and she looks ravishing. Ellie has on a beautiful blue dress, and Gracie is wearing dark pink. They all look gorgeous tonight."

The boy named Nicky smiled. "What about you? What are you wearing?"

"Me? Oh... I'm just wearing my uniform.

"You are?"

"No. I'm just kidding. My dress is red."

"You must look very pretty tonight. I bet Lieutenant Ardley can't wait to see you."

Tessa squeezed his hand. "Thank you, Nicky."

On the other side of the room, a soldier said aloud, "Save a dance for me, Ellie."

"Get better then," Ellie said. "When you're back on your feet, I'll dance with you."

"Is that a promise?" the soldier asked. He was about to say something more but a harsh voice interrupted him.

"There will be no dancing of any sort for you tonight, Lieutenant Swanson."

Everyone turned to see who was speaking. Fran Milton was standing by the door.

"I found out one person had taken an unscheduled leave. That's one more absence than we had originally planned for this evening. Lieutenant Swanson, I'll need you to stay to make sure we are adequately staffed."

The room quieted down as Captain Milton made her announcement.

"Wait," Tessa said. "Who has taken an unscheduled leave? Why does Ellie have to stay for this person?"

"It doesn't matter who," Milton said. "The important thing is we need to be properly staffed. I've decided that Lieutenant Swanson shall be the one to stay."

Alice, Irene, and Gracie all looked at Ellie. The patients in the room, too, were shocked.

"Come on, Captain," one of the soldiers said. "Let her go. We'll be fine for the night."

A few more mumbled and concurred.

Fran would not relent. "I've made my decision. This is a matter of hospital administration. Please stay out of it."

"Captain." Tessa stepped up to Fran. "You said you need Lieutenant Swanson to replace the person who had left without authorization. That's easy enough. You need one replacement. I'll stay. Lieutenant Swanson can go."

"Tessa!" Ellie gasped. Tessa shook her head at her, then looked at Milton.

Not expecting this turn of event, Milton stared back at Tessa, unsure of what to do but unwilling to back down. Everyone in the room watched and some started to plead on Ellie and Tessa's behalf again.

"Very well," Milton said in a huff. "You want to work too, you can both stay." Her harsh voice whipped across and silenced everyone.

Infuriated, Tessa glared at her. She grabbed her skirt and tightened her fists to control herself.

"Both of you, change back into your uniforms and start the evening rounds. Now!" Milton ordered, then said to Irene, Alice, and Gracie, "The rest of you, are you leaving yet or do you want to stay and work too?"

Irene, Alice, and Gracie mumbled inaudible responses and left the room.

On her way out, Alice patted Tessa on the back and whispered, "I'll tell Lieutenant Ardley you can't make it." Tessa nodded and forced herself to smile in response.

Milton followed the three nurses out of the room, leaving Tessa and Ellie behind in their disappointment and their patients in sympathetic helplessness.

As dusk turned to night, the army vehicles arrived one after another at Count Zeffirelli's villa, bringing officers and enlisted men, and nurses from the different hospital units. Some even carried civilian volunteers working for humanitarian aid efforts. The army band's music welcomed the guests as they entered. For one night, the villa's ballroom, which had lost its luster after years of being used by the German troops as an operational post, regained a shade of its former glory and reverted to a place for snazzy entertainment. A large banner with the words "Merry X'mas" hung above the ballroom's entrance. A fully decorated Christmas tree stood next to the long buffet table on which the army kitchen had laid an unexpectedly sumptuous spread of food. On another table, men gathered around hundreds of bottles of low-grade liquor of every sort. Their minds were already half gone in drunken bliss.

Standing by the side with Warren, Anthony glanced now and then at the ballroom entrance as they watched the crowd.

"Captain, Lieutenant." Jonesy came up to them with a bottle of wine. He poured a glass and offered it to Anthony. Anthony took it while Ollie gave Warren a glass.

"I have to give it to you," Warren said. "This is some party you two are pulling off."

"Thank you, thank you." Jonesy took a bow. "I don't mean to brag, but," he spread his arm out toward the ballroom's floor, "sixty-three Florence Nightingales here with us tonight, and we did not—let me emphasize, did not—even bring Lieutenant Garland with us when we invited them." He raised his drink.

Warren laughed and clinked his glass.

Jonesy sidled up to Anthony. "Don't get too excited now, Lieutenant, but Lieutenant Graham was there when we invited the 33rd Hospital brigade. When we told them we were having a party, and I told her you'd be here waiting for her, she had this look on her face, like she was ready to..."

Anthony swiped the back of his head.

"Oww! That hurts!"

"You're drunk," Anthony said, then laughed. "You say anything more and it's going to hurt even more."

"Come on, Jonesy," Ollie said, "let's go ask some ladies to dance." They took off as Alice came up to them.

"Lieutenant Ardley," she said.

"Alice?"

"I'm sorry to tell you this, but Tessa's not coming."

"She's not coming? Why?"

"Captain Milton. She's our head nurse. A real bitch." Alice lowered her voice and made a face. "I don't know what's gotten into her tonight. She showed up when we were all leaving and ordered Ellie Swanson to stay behind to work. Tessa, well, she tried to stand up for Ellie and asked to take Ellie's place. It backfired and Milton decided to make them both stay and work."

"You're kidding me!"

"No. I'm very sorry. I told Tessa I would let you know."

While news sunk in, he thanked Alice. She gave him a sympathetic look and walked away.

"That's terrible," Warren said. "I'm sorry."

Anthony looked at the roomful of people. The party had lost all its appeal. "I'm leaving," he said to Warren.

"Where are you going?"

"To the hospital. She can't come here. I guess I'll have to go to her." He gave Warren his glass. "I'll see you later."

Warren raised his glass in a toast as Anthony took off. "Merry Christmas."

Farther away at a table, Jesse watched Anthony depart while drinking with a group of nurses and officers. He wondered why Anthony was leaving. Where was Tessa? Many of the nurses from the 33rd had arrived. Tessa should be here by now. If Anthony left, did that mean those two had changed their plans?

He looked to the other side of the room. A lanky bald man with a gray beard and gold-rim glasses meandered about, looking lost in the sea of American men. His worn, outdated tuxedo needed an upgrade, but that was impossible given that Naples had been under German occupation for the last few years. No one noticed him. Everyone ignored him even as he smiled at them.

Jesse excused himself from the table. There was a bargaining opportunity here, he thought as he approached the man. He could feel it. But what exactly was on the table? He had to find out.

"Conte Zeffirelli," Jesse said to the man.

The man looked at him, surprised. "Ah… oh… yes."

"May I introduce myself? My name is Jesse Garland."

"You're an American officer?"

"Yes. I'm a medic." Jesse put on his most sincere smile. "Thank you for inviting us tonight. It is very generous of you."

The count seemed pleased. "My pleasure," he said. "Anything I can still do to show my gratitude for liberating us from the Nazi scum." His voice turned bitter, unaware that Jesse was observing his every reaction.

"Lord." Jesse stepped closer. "I wonder, are you by any chance related to the Marchese de Sforza?"

As soon as the count heard the name, his hand trembled, causing a turbulence in his wine glass that only Jesse noticed. The count put his other hand on Jesse's arm, his mouth agape. "Leopold! Do you know him? Where is he? Do you have news about him?"

Jesse glanced at the count's hand on his arm. "No recent news, I'm sorry to say. He and I haven't corresponded since I was deployed, but I do know him. Very well in fact." He in fact did not know the Marchese. He had seen the man a few times in a private club in New York and had heard about him from the other club members. It was a wild card to bring up his name, but it was worth a shot. "The Marchese lives in New York now. He was lucky he escaped before the Nazis got a hold of Bologna and his fortune." He watched the count's shaken reaction, then added, "His son and I were classmates at Yale."

"Leopold and I are distant cousins," Zeffirelli said. His face had lightened up as if he had woken up from a bad dream.

"When I left New York, the Marchese was working all available channels to get the Italian nobilities out of the country and to help them to recover all their assets," Jesse said. He was making this up. The Marchese, as far as he knew, was doing no such thing. The pathetic, selfish man was nothing but the last of a dying breed trying to hold on to the remains of his glory in a world that was rapidly changing and moving beyond him.

"I lost everything." The count stared at Jesse, like a castaway lost at sea who had seen a float, "I've been cut off from all my Swiss bank accounts. My money here too, it's all gone. All the Italian banks are gone. My art and antique collections," he looked up at the wall of the ballroom, his grip on Jesse's arm tightened, "the damn Nazis took everything from me."

"That's a shame, my Lord," Jesse said. "I'm sorry to hear that." He intentionally cooled his tone to sound detached with just the right note of sympathy. He did not want to appear too enthusiastic. He could not let the count know he wanted anything from him. He wanted the count to be the one in need.

The count reacted just as he expected. "Are you still in touch with Leopold? Do you think he could help me? My overseas assets…"

"I'm sure the Marchese will be thrilled and relieved to hear from you if I could reach him. The thing is," Jesse lowered his voice, "the army censors all our communications with people back home. Where your assets are and who owns these assets are not the kind of information you want everyone to know." He glanced around the room, then leaned into the count with a more hushed and serious tone. "To send the kind of information you want me to pass along, and to make sure the information goes only to the right hands, I'll have to grease the wheels with the right people. If you've lost everything, I'm afraid it's going to be difficult." He drew back and studied the count's expression. The man was weighing something in his head. Obviously now, the count did not lose everything. He still had something, but what?

"I have something here the Germans never found," the count whispered.

"What?"

The count looked around him, then said, "Follow me."

He followed the count to the basement through a long corridor to a room at the end. A musky smell hit them when the count opened the door and switched on the light. The light was dim, but Jesse was able to make out it was an old storage room. The wallpaper was either stained, torn, or peeled. The parts of the walls not covered by wallpaper were chipped. The few paintings still on the walls were hung crooked and the colors of the artwork had faded. Used and broken furniture, wooden boxes, and other old items of no value were scattered across the floor.

The count walked up to a bookshelf lined with a collection of rotting books.

"These are all I have left. Those Nazi scum never knew they were here," the count said proudly. He pushed the bookshelf across the wall to reveal another door behind it. He unlocked the door and went inside. Jesse went in after him.

Unlike the storage room that served as a façade, the hidden room was clean. Jesse looked around. The walls were lined with shelves and shelves of liquor. There must have been hundreds of bottles. Amazed, Jesse took a walk around. He took a cognac off a shelf, examined the label, and stared at the count. "Is this…" He couldn't believe what he was holding.

The count nodded and broke into a smile. "My private collection. I dare say you won't find many of these anywhere on this continent right now."

Jesse could not believe his luck. In this upside-down world where the rules of civilization had gone by the wayside, these liquors were even more valuable than cash. They would be good chips to have, a definite insurance policy in case he needed something to offer for a trade. Anyhow, if nothing else, he had just acquired himself a continuous supply of fine booze for the foreseeable future.

"This will make things easier," he said to the count. "You can count on me, my Lord. I promise you, I will find a way to contact the Marchese to let him know your situation. And then, we'll see what we can do to recover your assets. A great man like you deserves all the help he can get." He looked at the liquor bottle in his hand again. "These, of course, will get you a lot of help within the U.S. Army communications channels and beyond."

The count nodded. Jesse knew then he had sealed the deal. At this moment, the man would give him anything he asked for. There was nothing easier to bait than a man who was greedy and desperate. Someone in such a predicament would only hear what they want to hear and believe whatever they want to believe.

"What I'll need you to do is to send me some of these fine spirits whenever I get a message to you. It pains me to have to ask you to do this. You have a wonderful collection here. I hate to see you part with these, but it's the only way I can get the communications officers' cooperation to secure our messages to your cousin the Marchese."

"Yes! Yes! Thank you, Mr. Garland!" the count said. "Here." He pushed the cognac Jesse was holding further into Jesse's hands. "Take this. My token of gratitude." He had the look of someone holding onto his last hope.

"Thank you," Jesse did not refuse. "Shall we take this upstairs to celebrate? A toast to your upcoming reunion with the Marchese de Sforza?"

The count readily agreed.

Back in the ballroom an hour later, the count sat among a group of American soldiers, all of them drunk as they passed around the last drops of his bottle of aged cognac. Sober, Jesse stood by and searched the room again for Tessa. There was no sign of her or Anthony anywhere. He lowered his eyes and let out a quiet, self-deprecating laugh.

"Jesse." A woman appeared next to him. He looked up. It was Irene. She came next to him, lit a cigarette, and exhaled with her arms across her chest. "Why don't you join us?" she asked.

Jesse shrugged. "Guess I needed a moment to reflect on the meaning of Christmas. Pray for peace on earth, all that good stuff."

She raised her brow and ignored his joke. "You having a good time?"

"Always!"

She waited for him to ask her to dance. When he didn't, she glanced at the table not too far from them. "Looks like you got yourself another admirer. Gracie over there's been staring at you all night."

"Who's Gracie?"

"The new nurse who arrived with Tessa a few weeks ago."

Irene tossed her head toward Gracie's direction. "She's from Milwaukee."

He looked over to the table where Alice was talking and laughing with a group of nurses and soldiers. Next to her, a sweet looking girl with a heart shape face quickly turned away to avoid his eyes.

"Not interested," he said. "Too small town for me."

"Milwaukee's not that small."

"Small enough."

The band switched from fast jazz to slow songs and the men took all the nurses at the table to the dance floor, leaving only Marcy Sanford alone by herself. Marcy fidgeted and looked about, then went to the buffet table and began collecting the small plates with leftover food and used utensils.

"She's very cute," Irene continued, still talking about Gracie.

Bored by the subject, Jesse gave her one of his trademark seductive smiles. "You know you're the only one for me, Irene."

"I wish I could believe that," she said, her voice subdued and resigned, her eyes still full of longing.

He brushed her chin with his fingers and walked away.

He went to the buffet table where Marcy Sanford was busying herself with cleaning up the others' mess. A short woman about five feet tall, the evening dress looked all wrong on her. The long skirt wiped the floor as she moved. Several times, she nearly tripped over it. The soft satin fabric accentuated the plumpness around her waist and her unruly curls had fallen out from the hairpins again. But she tried. She even put on lipstick tonight. He had never seen her wear lipstick.

"Hello, Marcy," he said to her. "Merry Christmas."

"Jesse! Merry Christmas!" Her eyes instantly lit up when she saw him.

"You don't have to do that," he said, frowning at the plates in her hands. "Let the boys clean up tomorrow."

"Oh, it's all right," she waved her hand in dismissal. "I don't mind helping."

He watched her return to clearing the buffet table. "I hear you're leaving us after this week."

"Yes. My tour of duty's over. I can't stay anymore. My mother's dementia's getting worse. I have to go home and take care of her."

Jesse's eyes softened. "I'll miss you."

"You're very sweet to say that." She put the stack of small plates she was holding on the table. "Jesse, thank you for always being so kind to me. Sometimes, I feel so lost here. Everything can get so depressing. It means a lot to me that you always come by to see me."

He smiled. "Can I invite you for a dance?"

"Oh-ho! No!" She laughed. "You go dance with one of those beautiful young ladies out there. It's very nice of you to ask, but you don't need to amuse an old lady."

"You're not old, and I'm serious. Can I please have a dance? It'd be my honor."

Marcy looked at him, unsure and hesitated.

"Please? If you say yes, it'll be the best Christmas present I'll receive this year."

Marcy laughed again. "Okay. One dance. But you really don't have to do this."

"I want to." He took her hand and led her to the dance floor, then guided her with simple steps.

"I haven't danced with anyone since Bill passed away four years ago," she said, her voice choking up a little.

"Then I envy the lucky fellow you're going to meet and dance with all the time when you get home."

Her eyes teared up. "I'm going to really miss you, Jesse."

He smiled again.

"You take care of yourself, okay? When this war and everything is over, you go home, find yourself a nice young lady and settle down. You take real good care of yourself now after I'm gone," she said as the song came to an end.

"Goodbye, Marcy."

"Goodbye to you too, Jesse. And good luck."

When their dance finished, he left the ballroom and headed out of the villa. Outside, he lit a cigarette.

Another Christmas. Another year. Every year was the same. Even here in Naples thousands of miles away from New York, nothing was real. No one wanted him to be real. He couldn't be real.

How much longer must this charade continue?

A merry group of people was getting into a truck. He threw his cigarette butt on the ground, snubbed it out with his foot, and went over to them and asked the driver to drop him off at his base camp. The driver agreed and he hopped in.

CHAPTER THIRTY-EIGHT

AT THE HOSPITAL, Tessa and Ellie grudgingly made their rounds. The work they were doing was redundant. Captain Milton was making them do unnecessary busy work to punish them. For what reason, they did not know.

Ellie, at least, had made peace with their situation and took the opportunity to go around each patient's bed to wish them a happy Christmas. Tessa could not bring herself to be as forgiving. She went to each bed, mechanically taking each person's temperature and blood pressure. When she finished, she stomped out of the patients' ward to take the equipment back to the storage. The more she thought about what happened, the more irate she became. She tensed her hands around the rolling cart of medical tools as she pushed it along, passing everyone in the corridor without looking at them.

"Why such a cranky face on Christmas Eve?" someone asked behind her.

Her heart opened as soon as she heard his voice. With a wide smile on her face, she turned around. "Anthony!"

Anthony came and gently took her hand, intertwining her fingers into his own.

"You've come," Tessa said.

"We said we'd spend Christmas Eve together, remember? Alice told me what happened. I came straight away." He moved closer to her. "The party's no fun without you."

All her anger with Milton dissipated. "What will you do here?" she asked him. "Follow me around all night?"

"Nothing I want to do more in this world."

Ellie had now finished with her round. "Tessa!" she found them in the hallway. "Lieutenant Ardley, you're here!"

"Merry Christmas, Ellie," he said.

Ellie walked up to them. "Tessa, I was thinking, since we're here anyway, wouldn't it be nice if you and I go around and sing Christmas carols for the patients? It's not as exciting as the party at the count's villa, but it'll cheer everyone up." She looked to Anthony. "Maybe you can join us too, Lieutenant?"

Before he could answer, Wesley Sharpe appeared. "Ardley?"

"Lieutenant," Anthony said, equally surprised to see him. "Merry Christmas."

"What are you doing here?"

"Lieutenant, this is my girlfriend, Tessa Graham. She's working tonight. I came to see her." He turned to Tessa. "Our First Lieutenant, Wesley Sharpe."

"Can we help you with anything, Lieutenant?" Tessa asked.

"Nah. I came to visit the boys to wish them a Merry Christmas. I thought it'd be a good time to do that with everyone else away at the party."

"You didn't go to the party?" she asked.

"Parties aren't my thing. If you don't mind, I'll go around and look for the familiar faces."

"Actually, Lieutenant," Ellie said, "we're talking about going through the wards to sing Christmas carols for the patients. Would you like to join us?"

"That's a wonderful idea. I would love to."

"You would?" Anthony asked. "You sing?"

"Why's that such a surprise? I was a choirboy. I used to be in an a cappella group back in West Point too."

"No kidding!"

"Now we are a real choir with four people," Ellie said.

"Wait!" Anthony said. "Tessa's a fantastic piano player. What if we get a piano here? We can have a concert right here in the lobby."

"Get a piano here? From where?" Tessa asked.

"The one over at the club where the army band plays. It's only ten minutes' drive from here." He looked at Wesley. "What do you think? We can use one of the transport trucks outside and bring the piano over here?"

"There's no one to tune it," Tessa said.

"I know how to tune a piano," Wesley winked at her.

"I didn't know you're musical," Anthony said to him as they took off.

"This is wonderful," Ellie said to Tessa. "Tonight's turning into a fun one after all."

Tessa agreed. "Let's tell all the patients to gather in the lobby. And the ones who can't walk, let's see if we can find help and bring them there too, or at least some place closer so they can listen."

The announcement of an impromptu Christmas concert roused everyone into excitement. By the time Anthony and Wesley returned with the piano, hundreds had already gathered in the main lobby. What's more, Anthony had brought with him a stack of sheet music of Christmas songs the army band had left behind.

They set the piano in the middle of the lobby and gathered around to sing as Tessa began to play "Angels We Have Heard on High." Soon, the patients too joined in and Anthony sat down next to her.

Between songs, she glanced at him. Sometimes, she almost felt as if she must check again and again to make sure he was still with her.

In her mind, the struggle against the dark unknown forces out there oppressing them continued. *Don't take him away from me*, she warned them in her thoughts. She had fought her way to get here. She wanted him by her side like he was now, always.

Don't take him from me.

Aaron Haley returned to the hospital to find the lobby full of people singing Christmas carols. He had gone to the party at the count's villa earlier with the hope of seeing Ellie there. All evening, he tried to think of the right way he should conduct himself when he saw her at the party. He couldn't very well approach her like an ardent suitor and ask her to dance. No matter what Tessa Graham said, he still felt he was too old for Ellie. Besides, it had been years since he had even thought about approaching a woman. Everything felt awkward and laughable.

Maybe he could just give her a little Christmas present.

At the party, he looked everywhere for her but couldn't find her. He couldn't find Tessa either. He waited and waited for Ellie to show up. She was a conscientious worker. Maybe she got held up. He had no idea why Ellie and Tessa were both absent until he found Alice and she told him what happened. His entire trip and all the waiting had been for nothing. Disappointed, he decided to return to the hospital, hoping to catch Ellie and to wish her a Merry Christmas before the evening ended.

It came upon a midnight clear
That glorious song of old...

The welcoming sound of everyone singing was a pleasant surprise.

He walked into the lobby. Right away, he saw her. She was standing by the piano and leading the singing. She looked so serene, such a calming and pretty sight among all the wounded. He walked toward her, but stopped when he saw Wesley Sharpe standing next to her. Wesley showed her something on a sheet of music, then leaned in and said something to her ear. She smiled in response. The two then looked at the music sheet they shared and started singing again.

...Beneath the angel strain have rolled
Two thousand years of wrong
And man at war with man hears not
The tidings which they bring...

Watching Ellie and Wesley sing, Aaron reached into his pocket where he carried the hand-carved dove he had made for her and closed his hand around the ornament.

She should be with someone like him, he thought, looking at Wesley. A vigorous young man like that would be better for her.

He stood at the spot and pondered whether he should stay or leave. He was still making up his mind when the next song, "I'll Be Home for Christmas," began. A patient in a cot near him started crying. He knew the patient, Buddy Muller. Buddy got thrown out of a truck in a mine explosion two weeks ago. His injuries were serious, but worse was the loss of his three closest friends in the army in that incident. Buddy was the only survivor. As the song continued, tears flooded down his face.

Aaron looked at Buddy, then at Ellie and Wesley again. Dejected, he put his hand on Buddy's shoulder and gave him the dove in his pocket. Buddy stared back at him, his eyes wet.

"Merry Christmas," Aaron said to him.

Buddy took the dove. "Thank you, Doctor." He held the dove in both of his hands like he was trying to hold on to hope.

When the song was over, Ellie spotted Aaron in the crowd. Surprised and happy to see him, she walked over to him. "Won't you join us, Doctor?"

He followed her toward the piano. Wesley gave him a sheet of lyrics and they began singing along to the music of "What Child is This." Hesitant at first, Aaron whispered the words until Ellie put her hand lightly on his arm. The feel of her touch sent a wave of warmth to his heart. He glanced sideways at her. Her head was down and she was concentrating on the singing, but her hand still rested on his arm. Reassured, he joined in the singing with a full heart.

The evening of Christmas carols closed with "Silent Night." Sitting beside Tessa, Anthony said a silent prayer. He hoped the angels and the Lord on high would hear him. He hoped they would hear the voices of all the wounded soldiers right now in this building, all of them singing their wishes for peace.

How many more men must be harmed like those who surrounded them tonight before the war was over? He prayed he would do right by the ones who fate had entrusted him to protect. He prayed the Almighty would guide him along the way.

He prayed that all the atrocities would end, and he and Tessa could leave all this behind.

May all things change for the world when the next year began, and when next Christmas came, the two of them would be sitting together by the piano at home.

— *To be continued* —

Rose of Anzio Book Three
Desire

Rose of Anzio Book Three - Desire

Get your copy now on Amazon

ROSE OF ANZIO
Book Three ~ Desire

"We have so much ahead of us, Tessa. What we have ahead is this sea. It'll be the same sea we're looking at now, vast and beautiful. It's already here, waiting for us. It won't change. The war can't take it away."

The Rose of Anzio Series

Available on Amazon & Kindle Unlimited

Get your copy now!

CITATIONS

The following parts of *Rose of Anzio – Jalousie* are either inspired by or based on factual accounts contained in *Bob Gallagher's WWII Stories*. Mr. Gallagher was a GI during WWII and had written a wonderful and fascinating memoir of this time served as a new recruit at training camp and a corporal of the Third Army's 815 Anti-Aircraft Artillery Battalion. Mr. Gallagher passed away on January 23, 2013. His story can be read online at: http://www.gallagherstory.com/ww2/index.html

My sincere gratitude to Mr. Mark Gallagher, son of Mr. Bob Gallagher, for authorizing me to use his father's story as a primary resource for the historical background and inspiration for *Rose of Anzio – Jalousie*.

1. **From *Bob Gallagher's WWII Stories* Chapter 2 – "Drafted"**
   Jalousie: Chapter Four

   - Camp Grant as the first destination of army recruits from Chicago
   - Procedures for receiving uniforms and other army issued items upon arrival

- Description of barracks
- Anthony's Letter dated January 29, 1943: experience at County Draft Board as to branch assignment procedures and related rumors; initial drills and training at Camp Grant; recruits' duties at camps; subsequent transport to California for additional training; training at camp in California; quality of food at camp

2. **From *Bob Gallagher's WWII Stories* Chapter 3 – "Camp Haan - California"**
Jalousie: Chapter Eight

- Army recruits hiking and the loads they carried during the hikes
- Randomness of training activities; penalty for asking questions
- Sergeant Hinkle
- Requirements for dress code
- Latrine duties
- Army training encouraged mediocrity

3. **From *Bob Gallagher's WWII Stories* Chapter 6 – "Camp Irwin and the Mojave Desert"**
Jalousie: Chapter Nine

- Target practice at California desert

4. **From *Bob Gallagher's WWII Stories* Chapter 4 – "Hooray for Hollywood"**
Jalousie: Chapter Twelve

- Anthony's Letter dated April 5, 1943: weekend pass to visit L.A.; visit to dance club in L.A.; presence of U.S. and foreign servicemen in clubs

Sign up for a free story

Enjoyed reading my stories?

Subscribe to my email list and receive a free copy of the story *Christmas Eve in the City of Dreams*, a story about Jesse Garland, the favorite character of readers of the *Rose of Anzio Book One-Moonlight* who will appear in *Book Two-Jalousie*, plus news on book releases, artwork, and more.

http://Alexakang.com/rose-anzio-news/

ACKNOWLEDGMENTS

Rose of Anzio began as a personal challenge for me, but over the course of last year, I discovered that writing a full-length novel (four novels, in fact) is a group project. Words alone cannot express my gratitude to everyone who had encouraged me and helped me bring this series to its completion. I am still amazed at the time and efforts of those who volunteered to help me make this story stronger and better.

Thanks to Anneth White, who first encouraged me to write this story and continuing to inspire me by following it faithfully throughout. Thank you to Pamela Ann Savoy, who gave me great feedback on story ideas and development along the way, and took time out of her super busy schedule to proofread my work as I wrote. Thanks to Eleanna Sakka, whose shoulder was always available for me to lean on every time I hit the wall. My utmost gratitude to Mylius Fox, author of the thriller novel *Bandit,* who reached out to teach me the ropes of self-publishing, and gave me valuable advice and support throughout the process. Also, a very special thank you to Ms. CandyTerry, who gave me a huge amount of moral support, as well as the first platform for me to introduce this story. Thank you also to Mr. Mark Gallagher, for authorizing my use of his father's story for some of the historical facts retold in this book.

My heartfelt thank you to both Kristen Tate, my content editor, whose suggestions and insights helped me improve my story significantly, and Geoff Byers, for his tremendous help and advice on how to create and construct my battle scenes throughout the entire series so I could keep the story as realistic as possible. Thanks to Stephen Reid, for making sure Tessa speaks proper British English. Thanks also to my copy editor Fiona Hallowell, and proofreaders T.J. Moore and Patrick Cunningham, for making my story a truly polished piece of work.

Last but not least, thanks to my husband, Dan, for his unending amount of patience and support.

ABOUT THE AUTHOR

Alexa is a WWII and 20th century historical fiction author. Her works include the novel series, *Rose of Anzio*, a love story saga that begins in 1940 Chicago and continues on to the historic Battle of Anzio in Italy. Her current series, *Shanghai Story*, chronicles the events in Shanghai leading up to WWII and the history of Jews and Jewish refugees in China. Her other works include the WWII/1980s time-travel love story *Eternal Flame* (a tribute to John Hughes), as well as short stories in the fiction anthologies *Pearl Harbor and More: Stories of December 1942*, *Christmas in Love*, and the USA Today Bestseller *The Darkest Hour*.

I would love to hear from you.
Contact me or follow me at:
www.alexakang.com
alexa@alexakang.com

You can also find me on Facebook and BookBub

Printed in Great Britain
by Amazon